INTRODUC

Woman of Valor by Jill Stengl
Helen Walker has come to Marston Hall in 1631 to care for three neglected children and a household in disarray. Oliver is the horseman who admires her loving way with the children. But is she good enough for this hired man?

Apple of His Eye by Gail Gaymer Martin
Sarah Hampton is curious and independent for a Victorian young woman of her day. John Banning is a farmer who also works as an orchard keeper at Hampton Manor. Though Sarah's father respects him, John would never be invited into the home as a guest. How will her family react when she tells them she loves him?

A Flower Amidst the Ashes by DiAnn Mills
Margaret is a member of the Royal Air Force and Andrew a pilot in 1940 when they meet in London. She becomes his vision of a flower against the background of war horrors. But is it fair to seek more than friendship amidst the uncertainties of war?

Robyn's Garden by Kathleen Y'Barbo
Robyn Locksley is employed at Lowingham Manor and in charge of maintaining the historic gardens. When one of her family heirlooms is mistakenly sold to an American businessman, she must decide whether to fight the man for what belongs to her or use the money to help fund a trip for special children. Could the American have another option in mind?

The ENGLISH GARDEN

Centuries of Botanical Delight Brought to Life in Four Romantic Novellas

Gail Gaymer Martin
DiAnn Mills
Jill Stengl
Kathleen Y'Barbo

BARBOUR
PUBLISHING

Woman of Valor ©2001 by Jill Stengl.
The Apple of His Eye ©2001 by Gail Gaymer Martin.
A Flower Amidst the Ashes ©2001 by DiAnn Mills.
Robyn's Garden ©2001 by Kathleen Y'Barbo.

Cover art by Corbis

Illustrations by Mari Goering

ISBN 1-59310-833-8

All Scripture quotations, unless otherwise noted, are taken from the King James Version of the Bible.

Scripture quotations in *Robyn's Garden* are taken from the HOLY BIBLE, NEW INTERNATIONAL VERSION®. NIV®. Copyright © 1973,1978, 1984 by International Bible Society. Used by permission of Zondervan Publishing House. All rights reserved.

"There'll Always Be An England" Words & Music by Ross Parker & Hughie Charles. Copyright © 1939 by Dash Music Company Limited, 8/9 Frith Street, London W1. International Copyright secured. All rights reserved. Reprinted by permission of Music Sales Ltd.

Published by Barbour Publishing, Inc., P.O. Box 719, Uhrichsville, Ohio 44683, www.barbourbooks.com

Our mission is to publish and distribute inspirational products offering exceptional value and biblical encouragement to the masses.

 Member of the
Evangelical Christian
Publishers Association

Printed in the United States of America.

The ENGLISH GARDEN

Woman of Valor

by Jill Stengl

Chapter 1

Norfolk County, 1631

O ut, Woman. This be as far as my coach goes. The road past here is all mud." The driver wrenched open the coach door, placed the step in front, then proceeded to haul down Helen Walker's small trunk and dump it upon the side of the road.

"I paid you to drive me to Biddlesham Fen." One hand on the doorframe, Helen peered out.

"And here you be." The driver waved a gloved hand to indicate marshy fields on every side. "This crossroads is nigh the village. Make haste, Woman. There be a fog comin' in."

Helen opened her mouth to protest further, but the coachman narrowed his eyes and lifted a brow. His bristly, pock-marked face reminded Helen of an ill-tempered pig. Shaking in every limb, she stepped down. Her shoes sank into mud. Lifting her petticoats, she sloshed over to her trunk.

"God be with you." Kind words, spoken in a voice of lead. The driver climbed back to his seat.

"You cannot leave me here!" Helen cast a fearful glance skyward. Across the way, strategically placed at the crossroads to catch the attention of any traveler, an iron cage swayed in the crisp spring breeze. Racing clouds released a brilliant sunset ray to highlight its resident criminal's decayed condition. Helen clapped a hand over her mouth.

Without another word to her, the driver coaxed his team into a sidetrack, turned the small coach around, and headed back to Thetford.

Gaping in disbelief, Helen watched until the coach passed out of view. Casting a glance down each vacant road, she felt tightness in her belly. A wind gust cut through her woolen cloak and stung her cheeks. Ropes and chains creaked. A ghastly shadow bobbed near Helen's trunk until a cloud mercifully obscured the sun. Helen kept her gaze averted from the atrocity across the way.

Clutching her cloak at her breast, she sat on her trunk, closed her eyes, and begged God to send help quickly. "Not that I believe You unaware of the situation, Lord. I know that Your eye is upon them that fear You and hope in Your mercy. I ask to be delivered from all my fears and to have my feet placed upon solid ground." She peeked at her soggy shoes, then squeezed her eyes shut. "As You know, my cousin expects to meet me in the town of Biddlesham Fen tonight and—"

A mournful cry drifted across the fens. Helen's mind told her it was a bird, but her imagination insisted it was the ghost of her putrefied companion. Her face crumpled as she fought back hysterical tears. *Am I doomed to spend the night in this place? I would walk to town, but I do not know which path to take. God, You promised not to allow trials too great for me to bear! Why did I ever leave Surrey? I might have married Wilmer the butcher and raised his six children. Anything would be better than going mad here in this marshland with no one to see or care!*

A rhythmic beat caught her attention. Was the poor wretch on the gibbet rattling about again, or was a horse coming?

Screwing up her face, she peeked with one eye. A horseman approached from the north. Relief slackened Helen's taut nerves until she realized the rider could be a highwayman. . .or worse, a phantom.

Trotting hoofs splattered mud. The puffing horse pulled up several feet from Helen, sparing her skirts. Huddled within her cloak, she cast an anxious gaze upon the rider. He looked substantial enough in brown leather doublet, plain gray breeches, and cuffed boots. Unlike many men of fashion, he wore his hair short—falling just above his shoulders—yet a flowing cape gave him a dashing air.

"Helen Walker?" The brim of his hat shaded the man's face. Helen beheld only an imposing hawk nose and a clean-shaven chin. Could this be. . . ?

"Cousin Cyril?"

"Surely you did not expect him to meet you in person. Have you been waiting long? I never thought of a trunk. Need a cart for that." His mount, a fine palfrey, stamped a hoof and whipped its cropped tail from side to side.

"Where is my cousin?"

"Who, Biddlesham?" He sounded scornful. "The *master* is away on business. We will not see him for a se'ennight, I expect."

"I–I see," Helen replied.

After a short pause, the horseman said, "I shall return for the trunk tomorrow." He dismounted in one motion and handed her his horse's reins. Helen and the horse regarded one another uncertainly; then the animal lowered its head to graze.

Helen's rescuer hauled her trunk into the brush and concealed it. Helen disliked the idea of leaving her possessions unattended overnight, but she was in no position to object.

"I shall give you a leg up. You will ride behind me."

Helen accepted his outstretched hand and, rising, gazed into his eyes. "I must ride a-pillion?" she said, hating the wobble in her voice. Something about the man sent warning signals racing through her veins. She clutched her cloak at her throat.

"You will be safe."

The padded pillion strapped behind the saddle gave little confidence of solidity, but Helen had no choice. Placing a hand on the man's shoulder, she let him boost her to the seat. The horse shifted beneath her. Her skirts tangled around her legs, and for a flustered moment she sat astride, hands gripping the cantle between her knees.

"Put your feet to the off side; you will find a platform." Once again she detected amusement in the man's voice.

Smoothing her rumpled petticoats, Helen drew a deep breath in an attempt at composure. Her rescuer climbed back into his saddle. His broad back was close; his cape nearly engulfed her. Pushing it aside, she clutched the saddle's high cantle and tried to rise above her circumstances.

Warmth emanated from both man and horse. Helen's nostrils twitched. Along with the expected pungency of horse, leather, and male body, she caught a spicy fragrance that made her think of summer and gardens. "Better hang on to me," he said.

The horse started walking. Helen found it easy enough to balance her body, but her mind reeled with alarming speculations. The man's elegant carriage, cultured voice, and the hint of gallantry in his manner were at odds with his plain garments. Was he, in fact, a highwayman? Was she allowing herself to be abducted? Her head felt light from exhaustion even as a thrill swept through her.

"What is your name?" she demanded.

"Oliver Kirby. This wind is pushing the fog inland. We must hasten." The horse moved abruptly into a canter. Falling backward, Helen grabbed at Kirby's shoulders and hauled herself against him. Terror clutched her throat.

"I told you to hang on. Wrap your arms about my body."

Helen obeyed, keeping her hands fisted. His blowing hair tickled her face. His cape was cold and damp from fog or rain. She wanted to lash out at the man, but she held her tongue. He might decide to set her down beside the road and let her fend for herself. Which would be worse, abduction or desertion?

It was entirely improper for a lady to be so close to a man, on or off horseback. *What would Papa think if he were to see me now?* But the situation was oddly exhilarating—Oliver Kirby's shoulders looked enormous from this angle, and it was not unpleasant to lean against his solid back. He seemed cleaner than most men; she hoped he carried no lice.

Kirby? The name was familiar.

Not far ahead, the road disappeared into a murky gray cloud. A similar cloud of uncertainty oppressed Helen's soul. *Dear Lord, guide me into Your paths. I know not what to do! Are You here with me?*

"So you are the master's cousin?" Oliver Kirby called back.

"Aye, Master Kirby, we share grandparents." She lifted her face and voice against the wind.

"I am not your master; I am but a hired servant. Call me Oliver, as befits my station."

Astonishment rendered Helen silent. A hired servant? Surely not! To address such a man by his given name would seem brazen.

"What of your other family?" he asked.

"My parents died one year since."

"I am sorry. The plague?"

Helen was surprised to hear genuine sympathy in his deep voice. "Nay. They were both stricken in years. I was the child of their old age."

"And you have traveled here alone from. . .London?"

"Surrey. I traveled first on horseback in a caravan, then by river to Thetford. There I hired a coach."

"And the driver left you at the crossroads? The swine."

Helen thought this characterization apt. "Does my cousin often travel on business?"

"He has always liked to travel, both for business and for pleasure. These past few months he travels even more."

Helen found it difficult to imagine anyone traveling for pleasure. "Since his wife Sarah died, you mean. Her death devastated him, I know from his letters. But are there not three children yet living? Surely he must care for them," she protested.

Helen felt Oliver's shoulders move. "Now they have you." The horse slowed to a jog, then a walk. "It becomes too dark for the horse to run. Wrap my cloak about you. I hear your teeth rattle from the cold."

Helen thought he might actually be hearing the pounding of her head or the throbbing of her backside. She was far too chilled to disobey. Enveloped beneath the silk-lined cloak with only her face exposed, she refrained from further conversation.

Mist drifted along the ground. Above, lowering clouds concealed every star. Not one bird chirped a friendly good evening. No foxes yapped; not even a dog barked. Helen heard only the horse's muffled hoofbeats. She could feel Oliver's steady breathing. His back was warm. Helen could not determine which of her reactions to him took precedence, trepidation or security.

An unearthly cry floated through the fog. The horse snorted in response. "No self-respecting highwayman would be out on such a night," Oliver said firmly, as if to convince himself. At first Helen thought he was addressing her, but when he continued speaking she realized that he was talking to the horse. "Almost there. Soon you'll be back in your warm stall. However, you must be patient while I deliver the governess."

What manner of man spoke to a horse as if it could understand?

"We have arrived," Oliver announced.

The horse continued walking up a tree-lined drive, through an open gate, past several outbuildings. Torches lit the approach, yet light shone in only two of the manor house's many glass windows. Helen extricated herself from Oliver's cloak and scanned the looming brick building. "This is my cousin's home?"

Without bothering to answer, he dismounted and reached for her. She placed her hands on his shoulders and swung her legs over the saddle. His gloved hands nearly spanned her waist, sending hot waves of alarm through her body.

Oliver tossed the reins over the horse's neck and gave its haunch a slap. The animal trotted away, disappearing into the mist. "Enter." Taking Helen's arm, Oliver hurried her toward the house.

"Where are the other servants?" Helen planted her feet. "Where have you brought me?" Frost showered from her hood when she gripped it beneath her chin, and her quickened breath added to the surrounding fog.

He made no attempt to conceal his annoyance. "This is Biddlesham Hall, I warrant it. Wherefore no one has come to greet you, I know not. . .although, household matters have been in disarray since the mistress passed on and the house-steward left us. Now if you will but step inside, I shall find a maidservant who will relieve your fears."

Helen lifted her chin and tugged her arm from his grasp. "I am not frightened," she quavered.

"Oh, not in the least." He opened the door and ushered her inside.

The great hall was dark except for glowing coals on the hearth, which did nothing to warm the icy expanse. A portrait hanging over the fireplace fixed Helen with a disdainful stare. She shivered. How could anyone live in such a tomb?

"The fire needs stoking."

Helen followed at his heels to the stone hearth and watched while he blew the fire back to life. When the flames were crackling and bright, Oliver turned to face her, brushing off his breeches. "I'll go find Jenny or Maggie to show you to your room. Or Gretel. She is the housekeeper and a veritable dragon." A smile did little to soften his features.

Still gripping her cloak at her throat, Helen nodded. Frightening though it was to be so close to a man, the surrounding darkness was worse. How she longed for something, anything, familiar and secure!

"Once I find someone to show you to your room, you will feel better."

The words were kind, yet Helen sensed contempt. She crept toward the fire and lifted shaking hands to seek its warmth. "I am grateful. You are very good."

"Sit yourself nigh the fire. I shall return forthwith."

Helen felt panic rise in her throat. "Mayn't I come with you?"

He blinked. "To the kitchen? I suppose you may. You will need to learn your way about the house."

As one in a dream, Helen followed him along a hall to the back door, then along a covered walkway to the detached kitchen. Two elderly servants looked up from their tankards when Oliver entered. "Where you been, Master Oliver?" The plump man sounded well into his cups.

"Don't call me master," Oliver growled. "This is Helen Walker, the new governess. Helen, meet Cook and Gretel. Has anyone prepared the nursery room? Where is Maggie or Jenny?"

The iron-eyed woman called Gretel said, "If you ain't a master no more, you've no call to bark orders like one." She summed up Helen in one glance. "Puny, ain't she? Whiter than a ghost. I forgot she was coming."

A huge mastiff rose from the hearth and shoved its muzzle into Oliver's hand. Helen backed toward the doorway. Her mouth went dry. At any moment the dog might see her.

Oliver patted the animal absently. "Where are the maids?" he asked again.

"This is Friday; the others are gone to town or their homes, as you might recall if you would but settle your mind for a moment."

Oliver rubbed his chin. "Then you must help, Gretel. Helen needs a woman's care lest she take a chill and die ere she claps eyes upon the children."

Gretel's scraggly eyebrows rose. "She's a servant, same as us. Let her make up her own room, I say." She glared at Helen. "You'll find clean bed linens in a chest. The mattress is fresh stuffed."

Helen could not drag her gaze from that dog. Her feet were lead weights. Her mind seemed detached from her body.

Gretel tossed back her drink and wiped her mouth on her own plump shoulder. "If you're hungry, take whatever food you find."

At that moment, the mastiff noticed Helen. With a thunderous bellow, it rushed to investigate.

As from a distance, Helen heard Oliver shout at the dog. Enormous white teeth in a slavering red mouth loomed like approaching death. Her body went slack. First the beamed ceiling then the flagstone flooring flashed before her eyes. Dimly she expected to impact upon the stones, but something broke her fall. A deep voice repeated, "Helen?"

Chapter 2

Helen opened heavy eyelids and blinked. No light met her straining eyes. She lay adrift in total darkness. Panic filled her chest. *God? Are You here?* A quilt fell away when she struggled to sit up. Billowing softness surrounded her.

She sat in a feather bed, fully clothed.

At last, her eyes caught the dim glow from a banked fire. A muffled wail brought her fully awake. Somewhere nearby a child was crying. Helen flung off the quilt and put her feet to the floorboards. Groping with shaking hands, she discovered a bedside table, a tray, and what felt like cold meat and a roll. There it was—the hoped-for candle.

Helen slipped out of bed and knelt on the hearth, touching her candle's wick to the coals. Her heart pounded and her hands trembled—she could scarcely grip the taper. At last the candle flared to life, and Helen pressed it firmly into its holder. Protecting the feeble flame behind her cupped hand, she searched her chamber for a door. Did no one else hear those pitiful cries?

Two doors led from her bedchamber. The weeping came from behind the door nearest the windows. When Helen pushed it open, the creak of its hinges sent chills down her spine.

The stench of bodily waste made her clap a hand over her nose. Disgust overcame her fear of the dark. Did no one empty chamber pots in this house? Steeling herself, Helen lit a sconce on the wall and set her candle on a stool. As light filled the chamber, her knees gathered strength and her breathing deepened.

Three small beds lined the walls, each with a blanket-covered lump. The farthest lump reared up to reveal wide eyes in a round face. As Helen approached the child's bed, two skinny arms reached for her. She dropped to her knees and took the child in her arms. "I am Cousin Helen. Did you have a bad dream?"

The small head nodded against her shoulder. "A bad dog eated me, Cousin Helen."

Helen could relate to that nightmare. She patted the bony little back and encountered one source of the foul odor—the child's bedclothes and shift were soaked. " 'Twas only a dream, little one. I think you will sleep better if we get you into dry clothing and a clean bed." Helen lifted her small charge and stripped the trembling body of its clinging gown. Every rib showed beneath the child's pale skin. Scars dotted her body. Helen's memory began to return. "You are Patsy?"

Patsy nodded. Her lower jaw shook with cold. "I can sleep with Avril."

"Where are your clean clothes?"

Patsy wrapped both arms around her thin body and shivered.

"Patsy, where do you keep your clothes?"

Realizing that the little girl would not or could not give her an answer, Helen began to search the room. She found a clean shift, several sizes too large, on a wall hook. "This will have to do."

"That is Avril's. She will be angry," Patsy stated as Helen enveloped her in the gown. The child's eyes were large and apprehensive in her thin face. Her hair appeared to have been chopped off at chin level.

"We will worry about that tomorrow, little one. Now is the time for good girls to sleep."

"You will be here when I wake?" Patsy reached small fingers to touch Helen's face. "I like you, Cousin Helen."

Helen scooped Patsy into her lap and rocked back and forth. "And I like you. I will be here in the morning. I am your new governess. I will care for you and Avril and your brother from now on." At the moment, the boy's name escaped her.

"My brother is Franklin. Joseph died of the spots. He was my other brother. My mother died too. Our old nurse went away and got married. Do not die, please, Cousin Helen?"

"I shall strive to remain alive for a long while yet, Patsy." Helen began to hum a little tune, pressing her cheek against the child's matted hair.

"I am hungry." Patsy's cheeks were sunken. Helen decided it would be wise to give her food whenever she craved it. She led Patsy into the other chamber and allowed the child to eat heartily from the loaded tray on the bedside table. After building up her fire and setting lighted candles about the room, Helen nibbled on a date and watched the little girl drain a cup of milk.

Her stomach nicely rounded, Patsy popped a thumb into her mouth as Helen carried her to Avril's bed. The child was asleep before Helen tucked her in. Avril frowned in her sleep and rolled toward the wall. The older girl's hair was as tangled and dirty as Patsy's—shorn during the recent bout of illness, Helen surmised. Had no one cared for these children since their mother's death?

Helen snuffed the light and returned to her chamber. She blew out her candles, leaving only one lit beside the bed. After removing her gown and petticoats, she crawled beneath her quilt, mentally listing the changes she would make on the morrow. "Dear Lord, give me strength to bring Your glory and love into this house," she whispered. "And please help me to endure this wretched darkness."

Morning light awakened Helen. Delighted to see streaks of sunshine on her bedclothes, she climbed out of bed, pulled back the heavy draperies, and let light stream into her chamber. After stretching her stiff arms and shoulders, she poured water into her basin and began to splash her face. "Good morning, Lord Jesus."

She unbraided her hair and began to comb out its tangled length. Last night's fog had made ringlets out of the fringe on her forehead and around her ears. Helen tried to comb them out, creating puffs of curls. Lacking a mirror, she could only feel the disarray she had caused.

Someone knocked at the door. Probably a maid. "You may enter," Helen called.

Silence. Curious, she opened the door, then slammed it shut. Waiting in the hall was the man with the scornful smile and hawk nose. She had just shocked the life out of him, no doubt, answering the door in her smock, with her hair hanging loose! "One moment, please."

She pulled on her wrinkled gown. Tossing aside an assortment of petticoats, she hunted for her cap. *Where was I when I took it off?* Pausing abruptly, she wrinkled her brow. *I don't remember coming to this room last night. How did I get here?*

Another knock at the door. "I have your trunk," he explained in an overly patient tone.

The cap was nowhere in sight. Helen sighed. *I recall there was a huge dog. . . Or did I dream it? Or was that Patsy's dream?*

The next knock was harder.

Helen lifted the latch and pulled the door wide open.

"God give you good day, Helen Walker. I trust you slept well after your disturbing experience."

As usual, his deep voice hinted at derision. Helen's face burned. "My disturbing. . . ? Oh, aye. Thank you, um. . ."

"Oliver," he supplied. "I promised to bring your trunk today. Where would you like it placed?"

She stepped back and fixed her gaze upon the floor. "Against the wall between the windows, if you please. You must have risen before dawn. You are exceeding kind." She could not bring herself to address him by his first name. Did governesses often allow male servants to enter their bedchambers? Helen found the situation uncomfortable.

He hefted the trunk, crossed the small chamber without bumping into any furniture, lowered the trunk, and shoved it against the wall. "Is there anything else you'll be needing?"

Helen remained near the open door. She tried to sound friendly yet indifferent. "I'm sure I shall straightaway learn to feel at home here now that I have my trunk. It contains not only my clothing, but also my Bible and other items that belonged to my parents. Everything I own is packed inside."

"I, too, cherish a Bible among my belongings. Its translation was one of the few beneficial acts our late king accomplished. Do you read it often?"

She was startled into looking at him. "Every day. Are you a disciple of Jesus Christ? I mean, do you truly know God?"

This time Oliver lowered his gaze. "I do. Knowing Him is my only boast."

"And does the vicar in this parish teach from the Scriptures?"

"He does. There are many true believers in the community." Oliver shifted uneasily. A flush stained his high cheekbones. "You find it difficult to believe that I am a Christian."

Helen floundered for a moment. Ignoring his comment, she tried to speak brightly. "I must confess, I feared that I would find no one in East Anglia with whom to fellowship, but God has provided for my every need just as He promised. Please accept my apology. I was uncivil to you last night. Had I known you were a Christian, I would not have mistrusted you so."

Helen could not read his expression.

"It is I who should ask pardon," he said softly. "I should have perceived that you were nigh unto swooning and been more solicitous of your welfare."

"Swooning?"

He shook his head slowly, his eyes searching her face. "You do not remember?"

Helen swallowed hard. "Wha–what is it I should remember?"

The door to the nursery creaked open, and Patsy staggered into the room, rubbing her eyes. She lifted the hem of her borrowed gown to keep from tripping over it.

Oliver greeted her. "What have we here? Good morrow, little lady."

Helen would never have believed the man could speak in such affectionate tones. He seemed to welcome the child as a reprieve.

Patsy blinked up at him. "Uncle Oliver, wherefore are you here?" Then she caught sight of Helen. Her face lit up, and she dashed across the room to fling herself into Helen's open arms. "You're not a dream!"

"No, Darling, I am real," Helen assured the child, holding her close.

"Did you bring Cousin Helen for me, Uncle Oliver?" Patsy twisted around in Helen's arms to inquire. "She says she came to take care of us. I think God must have sent her. I prayed for a new mother, although Avril told me not to. Maybe Father will marry her and we will be a family again."

"This cannot be, Patsy, for I am your close relation," Helen hastened to inform the child. "Cousins may not wed by order of the church."

Patsy's face fell. "But I do so want a mother."

"I understand. Would you like to hear me read a story? I have a Bible in my trunk. It has the most wonderful stories you ever heard."

"I will take my leave, Ladies. Enjoy your cousin while you may, Patsy."

On that remark, Oliver closed the door behind him.

❧

Jenny entered the kitchen, carrying an empty tray. "Those children were eating like trenchermen when I left the nursery. Must have worked up appetites with all the screeching and howling that went on this morn." After discarding the tray on a worktable, she ladled pottage into a bread bowl and joined the other servants for the noon meal.

"She's a glutton for work, this governess," Maggie complained around a mouthful of pottage. "Such a wee thing to be spouting orders like a queen!"

"And how she did handle that Franklin when he tried to escape the bathin'!" Jenny added, giving a snort of laughter. "Took the lad by the back of his neck, she did, and popped him in the tub pretty as you please! Not even the late mistress could make that one do as he was told. I wonder how long it will be before the young knave starts his usual tricks and makes this governess wish she had never heard of Biddlesham Hall."

Gretel frowned and shook her gray head. "Weak as the children be, she'll be the death of them with this washing and this opening of windows. The master will return to find his offspring dead of lung fever, for certain."

"I do wonder what he will say," one of the gardeners agreed. "However, this Helen be a friendly enough wench. Leaned out her window to compliment me on the gardens today whilst I was trimming topiaries. Not above her station, that one."

Jenny scoffed. "So you say! Thinks she's mistress of the hall, she does. How my arms ache from toting water up and down, up and down so's she could wash."

Maggie laughed, displaying gaps between her yellowed teeth. "Puts me in mind of Oliver and his fancy for soap and water!" She dug an elbow into Oliver's ribs. He continued eating.

Jenny ranted on. "She had me digging through chests and trunks for clean clothing. Says she is taking the children out for fresh air. As if the nursery ain't awash with cold air from the windows hanging open all the day!"

"She will be good for them."

All eyes turned to Oliver. "What did you say?" Gretel demanded.

He rose and tossed his soggy bread bowl out the window to the waiting chickens and geese. Eyeing the other servants coldly, he said, "Helen is exactly what those children need—someone to love them and give them hope for the future. Attend upon me now: We must keep Diocletian out of Helen's way until the master returns. Quincy," he addressed the under-groom, "I place you in charge of the dog. Do you hear?"

Quincy nodded.

Gretel gave a cackle. "Gone soft on her, has our master-of-horse. Today I asked her how she liked being put to bed by Oliver, and she looked nigh unto swooning all over again."

Laughter rippled about the table, then suddenly hushed. Oliver cast a glare around the room. After one slap of his gloves against the tabletop, he strode outside into the brilliant sunlight.

Speculative glances and whispers followed his exit.

Helen paused to pray before selecting a pheasant leg from the noon trays. "Why did you do that?" Avril demanded, her gray eyes sullen.

"Why did I pray? I always thank the Lord for His provision. Look at this fine meal! Certainly we have much for which to thank Him." Helen smiled at the eight year old but received a blank stare in return.

Avril hunched her shoulders and munched on a crusty loaf. Soap and water had revealed a pretty child with pearly skin, luminous eyes, flyaway brown hair, and an aura of despair.

Franklin had not spoken a word since his enforced bath. Chewing with no effort to keep his mouth closed, he consumed only a few bites of meat and a handful of raisins.

Beside Helen, four-year-old Patsy gnawed on a cold meat pasty. Her exuberant hugs had lightened Helen's burden several times that morning.

Exhausted by the battle of wills and the physical labor, Helen began to doubt her own judgment. She now had three clean charges and a tidy nursery, but she feared she had created at least one lifelong enemy. Franklin's gaze held even more venom than Avril's, and the servants had seemed less than pleased by her requests for their extra labor. Had she not been the master's cousin, she suspected they would have refused outright.

To make matters worse, her thoughts kept returning to Oliver Kirby. He was, by his own admission, a fellow believer, yet his presence inspired in Helen a confusing blend of admiration and apprehension. Not that Scripture prohibited manliness while encouraging godliness; Helen had simply never before encountered a man possessed of both qualities in full measure.

If only she were well enough acquainted with Gretel to know whether or not to believe the housekeeper's astonishing report. Whenever she tried to envision her unconscious self in Oliver's arms, her mind flitted away in denial while her face grew hot.

Brushing her hands on her apron, Helen rose, strolled to the window, and looked down upon the terraced garden. Raised beds and pebbled walkways, paths that disappeared beneath bowers of interwoven tree branches, and a sunlit sweep of lawn reached as far as the distant woods. Pressing both palms against her warm cheeks, Helen drank in the perfume of evergreens and herbs.

Her heart expanded. "Thank You, Lord Jesus," she whispered. "If the children can learn to love me, I shall be content to live here. Please help me to find my place."

She turned back to the children with a bright expression. "After luncheon we shall walk in the gardens. It is a fine day, and we all need fresh air."

Chapter 3

One sunny afternoon more than a week after her arrival, Helen headed for the stables. Finding a groom cleaning stalls, she inquired, "Where might I find Oliver Kirby?"

The young man removed his cap. "In the pasture by the orchard, training the master's green colt. I'm Quincy the under-horseman, just so's you know. Your company will pleasure Oliver. He watches you take the children out to play every day. He says he's watching the children, but I know better."

Helen didn't like the way he smiled. "Thank you. Good day." Lifting her skirts, she picked her way through the stable yard, scattering chickens and ducks.

She met Oliver on his way back to the stable. Helen maintained a respectful distance from his lively mount. Oliver had removed his doublet, wearing only a full-sleeved white shirt above his loose breeches and cuffed boots. Although his hat bore no plume, he resembled the most dashing of cavaliers. Helen was uncertain which intimidated her more, Oliver or the horse.

"Braveheart, meet another valorous soul." Patting the colt's sweaty neck, Oliver grinned at Helen.

"I have come to enlist your aid," Helen announced in a nervous tremolo.

"Indeed? Where are the children?"

"With the head gardener. Guy is teaching them to plant parsnips. I would not leave them alone."

"My mind is now at rest. In what manner may I help you, Helen Walker? Will you climb up behind me here on Braveheart? We can better converse while in close proximity."

Wishing she could smack him, Helen backed away. "I will walk." She fell into step beside the tall horse, keeping a wary distance. "I find that the children have few outdoor playthings," she began.

"Franklin cares little for sport. Nevertheless, I will find a ball for you, and we can obtain hoops from the cooper. Is this the aid you require?" He sounded disappointed.

"Cousin Helen!"

Helen turned to see Avril running up the path. "Look what I found in the kitchen garden!" She held out a rock. "It has gold streaks in it. Guy says it isn't gold, but how would a gardener know? I want my doll to have it."

Helen heard stamping hooves and snorting behind her. Gripping Avril by the shoulders, she hurried the girl toward the gardens. "That would be nice, Dear. Now return to Guy—he must wonder what became of you."

Avril peered around Helen. "Franklin says he will ride away on Braveheart someday."

Squeals and grunts from the horse roused Helen's curiosity. She turned to find Oliver wrestling with the rearing animal. Hoofs, tail, and powerful quarters whirled past her at close range.

"Off the path!" Oliver ordered.

Helen pressed against a hedge while Braveheart thundered past. Avril sighed from the shelter of Helen's arm. "Is he not magnificent?"

"Aye, and his steed is fine also," Helen breathed.

❧

"I beg pardon for Braveheart's misconduct," Oliver said while hanging the colt's bridle upon a hook. "He is but newly broken to ride and finds it arduous to submit his will unto mine."

Still somewhat breathless, Helen simply returned his smile. Oliver touched her elbow and escorted her from the stable. "Avril is like unto a different child since your arrival."

Helen avoided looking at her companion. "Aye, she has become a veritable magpie. Poor child—how she mourns her hair! I assured her that it will grow as does her strength. The girls enjoy being clean and neat, and they love to learn and hear stories."

Oliver noticed an omission. "Has Franklin given you trouble?"

"I know not how to think of him. He keeps to himself. unless provoking one of his sisters. The child never smiles or laughs. He seems unnatural. Does he talk to you?"

"Seldom. Since Sarah's death he has retreated into himself. Does he respond to your attentions?"

"Embracing him is like embracing a stone. And one more thing. . ."

"Aye?" Oliver encouraged.

For once Helen did not feel as if Oliver were inwardly ridiculing her. She stopped and faced him, studying her hands. "I have discovered. . .problems in the nursery. Once the ropes supporting my bed gave way suddenly. One night there was little water in my pitcher—it was all on the foot of the bed. Once I found my clothing strewn about the room. I hate to suspect one of the maids of such childish tricks, but I also dread to believe that Franklin would be so cruel."

"Someone should have warned you. Be aware that Franklin has a knack for finding a weakness and exploiting it. If it helps at all, know that I am on your side in this conflict."

Helen smiled and looked up. "You have no idea how much it helps! I have felt alone here, with no one to pray with or talk to except the children."

Oliver regarded her for a long moment. His lashes were so thick and dark she could scarcely see his eyes. "You can talk with God."

"I do. He is my constant confidant."

"I believe you. But have you ever before confided in a man, Helen?"

"Only my father."

Oliver's lips twitched. "I thought as much. You are as jumpy as a fawn whenever a man approaches. Or is it only me?"

"I—I don't know what you mean." Helen slipped her

hand up to finger her neckcloth.

"Even as you illustrate my point." Oliver caught her fidgeting fingers. "Do you suspect me of dire intentions? A man tires of being regarded as a ravening wolf."

Helen tugged at her hand, her gaze fixed upon the brown hollow at the base of his throat. He allowed her fingers to slip through his grasp. "Why must you make sport of me? I cannot be at ease around someone who thinks ill of me no matter what I do or say!" Helen blurted while backing away.

She turned and ran toward the house.

Two days later, a breeze rippled the surface of the lake, sending sparkles of sunlight into Helen's eyes. Four white swans floated near a stand of cattails and rushes, ignoring the children's attempts to entice them with bread. Wildflowers carpeting the lakeshore shaded up a knoll into the verdant lawn. New leaves clothed overhanging tree boughs.

"Altogether lovely!" Helen breathed deeply. "This is my favorite artwork—God's masterpiece of creation."

"You smile a lot, Cousin Helen," Avril observed. "Do you find everything comical?"

Helen couldn't restrain a chuckle. "Not everything. But I do find joy and amusement in many things. The Bible tells us to 'rejoice evermore.' God wants His children to be joyful."

"He must be pleased with you," Patsy said, bouncing in Helen's lap. "Except that you're not a children."

Helen hugged the little girl. "In God's eyes, I will always be a child."

"I guess He's pretty old," Patsy stated.

Helen lay back on the grass and laughed aloud. "Patsy, dearest, you're a treasure."

Franklin knelt on the lakeshore, poking with a stick at something down in the water like any other nine-year-old boy might. But, unlike a normal boy, he did not join the conversation.

"Cousin Helen, are you going to marry our father? He said he would find us another mother."

Helen answered the challenge in Avril's eyes. "Your father asked me to come because you children need someone to care for you. I came because I need a family to love since my parents died and left me alone. The Lord provided for everyone's needs at once. If your father does choose another wife, I'm sure he will marry a woman who will love his children."

"If he marries again, will you have to go away?"

"Let's not worry about the future, Avril."

"Father doesn't like us since Mother died. Uncle Oliver plays with us sometimes, though," Patsy announced. "He throwed the ball to me yesterday, and I catched it bunches of times. Franklin said I never could."

Pleased that the subject of Oliver had arisen, Helen tried to question delicately. "Why do you call Oliver 'Uncle'?"

"He is our uncle," Avril said. "Our mother was his sister."

"He is your—" Helen was too surprised to continue. No wonder Oliver was so obviously a gentleman. No wonder "Kirby" sounded familiar—it had been Sarah

Biddlesham's maiden name. From everything Helen could recall hearing, Cousin Cyril had married into a propertied family of good repute. She longed to ask why Oliver now worked as horseman for his brother-in-law.

"May we wade in the lake?" Franklin asked abruptly. His knees were damp, and mud smeared his jerkin. "I want to catch tadpoles."

Helen hated to disappoint the boy the first time he requested anything of her, but. . .

"What's the matter, Cousin Helen? Don't you like tadpoles? They grow up into frogs." Patsy patted Helen's hand. "Franklin likes to catch frogs and toads and newts."

Helen struggled to turn her grimace into a smile. "How interesting! However, I fear it is too cold for wading as yet." Casting about for an alternative, she brightened. "You could climb these marvelous oaks." She plopped Patsy upon the grass and leaped to her feet, brushing grass clippings from her skirts and peeling off her gloves.

The children stared as Helen patted a sprawling oak's lowest branch. "Come," she coaxed. "Have you never climbed a tree? I often climbed trees during my childhood. From the branches of this one, I'm sure you could touch the sky!"

Helen helped Patsy find a secure place on one of the tree's massive support branches, while Franklin and Avril headed for a nearby oak. "Is this not enjoyable?"

Patsy grinned. "I'm a squirrel." She wrapped both legs around the limb.

"You're a bright-eyed red squirrel with tufted ears."

Helen patted the child's knee and savored Patsy's adoring smile.

"Cousin Helen, look at me!" A call came from the next tree.

Helen shaded her eyes and gazed at Avril. "My, but you're high like a bird on the wing!" she said. The girl smiled in satisfaction from a perch no more than ten feet from the ground.

Franklin appeared determined to out-daring-do his sister. Helen saw his foot slip and gasped inwardly, but the boy caught his balance and continued upward.

"Franklin, that is high enough. Can you touch the clouds from there?" Helen tried to keep alarm from her voice. "Franklin, please stop climbing now. Franklin?"

The boy ignored her. At last he settled into a fork between branches and hollered down, "Look at me!"

Helen forced admiration into her voice. "Franklin, you must be higher than the church tower! Can you see all the way to Cambridge?"

He laughed. "I can see all the way to France."

Studying his position, Helen nibbled a fingernail. "Maybe you'd better come down now. Let's explore the maze."

Avril obediently slid toward the tree's trunk. A gust of wind made the trees groan and sway, leaves aflutter. Helen heard Franklin give a yelp. "Are you all right up there?"

Not a word in reply.

"Franklin, do you need help getting down?" Helen lifted Patsy from her perch and, with the child on her hip, trotted toward the other oak.

Avril scooted down the trunk and landed with a thump on her backside. Hopping up, she brushed herself off and joined Helen. Her cheeks and eyes glowed. "What else may we do, Cousin Helen?"

"We must wait for your brother before we try anything else," Helen said. She peered upward, shading her eyes. The topmost branches swayed back and forth. "Franklin?" Moving to the other side of the tree, she caught sight of his face. His eyes were squeezed shut. Both arms and legs gripped the tree. "Can you hear me?"

No response. The sisters echoed her call. Their shrill voices filled the air. "Come down, Franklin!"

"You girls stay here with your brother while I go for help," Helen ordered quietly.

Franklin had sharp ears. "No! Don't leave me!" he screeched.

"I saw Guy, the gardener, mowing the grass only a short distance from here," Helen tried to assure him.

Franklin shook his head. "You can't go; I'll fall. You must come and catch me."

"But someone must get help. I cannot climb a tree!" Helen protested.

"Help me!"

The panic in his voice prevailed over fear and propriety. "Avril, find someone to help."

Avril nodded. "Do you want me to take Patsy?"

"Aye." Catching hold of a stout branch, Helen swung into the tree and began to work her way upward. "Hurry, girls!" Tree-climbing was not as easy as she remembered.

Her shoes slipped on the rough bark. Her cumbersome skirts snagged on twigs and bark.

A stout branch beneath Franklin's perch supported Helen's weight. Gripping another branch with one hand, she stood on tiptoe and touched the boy's ankle. "You could slide into my arms, Franklin. I am here to catch you."

Freckles looked dark upon his white cheeks. His face scrunched into a mass of wrinkles. "You're too small. You would drop me!"

"I am stronger than I look," Helen said.

"Helen?" A deep voice inquired from below.

Helen looked down. The world tilted. Oliver Kirby's upturned face appeared distant, and the girls' faces were small dots.

"I'm coming up."

Helen tried to focus on a distant hill, but that one downward glance had destroyed her equilibrium. No wonder poor Franklin was afraid to move! "Dear Lord God, please strengthen our fainting hearts and bring us safely back to earth," she prayed aloud. "Thank You for sending Oliver to our aid."

Closing her eyes, she slithered her feet along the branch until she could hug the main bough. Another gust of wind made the tree wave and groan. Helen's groan followed shortly thereafter.

"I'm right beneath you." Oliver said. "Can you move to that fork in the branch there? Otherwise I must climb around you to reach Franklin."

"I can move." Helen extended one shaky foot and tried to release her death-grip on the bough. Oliver guided her foot to a safe place, then shinnied up far enough to hold her waist while she shifted her weight to the other branches. He held her arm even after she was securely seated.

"I will be all right now. Please help Franklin."

"You are certain?" His fingers squeezed gently. Today he wore no gloves. His sleeves were rolled up, revealing hairy forearms. Resisting the urge to grab hold around his neck, Helen nodded.

Through a haze of dread, Helen watched Oliver coax Franklin into his arms. With the boy hanging like a sack on his back, Oliver climbed down the tree. Although Helen could not distinguish Oliver's words, his kindly voice gave her comfort.

"Come down, Cousin Helen. Franklin is safe now." Avril's shout penetrated Helen's fears.

Four faces looked pale against the green grass far below. Helen felt a tear spill over and hated herself. "I can't!" she whispered.

Oliver gathered the children around. Helen opened her eyes in time to see her three charges dash across the lawn, giggling and shouting. Patsy tripped over her dress and fell but she hopped up without a cry and chased the others.

Oliver scrambled up the tree. "I sent the children to gather wildflowers," he confessed while still several branches beneath her. She noticed how he avoided glancing upward lest he inadvertently look up her skirts. "I thought you might find it easier to descend without an audience. Are you injured, Helen?"

"No." A sob escaped. "I am a fool."

"I suspected as much," he said in that bantering tone

she despised. "How do you come to acknowledge it?" He panted slightly as he pulled himself to her level. His hands each gripped a branch, one on either side of her legs. His hair glistened with strands of gold and silver where sunbeams touched it. Deep lines framed his mouth.

Helen wiped away a tear. "I did well until I looked down."

He chuckled, showing white teeth. "You will notice that I avoid looking down. Such height would frighten any person of sense. Franklin chose the largest tree in the park for his first attempt at climbing."

"The fault is mine. I encouraged them to climb. I thought it would be good exercise." Knowing that sooner or later Oliver would have to touch her, Helen felt her heart rate increasing. His kindness was more unnerving than his derision.

"And so it is. You are the best thing to come to this manor in many a long year, Helen."

Doubting his sincerity, Helen looked into his eyes. They were blue, she realized. How dark they had seemed beneath his thick brows! Beautiful eyes in an otherwise hawkish face.

Releasing her grip on the branches, she reached a hand toward him. His palm was warm and rough. One of her feet slipped, but Oliver caught her by the elbow. "Take care. If you fall, I am here to catch you."

Oliver coaxed her to follow his lead. His arms and legs were like a safety net around her. He seldom touched her, but she felt his body heat at all times, he was so close. Helen frequently clutched at his arms and found herself leaning in order to feel his solid chest against her back.

"Hold to the tree, Helen. It is stronger than I," he reminded her more than once. Helen began to wonder if she were dreaming.

At last Oliver hopped to the ground and reached both arms toward her. Interpreting this as an invitation to jump, she let go of the tree and dropped. Oliver managed to break her fall, but her impetus landed him flat upon the grass. Locked together, they rolled over like a log and came to rest side by side. Helen stared into his eyes. "I beg your pardon!"

Oliver stared back. Silence stretched long until Helen felt her face grow hot. She attempted to get up, but Oliver's encircling arms restrained her as if she were a butterfly, using just enough force to keep her from fluttering away. She placed both hands against his chest, yet she did not push. His heart pounded against her palms.

Then he released her and quickly stood, facing away from her with his arms crossed. "Here come the children. I must warn you that Franklin will not like your knowing about his fear."

"And I am not pleased that he knows about my fear," Helen admitted shakily. "I hope this is not something he can use against me."

Laughing and chattering, two little girls trotted across the green lawn. "We brought you flowers, Cousin Helen!"

Avril dropped daisies into Helen's lap. Patsy showered her with dandelions and tiny blue flowers that had already wilted beyond recognition. Franklin approached more slowly, wearing a smirk that should have put Helen on her guard.

"Let's make daisy chains," Helen suggested. Crossing her legs to make a table of her lap, she began to sort through the flowers. She hoped the children had not witnessed that embrace. *Did it really happen or did I dream it?*

Oliver turned. "I must return to work. I am pleased to see you and the children enjoying these gardens. I have often lamented the fact that only Diocletian and I appeared to appreciate their beauty. The gardeners work hard to keep this place up."

Helen scanned her surroundings and slowly shook her head—the brilliant hues of spring bulbs, the pale green of new leaves like a mist upon every tree, the smooth lawns. " 'Enjoying' scarcely begins to express how such beauty affects me. This place is a tiny foretaste of heaven."

Looking up at Oliver, she added, "Many thanks for your aid, and God be with you, Oliver Kirby." His name was pleasant upon her lips.

"And with you, Helen Walker. Helping you affords me unparalleled diversion." His eyes twinkled, but this time Helen did not mind.

"Did Avril run all the way to the stables to find you?" She suddenly thought to ask.

"I was working with the colt again in the pasture just beyond the fence," Oliver explained. "I heard the shouting and came to investigate."

"Do you need help, Uncle Oliver?" Franklin asked.

Oliver gave Helen an inquiring glance. "Do you mind if Franklin joins me for an hour or two?"

"Not at all." To Helen's amazement, Franklin talked animatedly until he and Oliver disappeared around a hedge. "Does Franklin often help your uncle?" she asked.

Avril shook her head. "He doesn't help anyone, ever. But he likes horses."

Helen smiled while threading one daisy's stem through another. This day was a tremendous answer to prayer, even to prayers she had never dared utter.

"I like playing in the garden, Cousin Helen. May we play here every day?" Patsy tucked dandelions among Helen's braids.

Helen felt as if her chest might burst with the fullness of joy. "Aye, every sunny day!"

Avril chuckled. "You're making God happy again," she said. "You make Uncle Oliver smile. I wonder if you can make Father smile. He hasn't smiled much since our mother died."

Helen touched the girl's slender arm. "I can't make anyone smile, Avril. Only God can put joy into people's hearts."

Avril shook her head. "I still think He uses you to do it, Cousin Helen."

Chapter 4

S leep well, children." Helen kissed each child in turn. The girls returned her hugs, but Franklin endured his kiss and hug stoically. After blowing out the candles, Helen closed the nursery door and leaned against it. Tonight her room seemed friendlier, even though shadows flickered in every corner. The day's sunshine, flowers, and fresh air lingered within Helen's soul.

A heavy knock at her chamber door brought her back to the present with a start. "Master Cyril has returned. He requests your presence in his drawing room." It was Gretel's voice.

"Cyril has returned?" The man must have sneaked into his house like a thief, Helen decided. Although now that she thought about it, there had been unusual commotion in the house while she prepared the children for bed. "He wants to meet me tonight?"

"He awaits you now."

"I shall come presently." With trembling hands Helen smoothed her hair—picking out a few wilted dandelions—inspected her face, removed her apron, and straightened her skirts. At last her questions about Cyril Biddlesham would be answered.

She opened her chamber door to find Gretel waiting. By the light of the housekeeper's candle, the two women traversed a long hallway past the stairwell, past rows of Biddlesham family portraits, to the other wing of the house. Gretel rapped on a door and pushed it open, stepping aside to allow Helen's entry.

The chamber was well lighted, although smoke and a sickly-sweet odor filled the air. As Helen entered, her cousin rose from a chair, then bowed over her hand. "Well met, Cousin Helen." Looking down from his considerable height, he smiled, crinkling his blue eyes. A pointed beard concealed his chin while his cheeks were clean-shaven. Dark hair curled softly on his shoulders with one beribboned lock hanging upon his broad chest. The froth of lace edging his falling band collar and the gold brocade of his doublet merely emphasized his air of romantic masculinity.

"Cousin Cyril," Helen murmured. She saw a remarkable resemblance to Avril in his countenance. Absorbed in her examination of his features, she forgot to remove her hand from his grasp. One of his brows lifted, and his moustache twitched.

A rumbling growl stopped Helen's breath. Turning her face toward the fireplace, she beheld the mastiff of her nightmares standing on the hearth. Its dripping flews quivered to reveal ivory tusks.

"Down, Boy. Cousin Helen is family." Cyril patted her stiffened shoulder. "Never fear; Diocletian will not harm you. Reach out to him."

Helen could not move. Hackles bristling along a spine the height of Helen's waist, the dog held her in a fixed stare.

"Are you deaf, Child? Show the dog that you do not fear him, or he will despise you."

"But I do f–f–fear. . . ," Helen faltered.

"Nonsense. A nobler beast than Diocletian never lived. Reach out your hand and touch him."

Silently claiming every protection promise in Scripture, Helen obeyed. As soon as her fingers stroked his head, Diocletian relaxed. His heavy tail wagged, and his ears drooped.

Thank You, Lord.

"Now come and sit across from me here before you topple to the floor." Cyril indicated a second carved oak chair. "Tales of your endeavors have already reached mine ears. Is it true that you applied soap to my son?" Cyril took a clay pipe from the mantelshelf, sucked on it, and puffed smoke.

Trying not to cough, Helen settled into the chair. "Aye, Cousin."

"You must possess more fortitude than is now in evidence. Although, it is true, Franklin is a weakly child." A melancholy expression filled Cyril's eyes. "His brother was robust and intelligent, a true Biddlesham. If illness can take a boy like my Joseph, I hold little hope that the others will survive to become adults. However, I am thankful you have come to take charge of them while they live. Since your father was a man of the cloth, I'm sure you will help prepare their souls for eternity."

Helen scooted forward on the chair until her feet

touched the floor. "I see no reason why your children should not live to maturity, barring some unforeseen illness. I shall certainly strive to train them in godly ways and guide them into all truth. They are intelligent, resourceful children, especially Franklin. I believe that—"

Cyril continued as if she had not spoken. "For some reason, we have always had difficulty keeping a nurse or governess in our employ longer than the requisite year. Perhaps the problem is our remote location. . ." His voice trailed off, and he sucked on the pipe again.

Helen dared to break the silence. "I believe it would benefit Franklin to be oft in your company. The boy craves the guidance of a man. I will bring the children to call upon you each day at whatever time you choose."

Cyril puffed for a full minute before replying. "I have no desire to attend my offspring every day. It would, perhaps, be advisable for me to observe their progress each week. Let us say you bring them to me here in my drawing room for a brief interview each Saturday evening. I do wish to see them tomorrow morning, however, to inspect the progress you have made during my absence. I plan to marry soon; I am newly betrothed to the widow of a wool merchant from Ipswich. Courtship and business will demand the majority of my time in these coming months."

"You—you plan to marry? You never wrote of this intent. . ."

Cyril's lips twitched. "I was unaware of it myself until last week. The bewitching creature has convinced me that man was not meant to be alone."

"I see." Concern for the children filled Helen's

thoughts. Would the "bewitching creature" make a good stepmother?

Movement at her side startled Helen. Pressing one hand to her heart, she stared down into beseeching eyes. Diocletian laid his black muzzle upon her skirt, leaving streaks of drool upon the fabric. In her peripheral vision Helen saw his tail waving, but she could not lift her gaze from the dog's face.

"Hmm." Cyril sounded mildly pleased. "You have found favor in Diocletian's eyes—a rare honor. He must recognize a relative; there is a Biddlesham look about you. I dimly recall your mother, my aunt. She lived here until her marriage—a comely woman. Your father was a diminutive, bookish sort. Her acceptance of his suit puzzled the family. But then, in neither a vicar nor a governess is height a requirement." A sardonic smile curled his moustache.

Helen laid a trembling hand on the dog's head and saw the thick tail increase its tempo. A pink tongue, nearly as large as Helen's hand, swiped over the dog's lips and nose. The head on Helen's lap felt as heavy as Patsy's entire body. Although the hair on Diocletian's head was rough, his ears were warm velvet.

Perhaps her cousin was right and this dog named for a cruel Roman posed no threat. It was difficult to believe that a body so large, possessed of such teeth, could contain a gentle heart.

She spoke quietly. "My parents loved each other deeply—"

"Your parents married late in life." Cyril dropped into his chair and stretched his long legs toward the hearth.

Firelight reflected from his forehead. Helen now noticed his receding hairline and the lines framing his mouth and eyes. She heard the creak of stays whenever he moved.

"And I was their only child. We had a happy home in Wyttlethorpe parish. My father was schoolmaster as well as vicar, so I received an excellent education."

"The quality of your letters told me as much. I trust you will pass on that education to my progeny as long as you are in my employ. I do not wish them to attend the school in Biddlesham Fen village. It has been my observation that congregating in masses brings on illness. My apothecary advises keeping the children apart from others of their age and feeding large quantities of white meats."

"Milk and eggs?" Helen translated the term in puzzlement. "What benefit does he hope to acquire from such diet?"

"Their good health." Cyril puffed rapidly at his pipe. "Have a care; I do not relish being questioned, Cousin." Giving her a sidelong glance, he suddenly asked, "Have you seen our haunting spirit?"

Helen's blood ran cold. "Did you say. . . ?" Her spine stiffened. "Nonsense. I do not believe in ghosts."

"Be that as it may, an apparition walks the grounds of Biddlesham Hall. Some say the specter is my grandfather who walked every evening in the gardens. Since he is your ancestor as well, he might appear to you." A glitter in Cyril's eye told Helen that he baited her.

"Taunt me not with spectral tales. I am no child to be tormented so."

He grinned. "You seem a veritable infant, with those

trusting eyes and dimpled cheeks."

"I am twenty-eight years of age and no babe," Helen snapped.

His eyes flashed sparks. "And I say you are a child. I warned you not to question me. Have done with you!" With a dismissing wave, he slumped back in his chair and puffed smoke.

Helen slid from beneath the mastiff's jowls. "Good even, Cousin Cyril."

He glowered into the fire. "Sleep well, Cousin."

The dog escorted Helen to the door. Although she recognized the acceptance in his drooping eyes, the animal's presence made her knees go weak. "Good even, Diocletian," she murmured, reaching out to give his broad head a farewell pat. *You, at least, are a gentleman. Who behaved like a child just now? Not I and not you.*

"Take the dog down to the kitchen when you go," Cyril ordered without turning around.

After shooting a glare at her lounging cousin's back, Helen ventured to touch the dog's head once more. "Come, Diocletian."

The mastiff's head and tail lifted, and he rushed into the hallway, nearly knocking Helen off her feet. She heard soft laughter from the drawing room as she pulled the door shut. The passage was dark and silent, lighted only by an occasional wall sconce. Although she knew that men's disembodied spirits did not walk the earth— such a thing was entirely unbiblical—Helen found that her imagination had a will of its own. Lifting her chin, she swallowed her panic and trotted past all those closed doors toward the stairwell.

The dog waited at the back door when Helen caught up with him. "Here you are," she gasped. Diocletian was reassuringly solid and alive beneath her hands. He willingly escorted her to the out-buildings, waiting politely while she opened the doors.

A roaring fire warmed the kitchen. Cook lounged at the table with both feet on a bench. He gave her a glance, then looked again from Helen to the dog. He exclaimed something unintelligible as his feet hit the floor, and Helen wondered if the man might be foreign.

"Does the dog stay with you, Cook?" Helen asked.

"But the dog. . . We are to keep the dog away from you since he makes you swoon! How is it that you walk with him so calm?"

"My cousin introduced me to Diocletian tonight." Helen patted the dog once more, feeling pride in her accomplishment.

"Ah." Cook still looked mystified. "Master Oliver will not believe me when I tell him." His jowls flopped as he shook his head.

"You say the dog made me swoon? I do not recall. . ." Helen wrinkled her brow in the effort to remember.

" 'Twas the night you came. Master Oliver caught and carried you away. No one else was to touch! Romantic, eh? All the servants talk about how he watches over the little governess and defends you from harm. Always he keeps to himself, but now he finds reason to be near you. A good man he is for a good woman. It gives him shame that King James stole away his lands." Glancing furtively about,

Cook crossed himself and winked soberly at Helen.

Smiling to hide her confusion, Helen excused herself and backed out the door.

Once in her chamber, she prepared for bed, panting from her frenzied run up the dark stairs. When her dress and petticoats lay in a heap on the floor, she splashed her face and neck with water from the basin, then rubbed her face with a towel. "I wish Cousin Cyril cared more for his children. I had parents who adored me—a blessing I would not trade for any amount of wealth or beauty. Perhaps his new wife will be the mother for which Patsy prays. Lord, I must trust You to provide for these children."

She paced across the room while taking down her abundant hair. Her candle flickered. Helen stopped and stared until the flame straightened.

Ashamed of her inordinate alarm, she heaved a sigh. "As if darkness could harm me. Lord, why must I be so fearful? 'I sought the Lord, and he heard me, and delivered me from all my fears,'" she quoted. "You did enable me to overcome my fears many times today, Lord Jesus. There was the tree—although Oliver in effect had to carry me down, I don't believe he realized the extent of my fear. And I actually befriended a dog! Only You could provide such courage. Cousin Cyril did not appreciate the magnitude of my victory, but You do."

Instead of picturing her handsome cousin, Helen dwelt upon memories of Oliver's rugged face. Smiling, she pulled her hair over one shoulder and stroked its length. "I wonder if Oliver would like my hair. It isn't a pretty color, but it is soft." Warmth invaded her body and heart.

Leaning over, she braided her hair into a thick rope. "Oliver said I was the best thing to come here in many years." Not a particularly romantic statement, to be sure, but at the moment any positive remark from Oliver nourished her runaway fancy. "The servants say he watches over me."

A breeze from her open window made Helen shiver. After tying off the braid, she hurried to her bed and pulled back the quilt. Something dark lay upon the white ticking. Helen paused with one foot lifted. Teetering, she fell forward with hands braced on either side of the invading object.

At close range she beheld four outstretched legs, empty eye sockets, and a gaping mouth. A scream caught in her throat. Everything went dark except for that ghastly gray nightmare. She could not shift her gaze. Her body seemed frozen except for the throbbing beat in her ears.

At last she caught a gasping breath and flung herself away from the bed. Huddled on the floor with both arms wrapped around her folded legs, she rocked back and forth, whimpering. As her mind began to clear, her lips whispered psalms. " 'Yea, though I walk through the valley of the shadow of death, I will fear no evil: for thou art with me. . . The Lord is my light and my salvation; whom shall I fear? The Lord is the strength of my life; of whom shall I be afraid?' "

Wiping her eyes with the backs of her hands, Helen took a deep breath. "Certainly not of a toad. The creature has been dead for eons, from the look of it." She clambered to her feet, tripping on the edge of her smock. Her gaze avoided the bed. "But what shall I do now?"

A handkerchief provided her deliverance. Averting her eyes as much as possible, she gripped one of the toad's stiff legs with the folded cloth, carried it to the open window, and dropped it, handkerchief and all. The handkerchief unfurled and floated down like a falling leaf. Helen leaned over the sill but could see nothing of the toad in the bushes far below.

Stars glittered overhead, and nocturnal creatures chirped. Helen wished she were not afraid of the dark, for the gardens appeared enchanting by starlight. Spirals of mist drifted across the lawns and lurked behind hedges. In a few short weeks, the trellises and fences would be cloaked with sweetbriar and blooming vines, and the heady perfume of jasmine might rise even to Helen's window.

A dark figure near the lavender hedge caught Helen's attention. She recalled no bush or statue in that location. Craning her neck and squinting, she leaned farther out. Her hand slipped, and she gave a little cry before ducking back inside. *How foolish I am!* she berated herself while waiting for her heart to stop its thundering. *Come morning, I shall be able to see the statue clearly instead of breaking my neck while trying to see in the dark.*

A chilly wind made her reach to close the window. Her hand stopped short. Her widening eyes searched the lavender hedge in vain. The dark figure was gone.

Seconds later she was huddled beneath her quilt in the middle of the bed. The breeze caused by her wild rush had extinguished her candle, leaving Helen to shiver in complete darkness.

Chapter 5

As dawn lit the eastern horizon, Helen pulled her dress over her head, bound her hair, and donned a cap and shawl. After scooping up her Bible, she marched downstairs with eyes straight ahead, determined not to run like a rabbit from invisible predators lurking in dark corners of the house.

She lifted the bar and opened the back door. Gray morning light touched her face. Smoke trickled from the kitchen chimney—*Cook must already be at work.* Helen stepped outside into a wonderland of silvery mist, dewy grass, and sleeping flowers. A spider web shimmered between two shrubs, its weaver waiting patiently for the sun to awaken a prospective meal.

Helen searched the back of the house for her bedchamber window, then hurried to hunt through the bushes below it for her handkerchief. The square of white cambric was nowhere to be seen. Might a bird have carried it away? There had been no wind last night. She searched behind and beneath the topiary hedges to no avail.

Giving up at last, she entered the formal gardens in

search of a bench. Her footprints were dark on the grass, and the hem of her dress became damp. She saw other, smaller prints in the dew; a rabbit or a fox had traversed the garden earlier that morning.

Beneath a trellis she found a wooden bench. After wiping it dry with her apron, she settled down and opened her Bible. Daily readings had taken her to the book of Isaiah, where she had become somewhat bogged down. Beginning with chapter forty-one, she buckled down to read. Two verses on, her mind and her eyes wandered from the page.

She sucked in a deep breath and released it in a tremulous sigh. Another sleepless night consumed in terror of the unknown.

A bird began to warble from a nearby beech, and sunlight pierced the mist, turning dewdrops into diamonddrops. Helen's lips quivered; tears overflowed. Wiping her face with an already soggy apron corner, she mourned aloud. "Why, Lord, do I doubt You whenever darkness falls? I have no trouble believing while the sun shines; but as soon as trials enter my life, my courage fails. I read Your Word daily, yet I draw little sustenance from it. How I long to talk again with my father and mother, to emulate their wisdom and soak up their strength!"

In the silence following her outburst, Helen considered her words. *Do I have faith of my own, or have I relied upon my parents to have faith in my stead? Is God truly my Father? He is never a grandfather—I cannot depend upon my parents' faith to save me.*

Discouraged, she again began to read. The tenth verse

widened her eyes. She read it again, aloud. " 'Fear thou not; for I am with thee: be not dismayed; for I am thy God: I will strengthen thee; yea, I will help thee; yea, I will uphold thee with the right hand of my righteousness.' "

With a moist smile, Helen lifted her gaze to the sky. "Lord Jesus, You have promised to be with me always, even unto the end of the world. I know that You created all things and that nothing is too difficult for You. You promised to hold me in the palm of Your almighty hand. I shall not fear things that walk by night. I shall not fear the beasts You have created. I shall not fear the wrath or mockery of man. I shall not fear the future. You are the Lord, and beside You there is no savior."

She read on, finding promises and assurance in every chapter.

Some time later, sensing another presence, Helen lifted her head. Oliver leaned one shoulder against a stone archway and watched her. "I wondered when you would notice me."

Helen snapped her Bible shut and rose quickly. His hair dripped water, and his shirt clung to his damp torso. His booted feet were crossed, and his head was bare.

Was he impervious to cold? Helen gathered her shawl closer to her shoulders and tried to restrain a shiver that was not entirely induced by the morning chill. "How long have you been there?" she demanded.

"Not long. I, too, often come to the garden to commune with my Lord." Despite the twinkle in his eyes, Oliver's voice held a tender note that soothed Helen's nerves. "Upon returning from my daily ablutions in the pond, I saw your footprints leading away from the house and followed them here. I apologize for disturbing your meditation."

Helen shook her head and took a few hesitant steps toward him. The gateway he blocked was her only exit from the enclosed garden. "You wash in the lake?"

"I swim on all but the coldest of days."

"In your clothing?" she asked before thinking.

"Nay, to walk about in wet attire would invite illness."

After contemplating his answer for a moment, Helen felt her face flame.

Oliver laughed softly, then sobered. "Are you well, Helen? Does aught trouble you?"

Startled by his insight, she glanced up, met his probing eyes, and again dropped her gaze. "I have brought my troubles to the Lord. Now I believe all will be well. But I thank you for the inquiry."

Pushing away from the archway, he took a step toward her. "You carry a heavy burden on your slight shoulders. Franklin alone is more burden than many could bear. He is my sister's child; I would share that load with you if will allow it."

Emboldened by her concern for the children, Helen searched Oliver's eyes. He seemed sincere. "I am grateful for your offer," she whispered, unable to find her voice.

He approached and reached a cold but dry hand to touch her cheek. Helen closed her eyes. "You were weeping," he said. "Why?"

Helen swallowed hard. "I am learning how little faith

I have," she admitted. "I find it difficult to trust the Lord with my life. Always I have had my parents to depend upon; now I have only God. I know that He is sufficient and that only He can truly meet my spirit's deepest longings. Yet in the darkest hours of night, when fears assail me, I find it hard to realize His presence."

He nodded. "I struggle with similar trials, Helen. Since the day of your arrival, I have come to realize that others can see little of Jesus in my life. Your amazement that I, too, was a believer shocked me to my senses."

Her eyes widened. "Oh, but I did not intend—"

A smile touched his lips. "I understand that you meant no offense. I cannot imagine you intentionally hurting anyone. Your surprise was genuine, the very reason it was effective. You struggle against fears; I fight daily, hourly against overweening pride." Blinking, he studied the top of a distant oak. "It is a fierce battle."

Helen touched his arm. "I will pray for you, Oliver."

He lowered his gaze to her hand. It looked small and weak against his sinewy forearm. Embarrassed, Helen started to pull it away, but he quickly clapped his other hand over hers and held it in place. "And I will pray for you, Helen."

From the tiny white temple in the middle of the rose garden, Helen could see over the top of the maze and glimpse the pasture beyond. Two distant figures held her interest—a horse trotting in measured circles and the man on its back.

"What are you staring at, Cousin Helen?" Avril asked,

joining her at the window. "Do you like Braveheart? I like his two white legs and pink hooves."

"It is a beautiful horse," Helen agreed.

"Uncle Oliver used to own Braveheart's mother, Glorious. Father bought Glorious for my mother. He bought lots of Uncle Oliver's horses, then hired him to care for them. Glorious died last winter of the colic, and Uncle Oliver cried."

"Oh!" Helen exclaimed.

"He cried more when my mother died, though, because she was his sister. Everybody else in the family died except us children. Jenny says the Kirby family was cursed because they were papists. What are papists, Cousin Helen? Am I one too?"

"Nay. You mustn't attend to gossip from the servants. You live under God's protection, not under a curse. 'Papist' is a term used to describe Roman Catholics. I was unaware that Oliver was Catholic." The idea troubled her. His life must be in constant danger.

"He isn't, and neither was Mother. I'm glad Father bought the horses. He did it to make Mother happy—she was afraid Uncle Oliver would go to the New World after he lost his property. He won't leave as long as his horses are here. It looks wondrous fine to ride upon a horse. I wish we could go for rides sometimes. We never get away from the house. Even the gardens are walled in. Franklin says he is going to run away someday and become a highwayman."

"Oh?" Helen cast a glance over one shoulder at Franklin. Instead of studying equations, he was on the floor, absorbed in using a stick to tease a crawling beetle. Helen knew she should demand that he return to the bench and complete his lessons, yet she dreaded the inevitable battle. Patsy had fallen asleep on one of the benches, her soft lips parted and her cheeks rosy.

"You talk too much, Avril," the boy grumbled.

"Cousin Helen doesn't mind." Avril leaned against Helen's side. "This morning when we visited Father in his rooms, he told us he plans to marry again. Patsy told him he should marry you. Franklin said he'd go live in the stable with the grooms if Father marries again. He said he wants to grow up to be like Uncle Oliver and tend horses. He never wants to sell wool. Then Father got all red in the face and called you to take us away."

Helen's arm tightened around the girl's slim shoulders. Sighing, she buried her nose in Avril's fluffy hair and breathed in its lavender scent. "I thought he seemed vexed, and no wonder. He cares about you children. He misses your mother and brother. I believe he is frightened of losing you as well." At least she hoped Cyril cared. He must care. "I am sure his new wife will be a good stepmother. Your father chose your mother, didn't he? Therefore, he must be a good judge of women."

"I should have died instead of Joseph."

The low voice from behind gave Helen a shock. "Why do you say that, Franklin?"

He continued poking at the beetle. After a long silence he said, "Father wishes it was me that died. I heard him say so."

Pain gripped Helen's heart. "Oh, Franklin, you must have misheard him."

The boy shrugged as if to reject her pity. "He doesn't care about anyone but himself. He thinks we should be glad that he's bringing another woman here to take Mother's place. I hate him."

Helen silently prayed for wisdom. "You might feel that way now, but in time I believe you will come to love him again. From this day on, my prayer each morning and night is that your father will recognize the treasure he has in you children. He should be proud. Now, Franklin, I must insist that you complete your lessons, or we will never again use the temple as a schoolroom."

To her surprise, Franklin crawled back to the bench and resumed his equations—but not before Helen saw a wet spot appear on the wooden floorboards beneath his face. Tears burned her eyes as she began to comprehend the depth of Franklin's despair. *How can I help these children, Lord? What can I do? I need to talk with Oliver as soon as possible.*

❦

That night Helen found a snail making a trail of slime across her bed linens. She performed a dance of horror, waving her arms and screeching silently. This time, anger joined her disgust and gave her courage to deal with the situation immediately. After gripping it by the shell and holding it at arm's length, Helen dropped the snail out her window to join the toad.

She refused to look toward the lavender hedge. " 'I will strengthen thee. . .yea, I will uphold thee,' " she quoted to herself. A day of constant communion with the Lord had done wonders for her spiritual fortitude. Last night's terror now seemed absurd, yet she knew that even one unguarded thought could again send her reeling into the pit of fear.

How had Cyril known that the mere suggestion of a phantom would be enough to start her imagination spinning? Was her craven character so evident? Not that she suspected her cousin of staging a ghostly promenade; Helen knew she must have imagined the entire episode. Rogue that he was, Cyril would delight in discovering the success of his ploy. She resolved he would never know.

Like father, like son. Somehow Franklin had discerned her dread of crawling things and now intended to use it against her—just as Oliver had warned. Should she drag the boy out of bed and chastise him for the prank, or should she pretend it never happened? Would either choice dissuade him from further escapades?

"Lord, You know how I despise these crawly creatures. . .and now Franklin knows it too. What am I to do? I must talk with Oliver."

Chapter 6

Summer approached, bringing to the gardens the glory of blossoming fruit trees, climbing vines, and budding roses. Days of romping with her young cousins should have been among Helen's happiest, yet she struggled against discontent.

One Saturday evening during her free time, Helen sat in the terraced garden with her Bible open in her lap. Pondering and praying, she attempted to put her troubles into words.

"Lord, sometimes I catch glimpses of Oliver, and more than once I have discovered him watching me play with the children, but each time he hurries in the opposite direction without a word. I thought I must be imagining his avoidance, yet time has proven otherwise. I can date his attitude of formality to the day after Cyril returned to Biddlesham Hall. Has my cousin forbidden him to address me? I cannot imagine why."

She paused, thinking, then began to shake her head. "I was foolish to have read more than casual amiability into Oliver's remarks and behavior. He said nothing that could lead me to expect more from him." But then she recalled the strength of his arms about her and the warmth of his eyes and voice. "He said he would help bear my burdens, yet when I need him he is nowhere to be found." Her shoulders began to quake, and she mopped flowing tears with her apron. The Bible slid off her lap and fell closed upon the bench.

"I feel so dreadfully alone! Because I must always be with my charges, I seldom see the other servants. Cyril does not crave my company. He knows I disapprove of the way he neglects his children." Shaking her head back and forth, she whispered to herself. "I dare not question him about my future as governess to his children. Perhaps it is best this way—I am not fit for my position. You know all about Franklin, Lord." Helen rolled her eyes and dissolved into fresh tears.

Franklin daily became bolder in his disrespect. He had not yet attempted outright defiance, but Helen knew he was biding his time. Every night she found some token of his aversion in her bed—dead fish, living beetles, worms, spiders, newts, nettles, and burrs. Once she had pulled back her quilt only to release a bat from its confines. Eventually the creature had found its way out her open window, but not before fouling the rush floor mats and the clothes chest lid. Helen had cried herself to sleep that night.

Her voice quavered as she spoke once more. "I understand that You allow these trials for Your purpose. I beg only Your care, provision, and comfort for my wounded spirit."

When dark spots appeared upon her skirts, Helen at first thought they were teardrops. But pelting drops upon her cap and shoulders sent her running across the lawn with her shawl over her head. Inside the house, servants scurried about like so many ants. Maggie rushed along the hallway, bearing an armload of bed linens and quilts.

Helen found the children unsupervised in the nursery. Wooden blocks lay scattered across the floor. In the middle of the room, Patsy crouched in a heap, sobbing. Avril sat on her bed, cradling the rag doll Helen had made for her. Kneeling on a chest beneath a window, Franklin rested his chin on his folded arms and stared out at the pouring rain.

"What has happened? Why are you not with your father?"

Avril launched into an explanation. "Father sent us away. He said he could not endure children because he must prepare for Lady Lillian's arrival."

"Lady Lillian? Cyril's betrothed is coming here?" Helen gasped. "When?"

"Today. Jenny couldn't watch us because she was busy. She said we were to wait here for you. Then Patsy bumped Franklin's block castle and made it fall, so he hit her."

Helen helped Patsy to her feet and inspected her for injury. The child appeared more hurt in spirit than in body, so Helen laid Patsy upon her bed and smoothed tear-wet hair from the little girl's flushed cheeks. "I said I was sorry." Patsy's rosy lips trembled.

Rising, Helen tried to keep the irritation she felt out of her voice. "I am disappointed in you, Franklin. Patsy is smaller and weaker than you are. A gentleman never hits a lady."

"What can you do about it?" Franklin asked bluntly without turning around. His voice dripped insolence. "You'll be gone soon, when my father marries that woman."

Helen was unprepared for confrontation, yet she could not allow open rebellion to go unchecked. She gripped Franklin's shoulder and tried to make him face her. In one motion, he threw off her touch, spun around, and kicked her shin a glancing blow. "Leave me be!"

While Helen collapsed on the floor holding her leg, Franklin ran for his life.

"Are you all right, Cousin Helen?" the girls asked, wide-eyed.

Helen staggered to her feet, puffing in wrath. "I will live, but Franklin is doomed. Avril, watch over Patsy for me." She skimmed down the stairs and stopped in the great hall, uncertain of the boy's flight path. The front door stood slightly ajar. Helen rushed outside in time to catch a glimpse of the boy disappearing around the corner of the house, headed for the stables. Helen took off in pursuit.

Rain pounded on her face and soaked her cap. She slipped on the wet gravel and fell headlong, skinning both palms and her knee. Immediately she scrambled up and ran, panting and sobbing.

The interior of the stable was dark, in keeping with the dismal weather. Helen rushed through the open door and stopped, hearing Franklin's voice although she could not yet see him. Oliver emerged from a stall, restraining a squirming boy.

"She'll kill me! Don't let her get me, Uncle Oliver! She's a monster!"

Helen felt like a dragon at the moment, ready to breathe fire. Her face streamed water, her dress dripped mud, and her smock clung to her body, so wet that her skin showed through the fabric. Her neckcloth and cap had disappeared sometime during that wild dash. Pressing both hands against her chest, she shivered even as she fumed.

Oliver spotted her before Franklin did. Stopping short, he gave the boy a shake. "Whatever have you done to Helen, you young whelp?"

"Nothing, I swear it! She is crazy!"

Helen clenched her jaw and enunciated slowly. "He kicked me in the leg."

Franklin's head popped up, and he met her gaze with defiance. "I did not. She's just a poor relative that Father took in out of pity. She's afraid of everything. Why should I obey her?"

Helen flushed beneath Oliver's scrutiny. Without a word to her, he turned back to Franklin, gripping the boy by the front of his doublet. "While I have a word with your governess, you pick up a rake and shovel and begin cleaning stalls. The dung cart is nigh the back door. Ask Quincy where to begin."

Franklin's jaw dropped. "I shan't do it! I shall tell Father."

With one hand, Oliver hoisted the boy to his eye level. "You will, and without another word unless you wish me to find a switch. You and I will exchange words in the near future."

Franklin wilted and nodded. When Oliver released him, the boy slumped off to collect his tools. Oliver watched him move out of sight.

Helen wrapped her arms around herself and shuddered, dimly aware that her palms were stinging. While Oliver spoke with Franklin she had furtively attempted to pull her bodice higher on her chest, but it failed to conceal her drenched smock. Although most women would have considered her attire modest, Helen felt improper. Her neckcloths usually covered her almost to the chin. Embarrassment only fueled her fury.

Crossing his arms, Oliver regarded her soberly. "Tell me."

"Do not insult me by offering again to share my burdens," she said. "These many days I would have welcomed your listening ear, but no more."

Some emotion she could not identify rippled across Oliver's face. Stepping toward her, he reached out a hand. Helen slapped at it and backed away.

Oliver stopped short. "Helen, let me see your hands."

She looked down to see red streaks on her smock, blood from her scraped palms. Her bruised knee ached. Sobs kept her from speaking, which also fanned her wrath.

Oliver gripped her wrists, and Helen panicked. "Unhand me!" Flailing with both arms, she struggled to free herself. She lifted her foot to kick his shins but could not bring herself to hurt Oliver as she had been hurt. He had done nothing to merit such treatment.

"I set the boy to work, Oliver." Quincy, the underhorseman, sauntered into the walkway, recognized that he had blundered into an interesting situation, and paused to observe.

"Helen, my dear woman, calm yourself," Oliver said. "I mean you no harm."

"Dost wish that I should tie her down, Oliver?" Quincy offered.

"Get hence," Oliver growled, glaring at the younger man over one shoulder. When Helen's frenzy did not abate, he released her and held out both hands in entreaty. "I desire only to give you aid, Helen. Let me bathe and anoint your wounds."

His solicitous tone confused her further. Covering her face with both stinging hands, she wept. Words began to spew from her lips, garbled by sobs that jerked her frame. "I am a fool! You have shown me nothing but kindness, yet I misunderstood your intent. I am but a plain and humble spinster, never to expect notice from such as you."

One arm encircled her shoulders. His fingers pushed damp curls from her forehead, slid down to her ear, then cradled the nape of her neck. He rested his nose atop her head and sighed. "Nay, you are right to chide me. 'Twas I, not you, who played the fool. Lord, forgive my senseless pride," he groaned. "How blind I have been!"

Helen could not comprehend his words inasmuch as his touch was sending exquisite fire through her veins. Feeling vulnerable and indecent, she was in no mood to be patronized. This splendid man could never want her as his bride; therefore his caresses were not rightly hers to savor.

Oh, how I love Oliver Kirby.

The terrifying realization gave her strength to push

away. Shaking and panting, she stared into his face. "I–I scarcely know you! We are mere acquaintances. How long ere you once again forget my existence?"

"She carries the field there, Oliver. You've spoken nary a word to her these three weeks. All us servants noticed. Seems a heartless way to behave toward a choice wench." Leaning on the farthest stall partition, Quincy chewed the end of a long straw and gave Helen a broad wink.

"Begone!" Oliver wheeled upon his assistant. "This is none of your affair."

Helen made a dash for the open doorway and plunged back into pouring rain. In her wake followed Quincy's laughter.

A shadow fell over her. Still running, she glanced up to find a cape fluttering above her head. Oliver jogged beside her, holding his cape at arms' length.

Helen stopped in the middle of a puddle on the entry drive. "Leave me be!" she shouted, pushing at his arms.

"Not until you are safe inside," he shouted back. "You will come ill after such a soaking."

"And the children need me, I know," she said bitterly. She turned to run, but he caught her arm, tossed the cape over his own shoulder, and pulled her close. She felt his hands cupping her face; then his lips pressed against hers. Helen went limp. Her hands crept up his chest.

"I need you, Helen." He spoke against her forehead. His hat's broad brim protected her face from the rain; his embrace restored warmth to her frame. "Come." Pulling the cape from his shoulder, he wrapped it around her and escorted her to the front door.

She turned in the doorway, still in a daze. He smiled tenderly and touched her chin with his knuckle. "We will talk later when you are dry. I will send Franklin to you when he completes his labors."

She nodded and watched him fling the cape back over his shoulder as he strode toward the stables. Quivering hands covered her cheeks. Oliver had kissed her in plain view of anyone in the house who might have happened to be near a window. Fear and delight warred for prominence among her emotions.

❦

Lady Lillian's entourage was late in arriving. "Muddy roads slowed our travel to a crawl," Helen heard a hearty female voice proclaim as she watched and listened from the stair landing. The future mistress of Biddlesham Hall seemed to accept the delay without dint to her high spirits.

"Cyril, this place is a delight! What a magnificent hall! The ideal surroundings for a magnificent man. I brought my faithful old nurse Middy and a few retainers." Helen smiled at the description of a swarm of attending servants. "I hope we are no trouble."

Helen's smile widened. No trouble to Cyril, perhaps, but she could imagine the turbulence in the kitchen. At least Helen had no immediate worries, for Cyril desired only that she keep his children unseen at present.

While returning to her room, she thought she heard a door click shut. Franklin! Was that boy up to mischief again? Helen jerked open her chamber door to find. . . nothing. A small fire glowed on her hearth, and candles flickered in the draft from the doorway. She marched across the room, hauled open the nursery door, and extended her candle. The sound of peaceful breathing met her ear. Each bed held a motionless lump.

Shaking her head, Helen returned to her room and prepared for bed. Her scraped hands still hurt, and her knee was turning blue. Recalling Oliver's concern, she sighed. Reluctant though she was to pin her hopes upon a man who had proven himself less than dependable, she could not prevent dreams of marriage and family from creeping into her thoughts. Oliver had captured her interest from the first, she admitted. What woman would not find such a man irresistible? Not even his sarcasm had sufficed to discourage her interest.

Slowly she combed tangles from her hair, frowning in thought. What if Cyril and Lillian wished her to remain as governess to the children? Would Oliver want his wife to work at the manor? Not that he had proposed marriage, she reminded herself.

The idea of leaving Patsy and Avril brought pain to her heart. If only Cyril would learn to care for his children. Visions of her cousin as she had glimpsed him in the great hall that evening, clad in full regalia—lacy boot tucks, falling band collar, and beribboned lovelock—pranced through Helen's mind. The peacock. Why did he not cherish his children? Did the man even know the meaning of love?

And Lillian—would she love Sarah's children? Franklin might be lovable if he tried, but Helen pitied any woman in the position of stepmother to that child.

Catching herself in the midst of resentful thoughts,

Helen squeezed her eyes shut. *Lord, help me to respect my cousin, and please teach him to love his children. Bless Lillian, and help the children to like her. Much though I love them, they are not my children and I cannot direct their future. I cannot even direct my own.*

Helen wandered to the window and rested her forearms upon its sill. Tonight the garden was clear and calm. The rainstorm had passed; moonlight silvered topiaries, walls, and statues. She could hear the garden's fountain and the faraway cry of an owl.

Helen's thoughts drifted back to the night she had seen the "ghost." A little smile twitched her lips. *What a coward I am!* Since her arrival at Biddlesham Hall she had encountered many frightening circumstances—among them several daunting people, an enormous dog, countless crawly creatures, a mysterious apparition, pervasive darkness, a recalcitrant boy, and one terrifyingly attractive man. *Notwithstanding, I am yet living, sane, and functioning as a member of the household.*

Still contemplating this revelation, she pulled back her bed quilt to check for prior inhabitants. Her horrified gaze traveled around speckled coils to meet an unblinking reptilian eye.

Chapter 7

Dropping the quilt, Helen swallowed a wave of nausea. Franklin had outdone himself. Of all creatures, Helen most dreaded snakes.

Taking deep breaths, she told herself repeatedly that the snake must be dead or Franklin could not have carried it to her room. Using the edge of her apron, she scooped up the slender creature and shook the cloth until the snake lay coiled in its center. Just as she reached the window, her heart nearly stopped—it could not be. . . Surely the snake's tongue had not flashed out for an instant! Cold and inert, the scaly nightmare lay limp upon her apron, but Helen knew in her heart that the beast was alive. Not even a snake should be dropped alive from a first-floor window. She must carry it downstairs and release it into the garden.

Keeping one eye on the bundled apron, she donned her dress. At this hour she was unlikely to meet anyone in the hallway, but she would not take the chance.

The great hall was still lighted. Cyril and his guest must be sitting up late. Like a wraith she passed the doorway, but Cyril spotted her. "Cousin Helen, come and greet my betrothed."

Shrinking inwardly, Helen obeyed, clutching her bundle beneath one arm. Cyril and Lillian sat near the fire; a gray-haired woman occupied a seat in the shadows. When Helen stepped into the hall, Diocletian rose from the hearth and approached her, tail waving. Helen patted his head, but he insisted on more petting. Pressing his nose against her bundle, he snorted.

Without budging from his chair, Cyril waved an idle hand in Helen's direction. "Lillian, this is my cousin Helen Walker who traveled here from Surrey to care for the children."

Helen curtsied, and Lillian nodded. "Good even, Helen." The woman surprised Helen with a friendly smile. "I am pleased to make your acquaintance. Have the children retired for the night? I look forward to meeting them."

Helen's heart warmed. "They are asleep, Mistress. I will bring them to you on the morrow."

Lillian turned to Cyril. "She is a pretty thing, Dear. Far too attractive to remain a governess. I am certain she could marry well if given a respectable dowry." She spoke as if continuing a conversation.

"And I am sure your beloved Middy would be an excellent nurse to my children. I told you before, Beloved, that I am trying to convince my brother-in-law to take Helen to wife. The two would make an ideal match."

Helen kept her jaw from dropping with some effort. Fascinated by her bundle, Diocletian pushed against Helen's side until she staggered. He gave another snort.

Helen felt movement inside the apron. Her heart skipped.

"But is he the best match for our Helen? I have heard rumors about the Kirby family. Did not King James confiscate their estate?"

"Aye, but it was a trumped up affair. Verily, Oliver Kirby never was Catholic. No Kirby was Catholic to my knowledge. That tale originated with Lord Holmquist— a neighbor who coveted the Kirby lands and discerned a way to obtain them at no cost."

"And King Charles has never amended the error?"

Cyril waved his pipe. "He cannot be bothered."

"May I be excused, Master Cyril?" Helen quavered.

"Not as yet." Cyril turned back to Lillian. "I purchased many of Oliver's horses to pacify Sarah. He has remained in my employ these several years, yet I know that he longs to move on. I have heard him speak with animation of the New World, the Virginia colony."

Lillian's curls bobbed as she nodded. "Mayhap you could give him aid. It is unseemly to have a former gentleman working as servant, let alone the brother of your first wife. I would be uneasy in his presence."

Cyril puffed at his pipe and stared toward the vaulted ceiling. "An honest sentiment. I shall approach Oliver again. You may go, Cousin. Take Diocletian out to the kitchen."

"Blessed dreams, Helen," Lillian said.

Helen curtsied and hurried from the room with Diocletian at her heels. As she reached to unlatch the back door, something touched her wrist. She looked down and nearly screamed. The snake had found an opening among the folds of her apron. Its head emerged, tongue flickering. Cringing, she shoved the narrow head back inside and tightened her bundle.

Diocletian snuffled against her arm. Pushing his bulk away, Helen opened the door and stepped outside. At last she could be rid of her nightmare. But when she reached for the bundled apron she felt a sharp pain. Startled, she threw out her arm. The snake hung from her thumb.

The door closed behind her just as Helen emitted a scream releasing all the pent-up horror of weeks of torment. Waving her hand and shrieking, she ran barefoot across the lawn with the two-foot-long snake streaming behind her. Barking in a thunderous bass, Diocletian raced beside her until a scent in the nearby shrubs jerked his head to one side. He skidded to a stop while Helen pounded on.

"Helen!" Oliver called from somewhere behind. "Helen, what are you doing? Stop!"

Running blindly, puffing labored sobs, she blundered across pebbled walkways and velvet lawns. Oliver caught her around the waist. She stepped on his boot and lost her footing. He staggered and fell, bringing Helen down upon the wet grass with him.

Rolling over, he came to his knees and pinned Helen to the ground by her wrists. "Have you lost your mind, Woman? Did you run from the dog?"

Helen shook her head, still gasping and whimpering. At that moment, the snake released her thumb and slithered across Oliver's hand. He let out a yelp and pulled away. "A snake?"

"It bit me," Helen moaned and began to cough.

Oliver helped her sit up, then pursued the snake and snatched it by the neck. After a quick inspection, he released it. "A grass snake. Undoubtedly more frightened than we are." He glanced around. "It should escape before Diocletian returns. He is a poor hunter."

Helen tucked her knees and curled into a ball. "I care not what happens to it. Just keep it away from me!"

"Let me see where it bit you." He squinted at her hand, turning it back and forth in the moonlight. "Plenty of scratches, but no bite mark. Grass snakes have small teeth. Now come, get off the wet ground, my dear. Let us talk."

Helen allowed him to pull her up. "I have never before visited the garden after dark. Is it safe?"

Oliver placed an arm around her shoulders and led her to a bench beneath a bower of climbing roses. "Quite safe when taken at a moderate pace. I walk here with Diocletian every night."

Helen looked up. "You do?"

Oliver sat beside her. "Aye. Head dog-keeper I am as well as head horseman. Diocletian likes Cyril, but he spends more time with me and Quincy than with his master."

"You walk here every night—even in the rain and the fog?"

"Aye. This surprises you? The dog needs exercise."

"I believe I saw you near the lavender hedge one misty night and mistook you for a ghost."

"A ghost?"

Helen bowed her head. "Cyril told me that night of a spirit that haunts the garden. I know better than to believe in such things, yet the sight of you sent me cowering to my bed."

"Typical of Cyril. Was that the night you dropped a handkerchief from your window?"

"You saw me?" Helen's head popped back up. "Franklin had put a dead toad in my bed. I used the handkerchief to pick it up but accidentally dropped the kerchief out the window with the toad."

"A toad in your bed?"

"Tonight it was the snake. I find some creature in my bed nearly every night."

"I shall throttle that young rascal," he declared grimly. "I have oft seen you at the window of a night and wondered why. I thought. . ." He sounded embarrassed. "I confess, that first night I thought you saw me. But when I approached your window and called, you had disappeared."

"I was quaking beneath my quilts in fear of the haunting spirit." Helen chuckled at her own foolishness.

Oliver reached into his doublet and pulled out a lacy bit of fabric.

Helen touched it lightly. "You kept it? But why?"

"I thought you dropped it for me." His voice was gruff.

"But why would you want it?"

He shrugged, then leaned forward and rested his elbows on his knees, head bent. "Have you not guessed? I adore you, Helen Walker." Suddenly he rose and paced a short distance away. "I wish to ask your cousin for your hand in marriage and have the banns published as soon as possible. If this is not agreeable to you, let me know at once, and I will never again bother you with my foolish hopes."

Helen could scarcely speak. "Even though Cyril advised you to marry me?"

He turned abruptly. "You know? Oh, Helen, it was pride that turned me from you for a time. I would not allow Cyril to choose my bride, yet I was miserable without you."

"I thought my heart would break when you seemed to forget my existence."

He rushed back to kneel before her on the wet grass. "Then you do care for me? Today you said we were mere acquaintances."

"I spoke in anger. It is true that we do not know one another well, but we will have ample time for acquaintance while the banns are being read."

"And after we wed, for the rest of our lives," Oliver added. "Kiss me, Helen, and I will believe that you love me."

"Do you think it wise? We cannot marry for six months." Although she longed to kiss him again, the very intensity of her desire made her hesitate.

"Unless I carry you off to Newgate." The teasing note in his voice no longer annoyed her. He persisted, "Helen, I love you enough to honor you and keep you pure until you are mine in the eyes of God."

She touched his forehead with trembling fingers and traced his dark eyebrows. "Where will we live, Oliver? Here with Cyril?"

His eyes caught the moonlight. "For a time. I often

think of sailing to the New World. Would you be willing to embark on such an adventure?" He pushed his head against her fingers like a dog begging to be petted.

"With you, I would go anywhere. But what about the children?" Helen caressed his wavy hair.

"I hope to have several if you are strong enough to bear them."

She felt her face grow warm. "I meant Cyril's children. I shall miss them."

Oliver paused. "God will provide for them."

"I like Lillian. I pray she will be a good stepmother."

He sighed and clambered to his feet. "As do I. We must accept the fact that Sarah's children are Cyril's to raise, not ours."

A voice called from across the grounds. "Oliver, are you out here? Come straightaway!"

Hands cupped around his mouth, Oliver shouted back. "Over here."

Helen heard running footsteps in the grass. Quincy panted as he spoke. "It's the colt—Braveheart. He's missing. Gone from his stall, and a saddle missing too!"

Chapter 8

Mincing on tender feet, Helen rushed to the house. Cyril leaped up at sight of her face. "What is it? The children?"

She shook her head, still panting. "Your horse—Braveheart. He is missing from the stable. Oliver sent me to tell you."

Cyril's face hardened. "Begone, Woman, and tend to the children." Helen heard him conversing with Lillian as she returned to her room. A few minutes later, the front door slammed.

Helen sat limply on the cold bed, exhausted. Her fire burned low, and her candles had nearly guttered. She picked up a candle and entered the nursery. Avril slept with her mouth ajar and arms flung wide. Patsy resembled a lump of blankets. Helen patted the child and frowned. She pulled back the quilt to find. . .a lump of blankets. The little girl was gone.

Panicked, Helen checked Franklin's bed to find a similar bundle of bed linens. A moment later she had hauled on her shoes and started downstairs, flinging a shawl over her shoulders as she ran. Lillian and Middy were no longer in the great hall, and the fire burned low.

The front door opened and a figure stepped inside.

"Oliver?"

He pushed the door shut with one foot, and Helen realized that he carried Patsy's limp figure. She pressed a hand to her heart. "No!"

"Never fear; she sleeps. I found her in an empty stall."

Helen's legs gave way. She dropped upon a nearby bench. "I was coming to tell you—Franklin is also missing."

Cyril entered behind Oliver, carrying a lamp. Its rays lighted Oliver's drawn face and Cyril's marble countenance.

Helen hurriedly explained. "Cousin, I believe Franklin took the horse. Patsy must have followed him to the stable. He has often threatened to run away, but I never dreamed he would do it. But then, after today, I should have watched him more closely."

"What happened today? Lillian's arrival?"

Helen related Franklin's earlier behavior and punishment. "Although in the past Franklin has harried governesses and threatened to run away, I have reason to believe that this latest prank denotes desperation of soul."

"How so? The child lacks for nothing," Cyril protested.

Seeing cracks in his façade, Helen answered bluntly. "He believes you do not love him, Cyril, and his heart is breaking."

Her cousin looked to Oliver, who nodded silent agreement. Cyril drew a shaky breath. "I must find my son," he said and rushed back outside.

"Take her," Oliver ordered, dumping Patsy into Helen's

arms. "Fear not; I will ride with him. Pray, my dearest."

Helen met Lillian in the upper hallway. Burnished auburn locks streamed over the woman's lace dressing gown. Her voice held concern. "What has happened?"

"Franklin has taken the horse and run away. Oliver found Patsy in the stable."

Lillian opened the nursery door for Helen and helped her tuck the child into bed. Holding her candle aloft, she studied the little girl's face. "She is adorable."

Helen smiled. "She will love you."

Lillian returned the smile. "I pray so. I have long desired children but can bear none of my own. God has blessed me beyond measure. I will remain here and wait for Franklin's return."

Rejoicing even as she prayed for Franklin, Helen returned to her room, leaving Lillian with her new family.

❧

Helen lay upon her bed for hours, fully clothed and listening. Occasionally she dozed; frequently she prayed. Memories of Franklin flashed into her thoughts. How that boy loved horses! Why had she never approached Cyril about obtaining him a horse?

Helen awoke to gray darkness. Bumps, footsteps, and hushed voices from the nursery sent her rushing to the door before she had completely regained consciousness. She flung the door wide and stood blinking. Oliver laid Franklin upon his bed and pulled blankets over the boy.

By the dim morning light Helen saw Cyril bend to kiss Avril's cheek and smooth wispy hair from her forehead. Beside him stood Lillian, a shining angel in white lace.

Oliver left Franklin sleeping and approached Helen. "You are still awake?" he whispered.

"I was asleep. He is well?" She indicated Franklin.

Oliver grinned; Helen could see his teeth gleaming in the gray shadow of his face. "He is well. Your prayers are answered, Helen. Come, let us find a quiet place to converse and leave Cyril and Lillian with their children." Taking Helen by the hand, he led her into the hall and down the stairs. Unmindful of her bare feet and frazzled hair, she followed.

Oliver revived the fire in the wide stone fireplace, just as he had done the night of Helen's arrival. Watching him as he squatted on the hearth and blew upon the coals, she suddenly felt joy sweep over her. "I love you, Oliver."

He stopped blowing and chuckled. "Fine time to tell me so. Wait a moment until I can join you."

She made room for him on the bench and snuggled beneath his arm. "First tell me what happened."

Oliver picked up her hand and gently kissed its scraped palm. "We found Franklin and Braveheart together about four miles the other side of town. They were both unhurt. Apparently Franklin dismounted, then could not remount the horse without a mounting block. Braveheart is not yet fully trained, you know, and he would not long endure a young boy's futile attempts to regain his seat."

"And Cyril?"

"We talked tonight, during both the ride out and the ride home." Oliver sounded pensive. "It had been long since we conversed. I believe the threat of losing another child has shocked him into understanding how precious are his daughters and son. Cyril pledged tonight to be a better father—to love them openly and give them time and attention."

"It is truly the answer to my prayers." Helen sighed in delight. "Lillian loves the children already."

"Furthermore, your cousin gives our union his blessing and will have the first banns read this very morning in church. He has promised Braveheart and several of my mares as your dowry. We can establish a horse farm in Virginia as I have often dreamed."

"God is good to us." Helen laid her head upon Oliver's chest. "I will miss the children. I do love them, Oliver."

"Your love for them and your courage were the first traits I admired in you."

Her head popped up. "My courage?" She laughed. "What courage? Oliver, if you only knew. . ."

"I knew how terrified you were that first night, left alone on the fens with a rotted corpse. One glimpse of your sweet little face, and I wanted to scoop you up and assure you that nothing would ever frighten you again— yet at the time such behavior from me would have frightened you more than anything!"

When Helen smiled, Oliver gently touched the dimple in her cheek. "I know how difficult it must have been to leave the only home you had ever known and travel across the country to care for a strange relative's children. I saw the abject terror in your eyes when Diocletian rushed you that first night. I can only imagine your reaction to finding dead toads and snakes in your bed—"

"Among other things," she murmured.

"Then there was the oak tree, and the ghost. . . You have encountered terrors sufficient to slay many valiant souls, yet you persevered. And I? Far from protecting you forever, I abandoned you when you needed me most."

Helen reached up to stroke his cheek. "Yet you overcame your pride, Darling. We all struggle with sin. Sometimes the Lord prevails; sometimes our old nature prevails for a time. Do not condemn yourself—I think you are wonderful."

"Ah, Helen, your courage rises to every occasion, and you never give up. Not one woman in a thousand can boast such tenacity and valor."

"It was the Lord, not I," she admitted.

"I know." Oliver lowered his face until their lips softly met.

JILL STENGL

Jill lives with her husband Dean, their four children, a dog, and two cats in a log home beside a lake in northern Wisconsin. She keeps busy home schooling, teaching Sunday school, playing piano, drawing, and watching romantic old movies. Born and raised in Southern California, she enjoys the changing seasons in the Midwest and the chance to learn winter sports. Jill particularly enjoys writing about England after living there for seven years while her husband served in the military. Jill's E-mail address is: jpopcorn@newnorth.net

Apple
of His Eye

by Gail Gaymer Martin

Dedication

To my wonderful English cousins
in Rowledge Farnham in Surrey
Paul, Jennifer, Nicola, and Scott Gaymer

And to my Gaymer ancestors, founders of England's
Royal Warrant Gaymer Cyder,
whose true story inspired me.

"With men this is impossible,
but with God all things are possible."
MATTHEW 19:26

"Keep my commandments, and live;
And my law as the apple of thine eye.
Bind them upon thy fingers,
write them upon the tablet of thine heart."
PROVERBS 7:2–3

Chapter 1

Victorian England, 1851–52

S arah Hampton peeked through her lacy bedroom curtain into the flowerbeds along the garden wall. "Who is the stranger tending the flowerbeds, Dulcie?"

The young maid eyed the stranger. "The new orchard keeper, Miss."

"The orchardist? But. . .if he is the orchard keeper, why is he in the garden? Where is Benson?" Sarah was fond of the old gentleman who brought her apples from the orchard and rosebuds from the garden.

"He's ill, Miss," the maid said, fastening the buttons of Sarah's chintz morning dress, though the clock had already chimed twelve noon.

"Very ill?" Sarah asked, peering through the lace.

Dulcie shrugged. "Ill enough to need time to mend."

Sarah faced her. "Then the young orchard keeper will do the gardening until Benson returns, I suppose."

"You ask a passel of questions, Miss Sarah." The servant shook her head and patted the dressing table stool. "Now if you'll sit, I'll dress your hair."

"No, Dulcie, I'll just tie it back with a ribbon, please." She pulled a ribbon from a wooden chest on her dresser. "See. It's cherry, the same color as the ribbons on my dress."

Dulcie made a tsking noise. "Let me at least make the bow. Your mother will be after me if I let you out of your room looking like a ragamuffin. You're a young woman, now—enjoying your coming out."

"Piffle, I'm but a child." She waved the ribbon like a flag, wishing her coming out had never been thrust upon her.

The maid snorted at her comment and caught the red streamer in her hand.

Acquiescing, Sarah pivoted on the dressing stool, allowing the maid to tie the ribbon, but her mind rested on the new orchard keeper whom she'd seen from the window.

Filled with anxious curiosity, she yearned to run into the out-of-doors and see the man more closely. Even from above, he looked like a giant, much taller than her father who seemed a tower in Sarah's eyes.

Dulcie completed the bow, then turned to dispose of Sarah's discarded nightgown.

After one last look in the mirror at her white gown and bright ribbons, Sarah hastened from the room and down the stairs. With the dining room empty, she snatched a piece of bread from the sideboard, smeared it with jam, and hurried through the side door to the garden.

To her disappointment, the new orchard keeper had

vanished from the border beds. Intrigued, Sarah slipped through the garden gate and sank onto the stone bench inside the wall, cooled by the dappled shade. She bit into the thick slice of bread and licked the fruity spread from her lips, her gaze darting from one side of the garden to the other. Suspecting the stranger had gone to the orchard, she nibbled the bread and waited.

Having overlooked her morning prayers in her exuberance, Sarah closed her eyes and asked God's blessing on her family and country. . .and for strength to face her eighteenth birthday. Soon her parents expected her to be courted and married, but Sarah had little desire for the convention. She'd danced and accepted callers, but none had won her interest. Not one had sent her heart on a merry chase. Squeezing her eyes closed, she prayed for God to guide her to the man of her heart.

When she lifted her eyelids, a shadow had stretched along the ground to her feet. Timidly, she tipped her head upward and looked at the mountainous man. Her heart jolted with such force it took her breath away. She gaped at him as he neared.

His attention did not settle but passed her by. He moved away to distant beds and went about his business, adding compost around the base of the budding flowers. She observed him and ate her jam and bread.

Sarah had always talked with the older gardener, Benson. She'd known him from childhood, and with his white hair and leathery wrinkles, he seemed like the grandfather she'd never had. When she'd grown to nearly a woman, her mother scolded her for lingering in the garden and bothering the gardener. But he seemed kind, and Sarah loved to smell the earth and blossoming flowers, all God's handiwork.

Now, knowing she behaved improperly, Sarah couldn't help but stare at the tall, lanky man. While his size seemed almost fearful, his gentle face and handsome features calmed her scurrying pulse. He so concentrated on his work that he seemed to ignore Sarah until she wondered if he'd even seen her at all. But she could tell one thing: he loved the earth as much as she did.

Swallowing her upbringing and the last of her breakfast, she rose and stepped away from the bench into the sunlight, calling to him. "Good morning."

He dropped the trowel and jumped to his feet, towering above her head. Instead of speaking, he only gave a bow and tipped his cap, then retrieved the garden tool and returned to his work.

Feeling ignored, Sarah scowled. Yet, she understood his hesitation. The young man belonged in her father's employ and knew his station. Regardless, she longed to hear his voice, venturing it would be deep and vibrant, coming from the depth of his massive chest.

"Do you have a name, Gardener?" she asked.

He turned to her, removed his cap, then shifted toward the house and back again as if he waited for the hand of God to smite him if he should speak. "John Banning, Miss." His resonant voice sparked on the air.

"Don't be apprehensive, Mr. Banning. If my father is about, I'll explain that I spoke to you first."

He gave her a grateful look, slipped on his cap, and

turned back to his compost and trowel.

With daring, she moved closer and scooped up a handful of moist earth, breathing in the loom's rich aroma.

He faced her fully and a frown settled on his brow. "Please, Miss, don't dirty your hands." He pulled a kerchief from his pocket and handed it to her.

"Thank you, Mr. Banning. You're a gentleman." She brushed her hands with the cloth, but viewing the soiled fabric, she did not return it. Instead, she clutched the kerchief and drew in a deeper breath. "I love the earth. Everything in nature. You too, I would imagine."

He nodded, seeming to avoid her gaze.

"We come from the earth, you know," she said. "Ashes to ashes and dust to dust."

" 'And the Lord God formed man of the dust of the ground.' " John glanced her way, then lowered his gaze.

Sarah's pulse tripped. She studied the man's sensitive profile, feeling something sweet and lovely happening in her chest. "You've quoted from Genesis. You are a Christian man."

He nodded and wiped the perspiration from his brow with the back of his hand, his nervousness evident in his shifting stance.

Sarah tilted her head to capture his gaze. " 'And the Lord God said, It is not good that the man should be alone.' "

John faltered backward and shook his head. "I must return to my work, Miss."

Good sense washed over her, and she nodded, withdrawing to the garden wall and letting the man continue his tasks. But instead of leaving, she lowered herself to the bench and fingered his soiled kerchief. No grown man had ever been so gallant toward her. He had treated her as if she were a true lady.

In silence, she watched him work, wondering about his age and background. Did he live in Barnham? If so, why had she never seen him? Sarah let her mind play on his name. *John Banning?* She'd heard his family name before, but the time and place failed her memory.

Finishing, John gathered his equipment and strode across the garden toward the tool shed. He gave her only the faintest nod.

Sarah watched him go, the sunlight reflecting on his broad back, his dark hair curling at the nape of his neck. The man's gentle manner stirred her. She could see his love for the earth—his kindness, offering her his kerchief and his respect. Benson had been thoughtful as well, but he had not stirred such unknown feelings within her.

Recalling the fearful look in his questioning eyes, she admitted she'd been wrong to speak with him without a proper introduction. With a whispered prayer, she asked God's forgiveness.

❦

John stood inside the tool shed, staring into the darkness and calming his pulse. What had he been thinking to allow the young woman to carry on a conversation with him? He'd begun his employment only today and had not earned the family's trust.

Riddled by uncertainty, John wondered about the young woman. . .girl who'd pestered him. He assumed she was Sarah, the Hamptons' only daughter. Calculating what he could recall, he speculated she would be in the middle of her teen years—almost ready for courting.

Despite her presumptuousness, her lovely face had impressed him—her raven black hair and eyes the color of a hedge sparrow's eggs. Beneath her youthful innocence, her attention had jarred unwanted thoughts. She had been born a woman of rank, not one who should enter his thoughts in such a beguiling way.

His first glimpse of her had sent the nerves shimmering down his back. Like an angel, she had sat in the shade dressed in a white frock. Bows the color of ripe apples trimmed her gown and captured her long dark hair. He recalled the sunlight flickering through the foliage and sprinkling her with fairy lights.

Not only her loveliness, but her disposition, as well, clung to his memory. Though a young woman of breeding, she treated him as an equal. A man. Her direct gaze and love of the earth. . .love of God had wrought the strange feelings that tripped through him.

John pulled his mind from the charming girl, wiped off the tools, and stowed them. The shed held the afternoon heat, and he slipped off his cap, then reaching into his pocket, he sought his kerchief to mop the moisture from his brow. The cloth had vanished.

He remembered. He'd given it to her. *Sarah?* The name lilted through his thoughts. A woman of breeding. A woman with pluck, yet gentleness. He'd seen it all in her soft blue eyes. He drew in a ragged breath and stepped into the light. His eyes were blinded by the afternoon glow, and

John paused a moment before he closed the shed.

The Hamptons' gardens burst with life in the June sunshine. He had much to do to keep the hedges and shrubs pruned and trimmed, the flowers and vegetables fertilized, and the orchard maintained. Grateful, he knew a full crew would arrive in time for harvest.

Still, his work wasn't finished. In respect to his parents, he owed his father time and energy on the family property. His labor also served as rent for the use of the small cottage on the family farm. Though he was only twenty-five, John's back ached like an old man's from the bending and digging he'd done since he'd come back to Barnham.

He broadened his pace and stepped beyond the garden wall, but the sight caused him to falter. Near the side porch, Edward Hampton stood on the lawn with his daughter. John noticed his employer's impressive stature as he stood beside the petite young woman. Though nearly as tall as John, Hampton's girth and posture presented a man of dignity and prosperity.

Withdrawing his gaze, John hurried to pass by unnoticed but hesitated when he heard the man's voice.

"Big John. How did you fair your first day?"

John pulled off his cap and clutched it in his left hand. "Fine, Sir. Thank you. I'll return tomorrow early. There's much to do." He kept his focus away from the fair face that stared at him.

"Sarah, this is our new orchardist, Big John Banning," Hampton said, his eyes beaming as he gazed at his daughter.

"How do you do?" Sarah asked, without disclosing their earlier meeting.

"Very well, Miss. Thank you." John stepped back, longing to make his escape. "Until tomorrow, Sir." He tipped his cap and propelled his long legs to carry him away with haste, but once a safe distance away, he glanced over his shoulder and saw Sarah watching him.

🦋

"Why do you call the man Big John, Father?" Sarah asked, her focus still tied to the young man.

"His stature, my silly Sarah. Can't you see the man is a Titan?" He patted her arm and walked with her toward the house. "I've heard once during the yeomanry review in Norwich, the Duke commented on his great stature. Big John may be a yeoman, but he is a man to be reckoned with."

Surprised at her father's words, she suspected she saw admiration in his eyes. "Is he from Barnham? I recall the name Banning, but I have no recollection why." She grasped her father's arm as they ascended the stairs.

"Robert Banning, John's father, leases a parcel of my apple orchard. He produces cyder as we do." He pulled open the door and allowed Sarah to enter first.

"But their cyder is not the fine quality of ours, is it, Papa?" She grinned at her doting father, knowing what she said would make him laugh.

He chuckled. "My girl," he said, then paused. "Young woman, I should say." He stood back and gazed at her with a look of pride. "You know, Sarah, you've been presented to many eligible men of the community. You must consider yourself a woman."

"Fiddle-faddle. I love being your daughter, Papa. I need no other man to care for me. I'm not eager to be a woman. Let me be your little girl awhile longer." She sent him a playful grin, but in her heart, she meant every word.

Her father thrust a hand behind his back and shook his head. "My Sarah, I might be willing to keep you here longer, but your mother has other plans. She wants you to be a lovely bride one of these days." He stroked her cheek and strode from the room.

Sarah watched his departure until he vanished through the doorway. *A bride. A wife. A mother.* All those things were distant frightening dreams.

She had been prepared for adult proprieties. She'd learned proper etiquette and conversation in polite society. With her mother's encouragement, she'd learned to sing and dance, to read literature and speak a little French, and to do needlework. Now the season had arrived when she would be presented to the young men for courtship. Yet her heart was not in it.

Despite her assured proclamation, Big John Banning towered in her thoughts. His chestnut hair, his gentle eyes, his humble manner. A man of the earth and the sky. His shoulders in the clouds, his hands in the soil, and his feet secured to the earth.

Chapter 2

W hat is this cloth?" Dulcie asked, holding up
John's kerchief.

"It's the orchard keeper's. He offered it to
me so I could wipe dirt from my hands." Sarah eyed the
clean kerchief she'd washed and hung on the towel stand.
"I must return it to him."

"No, Miss, I'll return it. Your mother will be angry if
she finds you too cordial with the man."

"Piffle." Sarah snatched the handkerchief from the
maid's hands. "I will take care of it, Dulcie. . .and I'll
speak with Mother." She arched her eyebrow, hoping to
make her point with the servant.

Dulcie backed away. "It's your choice, Miss."

Sarah sank into her window seat and clutched the
white kerchief, while Dulcie finished her tasks and left
the room.

Spreading the cloth in her lap, Sarah brought the corners together to fold it but, instead, paused. Struck by an
idea, she rose and located her sewing box, opened the lid,
then plucked out a needle and brown silk thread.

To find more light, she carried the items back to the window seat and looked toward the garden wall. Today no one tended the garden. After she threaded the needle, Sarah selected a corner of the kerchief and began small embroidery stitches, creating John's monogram.

A tap on her door startled her, and she slipped her needlework beneath the pillow behind her back. "Come in," she called.

The door opened, and her mother stood in the threshold. Sarah watched her mother sweep into the room. Tall and trim, her straight back and long neck announced an air of elegance and breeding. "Why are you inside, Sarah? It's a lovely day. Come let us sit in the shade so we can discuss your party. Time is fleeting."

"We have nearly two months. . .until August." Eyeing her mother's determined face, Sarah's stomach tightened.

Her mother sank beside her on the cushion. "Preparations must be made properly. We must make our guest list and prepare the invitations. Then we'll select the menu." Her mother touched her hand. "I want to please you, Dear."

"You could please me by not insisting upon another ball. I've danced enough and accepted too many young men callers. None piqued my interest. I don't want to think about courting and. . .marriage. I would rather be a spinster, Mother. Please."

With fire sparking in her eyes, her mother bolted upward. "Sarah, what has gotten into you? A woman must have a suitable husband. Do you want to be an old woman with only servants for company in your old age?"

Before Sarah could respond, her mother sank to the cushion beside her. "Dear Sarah, you are a beautiful young woman, and you may take your time finding the young man who captures your heart. But we will hold your ball." Her look pleaded with Sarah. "Marriage can be a beautiful experience. Fulfilling. . .and exciting."

Her mother's face flushed, and Sarah wanted to ask questions. She'd never seen her mother's life filled with more than tending to servants and accepting a party invitation on occasion.

"And babies, Sarah. You'll want children." Her mother's features softened, and she caressed her daughter's cheek. "What would I have done without you to bring me such joy?"

Sarah looked at her mother's misty eyes and could no longer argue. She would have the ball. But what young man would capture her heart? Sarah's fingers slipped beneath the pillow and touched the cotton handkerchief. "I'll be down shortly."

Her mother wrapped her arms around her daughter's neck, pressing her cheek against Sarah's. "I'll go now. We'll talk outside." She rose and slipped from the room.

When the door closed, Sarah released a rattled breath and looked out the window, her mind wandering. For years, she had known the young men who attended the parties. Awkward, proper men whom she'd met at church and social functions. Breeding had trained them well, but each had lost the naturalness Sarah found appealing. None had left a lasting impression or sent warmth rushing through her veins like the poets proclaimed. None. . .

She faltered, remembering the unexpected sensation that riffled through her in the garden. The tenderness that tugged against her heart when she spoke to the quiet dark-eyed orchard keeper. Holding her breath, Sara panicked as a deep fear stabbed her. She came from landed gentry. John had been born a yeoman. A farmer.

Yet with stubborn persistence, she pulled the kerchief from behind the pillow and looked down at her stitches. With the J completed, she lifted the needle and finished the B. Yeoman or not, John Banning behaved as a gentleman. She broke the thread, folded the cloth, and tucked it inside the sleeve of her wrapper before disposing of the needle and thread.

Moving across the room, Sarah stopped at the door and grasped her courage. She must cooperate with her mother. . .behave properly as society and her parents expected.

Still she clung to her mother's words. *You may take your time finding the young man who captures your heart.* Sarah would take her time.

John hunched over the boxwood that formed a low maze in the formal garden. Pruning the new growth, he shaped the shrubs into perfect cubes. In each corner of the garden, the greenery formed four intricate patterns. In the hub of the adjoining paths stood rows of iris, delphinium, foxglove, and in the center, a sundial. The formality reminded him of society—everything in its appropriate place.

Concentrating on his work, John trimmed the outer hedges beside the displays of peonies and rosebushes.

When footsteps crunched on the gravel, he sprang to his feet. "Miss Hampton," he said catching his breath.

"Good afternoon, Mr. Banning. The garden looks grand."

She stood beside him with a pale pink parasol opened to block the sun. The color matched the trim on her pale gray dress.

"Thank you." Nervousness stiffened his stance, and he looked toward the opening in the gate, knowing her father would consider it inappropriate for him to converse with his daughter.

"I so much enjoy the sunshine instead of spending gloomy hours in the arbor. My mother insists I attend one more ball. Men are so blessed to be excused from such foolishness."

Startled by her comment, John hesitated. While she seemed to wait for his response, he sorted through words that would be proper for a man in his position. "I'm sure it will be a wonderful party. Your parents are eager to present you to the young men of the community." He swallowed, imagining the suitors who would gather around her, awed by her loveliness.

"Fiddle-faddle, I'll oblige if I must. But consider this, Mr. Banning. What do you do if you visit a shop for a new cap. . .and none meets your expectation?"

He struggled with her thinking, wondering how she had moved the conversation from admirers to caps. He could only answer her honestly. "I would not be interested in a new cap I suppose."

"Yes, that's my thinking exactly. If no suitor meets my

expectation, I'll not be interested."

Thinking of what had been said, John finally thought he understood. "I'm certain one gentleman will catch your fancy, Miss."

She shrugged and traipsed away toward a row of blossoming perennials. "Perhaps, but I can't imagine it."

Her voice caught on the breeze, and John hid the grin that curved his lips. He bent again to the trimming, though his concentration centered on the vision of gray and pink who strutted nearby.

"Look at the peonies," she called, moving closer to the row of flowering stems. "The ants have done their work. They're open wide and very delicate—like flounces on a ball gown."

Eyeing the fragile blossom, he could imagine Sarah dressed in a dainty frock covered with ruffles and lace, accepting the offer of a dance from a young gentleman. As she moved from flower to flower, her graceful manner delighted him. Her delicate parasol bounced above her head while sunshine spread around her feet like liquid gold.

Without thinking, he stepped to her side, bent down, snipped a blushing peony blossom from the plant, and presented it to her. Sending him a sweet smile, she accepted the stem between two long pale fingers and nestled it against the bodice of her frock.

Her direct gaze lowered to the blossom. "It's so beautiful. Look at the tinge of pink." She extended the petals beyond the shade of her parasol and in the full sun, the color seemed ethereal.

Before she drew the peony into the shade, a large

white butterfly lit upon the bloom. Sarah paused, and her face filled with delight.

John watched as the airy insect flitted above the flower, it's wings wafting like a lady's fan, intriguing and enticing.

When the butterfly floated away, Sarah gasped and drew in a full breath. "I forgot to breathe," she said, her laughter as airy as the insect. "Such a lovely moment. Thank you, Mr. Banning."

Her delight had given him a lovely moment as well. "You're welcome, Miss. . .but God provided the butterfly. I only offered you the flower."

"Indeed, but I still want to thank you." As if struck by a thought, she faltered and slipped her fingers beneath her lace-fringed sleeve. "Lest I forget. . ."

She withdrew a white cloth from beneath the pink ruffle, and John stared at it in amazement. Could it be his kerchief? And if so, why had she tucked it into her sleeve?

She presented the handkerchief to him. "Here. It is yours. Remember? You offered it to me to wipe my hands."

He stood frozen, unable to move.

"Don't fear, Mr. Banning. It's clean. I washed it for you." As if encouraging him to accept it, she jiggled her hand, and the cloth splayed downward, fluttering on the breeze.

He grasped the clean kerchief, noticing the neat stitching in the corner; the cloth could not be his. When he lifted the end, his pulse surged, seeing the letters J B. His initials. His monogram.

He pulled his amazed gaze from the white fabric and

looked at Sarah. "But this isn't. . .did someone—"

"I embroidered your initials. There is no B for Big. I hope you don't mind."

B? A soft chuckle rippled from his throat, followed by his concern. "I'm touched by your generosity, Miss. . .but it's not at all proper."

"Piffle, Mr. Banning. It's my way to make you beholden."

He tensed, speculating what she might mean.

"Now I'll expect flowers from you. Vases of them for my pleasure. Our ailing gardener, Mr. Benson, presented me flowers often. Might I expect the same?"

Shamelessly, John gazed at the woman, wanting to remind her Benson was elderly and married. But how could John tell her he could not give her flowers because he might also give her his heart?

Sarah carried the flower inside, filled a small vase, and carried it to her bedroom. Setting it on her dressing table, she sank onto her bed and gazed at the blossom. Her hands trembled with the awareness of her shameless behavior toward the young man. She had been flirtatious with the orchard keeper—totally improper and unforgivable to her parents. She prayed God would not find her indiscretion unpardonable?

Sarah lifted the hem of her skirt and slid her feet onto the bed. Through the lace curtain, a blue sky filled the window, and she lifted her prayer toward the heavens, asking God if the feelings that struggled inside her were the Lord's bidding or her own evil direction. No matter, she needed God's forgiveness.

"Sarah." Her mother's voice sailed through the doorway.

"Come in," she called, watching the door until it opened and her mother stepped inside, her mauve skirts swishing against the doorframe.

"Are you well? You look flushed." Her mother bustled across the floor and pressed the back of her hand to Sarah's cheek.

"I'm well. I walked in the garden, and I became heated." Sarah could never tell her mother what brought the blush to her cheeks.

"Perhaps that's all it is." Her mother rose and drew a cloth from the washstand, then wet it with water from the pitcher. Returning to Sarah, she pressed the damp towel against her daughter's forehead. "I have exciting news."

From the enthusiasm in her mother's voice, Sarah's interest was aroused. "What news, Mother?"

"Father has agreed we will all go to London to visit the Crystal Palace Exhibition. I suggested the holiday to celebrate your birthday."

"To London—but how long would we be gone?" Her mother's expression sent a fearful sensation skittering down Sarah's back. She should have expressed excitement, not disappointment. "How lovely. Thank you." She prayed she had hidden her obvious concern beneath her new exuberance.

"My—my, Sarah, for a moment you sounded as if you didn't want to go." She fanned herself with her hand, then rose and lifted the window to allow a cooler breeze to drift into the warm room. "There, now that's much better." She sent Sarah a gentle smile. "While in London, we'll purchase new gowns, especially for the ball."

Instead of returning to Sarah's side, her mother pulled back the curtain and peered outside. "The new orchard keeper is certainly making wonderful improvements to the landscaping." Facing the room, her gaze lit upon the flower on Sarah's dresser.

Sarah swallowed her guilt.

"Who gave you the peony, Sarah?"

Controlling her vulnerability, Sarah sat up and swung her feet to the floor. "It's from the garden."

"But you didn't pick the flower. Peonies have strong stems and must be cut," her mother said as her back stiffened.

Feeling helpless again, Sarah's shoulders sank. "I asked Mr. . . .the orchard keeper to cut the blossom for me."

"The orchard keeper?" Her mother's lips puckered with disapproval. "The Banning boy is a farmer."

"He is not a boy, Mother. He's a man. . .and. . ." Sarah realized her error too late. The words had already slipped from her lips and struck her mother's ear.

"Yes, Sarah, John Banning is a man. Please use good sense and proper conduct when dealing with such matters." With a final look, she turned and strode from the room.

Sarah stared at the empty doorway, then turned to the lovely peony on her table. Did good sense and proper behavior have anything at all to do with her? She cringed, knowing the unwelcome answer.

Chapter 3

Sarah passed through the garden gate and wandered among the flowers, longing to see Mr. Banning. His work took him to both the orchard and the gardens. Perhaps today, he labored among the apple trees.

She sensed he'd been avoiding her. As soon as she appeared near the stone bench, he scurried toward the shed or to another area of the garden. Still from a distance, she noticed his gaze turned toward her, and Sarah wondered if he felt the same stirring excitement as she did.

Her mother guarded her incessantly. They had spent hours together planning the August ball. At times, Sarah had longed to be stricken with some disease—the plague maybe—so the ball could be canceled. Then the seriousness of her wish struck her, and she would retract her thought, asking God to forgive her foolishness and to proffer a way to solve her dilemma.

In only a few days, her family would head for London. Her father, who had gone a month earlier on business, had viewed a small part of the amazing industrial exhibition and had told her about the wonders of the display. Though

Sarah looked forward to exploring the new Crystal Palace, she did not look forward to buying the gown for her ball. She loved new frocks, but the ball gown affirmed the immediacy of her birthday. . .and her August gala. If she were truly honest, she preferred to remain in Barnham near the orchard keeper, even though he pretended not to see her.

Sarah quickened her pace, returning to the garden gate, holding the spring-green parasol to cover her fair skin from the summer sun. Perhaps Mr. Banning had not come to the manor at all today. She shrugged and stepped briskly across the lawn, up the stairs, and closed the parasol.

When she entered the house, Sarah ambled down the hallway with no idea how she would occupy her time. Passing her father's study, his voice rang out to her. She spun around and stood in the doorway. "Good afternoon, Papa. It's a lovely day."

"You've been walking in the garden?" From his desk, he looked at her over his spectacles.

"Only a few minutes." Did he suspect her interest in the orchard keeper? She waited for his reprimand.

"Where are you off to now, Sarah?"

His questions caused a guilty shiver up her spine. She shrugged. "Nowhere in particular. Perhaps I shall read."

He slipped off his spectacles and rubbed his nose. "Would you do your papa a favor, please?"

Relieved, she stepped deeper into the room. "Certainly."

He slid on his eyeglasses. "Mr. Banning is in the conservatory. Would you tell him to see me before he leaves today? He can ring the servant's bell and have someone show him the way to my study."

Her heart leaped at the news. "Yes, I'd be happy to deliver your message." She monitored her excitement, longing to dance from the room and head for the conservatory. She forced herself to cross the floor and kiss her father's cheek before leaving his company.

Once beyond her father's gaze, she dashed past the family parlor and dining room, through the large formal sitting room, and out the French doors toward the conservatory. Stepping beneath the glass dome, she stood in place, making a circle and peering through the palms and ferns. When she heard a noise from the left, her attention focused on the greenhouse, and she followed the sound.

When she stepped inside, the orchard keeper lifted his head from his work.

"Good afternoon, Mr. Banning," she said.

He shifted, his gaze darting toward the doorway. "Why. . .have you come here, Miss?"

"Looking for you." Gesturing toward him, Sarah realized she still carried the parasol.

"Looking for me?" His jaw tensed. "But why?" His brows knitted.

"I will tell you soon enough, but first, I need you here." She beckoned him to follow.

Clearly concerned yet curious, John wiped his hands on a ragged cloth and walked behind her into the conservatory. Inside the dome, she sank to the stone bench and patted the seat beside her.

He eyed her frilly parasol.

"I came from the garden, she replied, answering his

questioning look. "Please sit here." She pressed her palm against the bench. "I cannot see you up there."

"Miss, I. . .I can't sit with you." He glanced toward the glass enclosure of the greenhouse. "I'm working." His thoughts jumped to the garden. Had he trimmed something improperly? What had been so urgent in the garden to cause her to search for him?

"Please," she said, looking into his eyes and causing him to tremble. "Father is in his study and mother is indisposed. Don't be apprehensive."

"Has my work displeased you?" He studied her face, seeing no unpleasantness.

"Your work? Not at all, Mr. Banning. I admire your ability in the garden."

"Then, why have you looked for me?"

"I have a message, but first, I am curious. I desire to know more about you."

"Me? No. . .Miss, being alone with you is improper."

"I'm weary of being proper, Mr. Banning. I'll go away if you will sit beside me for only a moment." She gestured again to the empty place at her side.

He eyed his dusty clothes, then her lovely green and white striped wrapper and matching parasol, her hair knotted and pinned at her neck. He should not allow himself to submit to her, but winning the battle seemed hopeless.

The young woman's determination awed him. Such strength and honesty in one petite frame. He sank to the farthest corner. His voice tightened in his throat, and he could not look in her eyes; they were too close. . .too intimate. "What do you want to know, Miss?"

"I wish you would call me Sarah." Her voice seemed more a whisper.

He could never call her by name. *Sarah*. It played in his mind like a love song. Perhaps she could ignore propriety, but his position allowed him no options.

"I understand your family lives in town," she said.

"A farm on the outskirts of town, Miss."

"Who tends the farm?" She plucked at the pleat in her skirt.

"I do. . .and four brothers, Miss."

She drew in a gasp of breath. "You toil here all day, then—"

"Yes, evenings and the hours I'm not in your father's employ," he said, recalling how weary his life had seemed before meeting. . .Sarah.

Her eyes widened. "Do you not have time for leisure?"

"On occasion," he said. But the occasion had been very rare. While her life abounded with social engagements, parties, and excursions, he toiled. . .but not forever. Someday he would own a business. . .if God honored his dream.

"Work is not meant to fill each hour," Sarah said. "I'm sure God has provided a verse to assure us that pleasure and leisure are important, too."

John searched his memory. "My knowledge of Scripture is limited, though I would presume the Lord allows some leisure."

"But. . .you quoted me a verse, don't you remember?" A frown marred her face. "I thought—"

"I know there is a God in heaven who controls the universe and directs the seasons, but. . .a man of my means has no time for church and little time for Bible reading."

She shifted to face him more squarely, a quizzical expression on her face. "Then how did you know the Bible verse the day we met?"

"From my mother. She always reminded us if God found the earth perfect enough to create people, then we should never be too proud to till the soil." His pulse raced as he looked into her tender eyes.

"Such meaningful words. . .your mother's." She lifted her head toward the light streaming through the overhead glass. As if kissed by heaven, the sun's rays beamed upon her.

"But why have I not seen you before. . .until that day in the garden?" she asked.

"I've been away working as an apprentice. I dream of owning my own cyder business one day. A cyder of such fine quality it will receive a warrant from the queen." Embarrassed at his admission, he paused. She would probably think him foolish to have such high hopes.

"Mr. Banning," Sarah said, her voice as tender as a whisper, "that's a wonderful ambition. Please don't call it a dream. Dreams don't always transpire, but ambition. . . that is different."

"Thank you kindly for your confidence," John said, rising. "Now I must return to the greenhouse." He extended his hand to help her rise.

"You are a gentleman, Sir," Sarah said. "I have more

than confidence in you—I have faith. I shall pray for God's blessing on your endeavors. With God, Mr. Banning, all things are possible."

John gave Sarah a polite bow and backed away, with her words hanging in his thoughts. *With God all things are possible.* Could she be correct? Would God be interested in a lowly man's hopes? Wouldn't the Lord be too busy saving people for eternity to worry about a simple man's plans?

He grinned, realizing he'd said plans, not dreams.

"Mr. Banning, I nearly forgot," she said, pivoting toward him like a lithe dancer. "My father requests you see him in his study before you leave. Pull the cord and a servant will show you the way."

Surrounded by ferns and palms and washed in sunlight, she sent him a bright smile and moved with grace through the doorway into the house. John stared at the empty opening, longing to be released from the feelings that stirred in his chest. She was a woman to be cherished.

Though she had vanished, he drank in her enticing scent of lavender and chamomile that clung in the air. Sweet. Young. Fresh. She appeared to be a dreamer as he was. He read it in her eyes. Though she tugged on his heart, he felt certain even God could not make this dream come true.

Saddened by the thought, he hurried back to his work, riddled with concern. Why did Mr. Hampton want to see him? Had he displeased the man? If God had a special plan for even the simplest of men, John prayed the Lord would be with him now.

The servant tapped on Edward Hampton's door, and when admittance had been granted, John entered. Hampton sat at a spacious walnut desk, matching the paneling that covered the walls.

"Please," Hampton said, rising and gesturing toward a chair, "have a seat."

John hesitated, scrutinizing his rough work clothes. "I'll stand, Sir, as not to soil the upholstery."

"Don't be absurd, Lad, sit." He gestured again.

"Thank you." John accepted the chair and waited, his hands twitching in his lap. He struggled to keep his eyes forthright and confident.

"Let me be direct. I have two reasons to speak with you. First, since your position at the manor, I have had no opportunity to discuss at any length the gardens and orchards with you. You mentioned you arrived home from an internship. I would enjoy hearing your new methods."

"My methods?" John faltered, amazed at his employer's interest.

"I trust you, John. You are a man of vision. You have come to me highly recommended. I've known your father for years and respect him."

John relished his sincerity. "I hesitate to interfere with my untested approach."

"Come now, I am only asking your thoughts," Hampton said. "First let us discuss the orchard. I would like your opinion on the cyder apples." He eyed John over his spectacles.

John hesitated, knowing his father leased acres of the Hamptons' orchard. "Sir, I'm not certain what you—"

"Let me be totally frank. I've heard from some of the townsmen that your family's cyder has a sweeter taste and higher color. Are you responsible for this?"

John nodded. "I have experimented with a variety of apples, Sir, and I am pleased with the balance of flavor."

"And I've heard you are producing a small batch of specialty cyder." He waited with the look of expectation.

"Yes, Sir. It is woodruff."

Hampton stared at his desk, nodding thoughtfully. "Woodruff? Yes, it has a distinctive flavor." He focused on John. "Let me consider what you've said, Big John. Now, tell me about the gardens. What news do you bring us?"

Reviewing methods he had recently learned, John described ways he'd been taught to improve the vegetable gardens. Then he recalled his excitement in working with new exotic flowers being grown in England.

Hampton drew back. "What of this 'bedding out' I've heard so much about? Have you seen the phenomena yourself? They tell me the origin is Aztec."

"That's correct, Sir. I have seen it used for growing plants to create the intricate mosaic pattern of flower beds."

"And pray tell, what are they?" Edward asked.

"Flowers bedded in varying colors that form pictures. Before returning home, I took a carriage ride past the new Crystal Palace in Hyde Park and saw the wonderful gardens there."

"Ah, yes, I did catch a glimpse. Did you go inside?"

"No, Sir, time did not permit a viewing. But it is a sight," John said, recalling the amazing glass building he'd heard covered seven hectares on the ground and thirteen kilometers of display tables.

"Would you like to see the inside, Big John?" Edward asked.

John studied his employer, wondering why he had asked about an impossibility. "Certainly, Sir. Visiting the industrial exhibit would be a man's dream."

"If you would like, you will have your dream. . .with one condition."

John closed his gaping mouth, embarrassed at his addled state. "Sir, I don't understand."

"I am asking you a favor. I have promised my wife and daughter a trip to London to see the Crystal Palace—a brief trip that will include a shopping excursion for the ladies. I can no longer travel with them, having pressing business here at home."

"How might I assist you?" John asked, his mind whirring with possibilities.

"I trust you, young man. Not wanting to disappoint my family, I would like you to accompany them to London. You and the coachman will be paid and accommodations arranged."

I trust you. Obviously, Mr. Hampton had no knowledge of Sarah's visits to the garden or conversations with him. The man had no idea how John struggled to control his feelings for the intelligent, lovely young woman. A woman presented and ready to marry.

John grappled with his employer's offer. Saying no seemed impossible, but spending such luxurious hours with Miss Banning would be John's undoing.

"So will you consider my offer, John? I will be ever in

your debt." Hampton slid his spectacles from his nose and ran his fingers along the bridge, eyeing him with a persistent gaze.

"I will do whatever you ask, Sir."

Hampton rose and rounded his desk, then clamped his hand on John's homespun shirt. "You are a good lad. I will inform my family."

Speechless, John could only nod. His mind raced with questions. Now he faced the reality of hours. . .days in the presence of the lovely Miss Hampton.

Chapter 4

Sarah studied her father's face all through dinner and sensed he had unpleasant news for them. His look sent a chill down her arms. The dining room hung with silence while the servants removed the china and silver, then brought on the sweet course, warm pudding with sugar and butter.

When all had retired to the kitchen except the butler, her father cleared his throat, and Sarah slid to the edge of her seat, waiting to hear the message that had bothered him through dinner.

"Excellent meal, Mary," he said.

"Thank you, Dear. Cook made the pudding especially for you. She knows you love it."

"I'll have to properly thank her." He cleared his throat again and clenched his fingers together against the table edge. "I have something to discuss with you both. It concerns our trip to London."

"Oh, dear, I hope nothing has occurred to change our plans." Mary daubed her mouth with a napkin.

Tension knotted along Sarah's spine and settled

between her shoulder blades.

"Unfortunately, there has been a minor change." Her father shifted with discomfort. "Lord Beckenridge will arrive in the village while we are to be gone. Since he must speak with me on business matters, I find it impossible to leave."

"But what of Sarah's birthday. . .and her gown?" Her mother's concern etched across her face.

"You and Sarah shall go as planned. I've made arrangements."

"No, Papa, not without you." Sarah prayed this was the long awaited solution for which she had hoped. No holiday from the manor. No new gown for the ball she didn't want.

"You will be in good hands. Both of you," he said.

When he straightened his back, Sarah observed her father's determination. No one could be quite so stubborn. . .except perhaps her own obstinate nature.

"But how without you, Papa?"

"John Banning will be your escort," he pronounced.

"Mr. Banning?" Mary said, her attention shifting from Sarah to her husband. "But Edward, is this appropriate? Should we not delay our trip and—"

"I cannot promise a journey to London before the ball, Mary. . .and you wanted to select Sarah's gown." He arched a brow at his wife.

"Well, yes," she murmured.

Sarah sat speechless. She could ask for nothing more wonderful. . .or more agonizing. For days she would be under her mother's watchful eyes. How could she avoid holding conversation with Mr. Banning during the journey?

"You have nothing to say, Sarah?" her father asked.

"I'm disappointed you won't be with us, Papa."

"You'll have a wonderful holiday without me." Her father moved aside his dessert and leaned forward on his forearms. "I have talked to this young man, Mary. John is a reliable fellow. I realize he is a laborer, but I see a future in the lad."

"You do, Papa?" Sarah's heart tripped.

"What do you mean, Edward?" Mary asked.

"He has learned some grand techniques while away, and he's shared them with me—ways to make our cyder more appealing to our buyers, and Big John has offered valuable advice about new apple trees I will add to our orchard."

Sarah sat back amazed at her father's excitement.

"We are removing the Sheep's Nose and Court Royal trees to make room for Yarlington Mill and Dabinett. The lad is filled with ideas." Her father stared beyond his family, his thoughts seemingly in the future. "I will reward the young man. . .somehow."

Her mother vocalized a disapproving harumph. "He is rewarded by a trip to London. I would think that is enough."

He gazed at her over his spectacles. "Mary, Sarah is present. We will discuss this later if you don't mind."

Watching her mother's shoulders tense, Sarah longed to ask questions. How could John be rewarded? Why did her father trust his wife and daughter to his care? But she knew better than to ask. At this moment, she could hardly contain her joy. Somehow she would enjoy John's company despite her mother's watchful glare. If she couldn't find a way, she would leave her destiny in her Heavenly Father's care.

❧

Sarah breathed a relieved sigh when the public carriage returned them to their London hotel. She'd spent tedious hours with the dressmaker selecting her ball gown and other frocks for the social engagements following her birthday celebration.

The trip from Barnham had been tiring and uncomfortable. She sat with her mother in the carriage while John rode outside with the driver. What made her think they would have an opportunity to converse? She wondered if her father had traveled with them if he might have allowed John in the carriage and enjoyed conversation, learning more about his ideas for the plants and orchard. A foolish speculation. If her father had come, John would be at the manor, tending the garden.

Encouraged, Sarah could barely believe how fondly her father had spoken of John. He saw John's worth—his talent and quick mind. Her mother, on the other hand, only saw a lowly farmer.

Because of the time constraints, Sarah's dresses would be delivered to their home, an extravagance Sarah thought unnecessary but her mother deemed important. When the carriage door opened, the driver helped them to the ground with their few packages.

Her mother paid the driver, while Sarah hurried

ahead of her to the lobby and waited by the staircase. She'd never considered her father would arrange for John and the driver to stay in a less choice hotel. She sighed. Another propriety.

Since they'd arrived in London, Sarah had garnered enthusiasm for the Crystal Palace. People spoke of nothing else. At least at the exhibition, she and John might have a moment outside her mother's vision to speak a private word. Sarah eyed the grandfather clock on the broad staircase. John would arrive in a few moments to take them to the exhibition.

Sarah darted up the stairs, her mother trudging behind her. On the first floor, she rushed to their suite and waited until her mother arrived, breathless, with the key.

Tossing the packages on the settee, Sarah poured water from the pitcher, bathed her face to remove the street grime, then looked into the mirror. Her face glowed but from more than the exertion of the climb. The excitement of seeing John had tinted her cheeks a rosy hue.

Her mother had plopped onto the tapestry lounge and fanned herself from the midday heat. Her mottled red cheeks softened Sarah's heart. Going to the washstand, Sarah dampened a cloth to soothe her mother's flushed face.

"Thank you, Sarah dear," her mother said, continuing to fan. "You must remember to use the language of the fan, Sarah. Practice lest you forget."

"Mother, I have watched ladies and their fans forever, it seems. I don't need practice. I'll do what is natural."

"Sarah," her mother's voice raised to an unfamiliar

pitch, "you will do what is proper. What has come over you, Daughter? Since you have approached eighteen years, you have lost your gentler ways."

"I'm sorry, Mama," Sarah said, crumpling to the floor beside her and pressing her cheek against her mother's skirt. "I know you and Papa have only my well-being in mind, but I am having difficulty accepting what I must do."

"You will enjoy it in time, Sarah."

Sarah doubted it, but she did not disagree. She had no desire to be admired and courted by the young men of the surrounding area of Barnham. Sarah swallowed her thought, not wanting John's image to surface in her mind.

Why did this man stir her like no other? She'd wrestled with her thoughts over and over. Though roughened by physical labor, John had qualities that the eligible young gentlemen of the area did not. Maturity, tenderness, ambition, ingenuity, and a simple godliness. Those qualities rose in her mind when she thought of him. Yet her eagerness frightened him. She saw the look in his eyes. She must garner self-control. John would certainly avoid her if she showed him her true admiration.

Her mother rose from the lounge and appeared to have gained composure to make their way downstairs. With eagerness, Sarah waited, and when a tap sounded on the door, she opened it.

"The driver is downstairs," John said. His focus locked with Sarah's for a heartbeat, then slid to the carpet.

"The carriage is waiting, Mama," Sarah called over her shoulder.

Since she had only seen John dressed for gardening,

Sarah admired his Sunday clothes. He looked more hand-some than she had ever imagined, and the sight warmed her. Hearing the rustle of her mother's skirts, Sarah stepped away from the door to grasp her parasol and reticule.

Her mother swished passed, handing John the door key. He stayed behind to lock the suite, then hurried forward to assist her mother down the long staircase. Sarah went ahead, imagining how it might feel to have John's arm linked to hers.

At the carriage, John assisted them both inside. His hand lingered a moment on Sarah's glove, and when she drew away, the pressure of his fingers lived in her thoughts.

The carriage rocked and bounced along the cobbled streets, and when traffic became heavier, Sarah noted they were nearing Hyde Park. The driver guided the horses down North Carriage Road, approaching the north entrance of the park leading to the Crystal Palace. Through the iron gates, Sarah saw the giant glass edifice with the flags of all nations floating above. Transepts jutted from each end of the building, and in the dis-tance, she viewed people on foot and riding in carriages traveling toward the entrance. As they neared, the sight astounded her—elegant palms, statues, flowers, and the gigantic fountains.

"It's lovely," Mary said, her voice sounding awed by the splendor. "Your father chose Friday for our excursion. It is the favored day of the gentry with tickets going for a half crown. With smaller crowds, we'll have time to linger over the exhibits."

"What will the driver and. . .Mr. Banning do while

we're inside, Mother?" Sarah's heart pitched, waiting for the answer.

"Your father is generous, Sarah. He has allowed them to attend today as well."

"Very generous," Sarah said, monitoring the thrill in her voice. She closed her eyes, sending a thankful prayer to her Father in heaven.

At the grand entrance, John stepped down and gave them assistance. While her mother spoke with the coachman and arranged an agreeable time to depart, Sarah longed to tell John she would find him inside, but her mother's keen ears would hear even the smallest murmur.

When all had been agreed upon, Sarah and her mother went on ahead while John followed. Sarah gave a longing look over her shoulder, listening to her mother's prattle about the vast array of magnificent displays.

The exhibit appeared more than they could enjoy in one day. They moved from one display to another, marveling at the merchandise from all over the world, but Sarah's thoughts were behind her. Occasionally, she looked over her shoulder to see John an acceptable distance behind them.

Focusing on the exhibit, Sarah inspected elegant furniture, ornamental silver pieces, decorative boxes covered with japanning or decoupage, and spinning machines weaving hand-spun cuffs, but always, her mind centered on John. Watching her mother's eyes widen, Sarah inched forward to admire the majolica ceramic earthenware—brightly glazed vases and sculptures in all sizes and shapes. When they reached the talk of the exhibition, the Patek

Phillipe watches, her mother halted to study the lovely timepieces. News had traveled that Queen Victoria had purchased two of the creations during her visit.

When her mother insisted she sit for a silhouette portrait, Sarah had a small respite, while John observed from a distance. She had been more intrigued by the daguerreotypes. The thought of her actual portrait etched on a metal plate intrigued her.

For high tea, Sarah followed her mother to the refreshment tables where they nibbled on tea sandwiches and scones with jam. Sarah observed fashionable women and men ambling past, overhearing their praise of the Crystal Palace and the exhibition, but she longed to discern what John concluded about the amazing array.

When Sarah felt she could endure no more waiting, her mother straightened her shoulders. "Look, Sarah, it's Lady Hughes and her sister, Penelope. Remember, they came with Lord Hughes to visit last spring."

"Yes, Mama." Only a year younger than Sarah, Penelope had provided good company during her visit. Her appearance gave Sarah hope.

Before her mother acknowledged them, the woman sent her a friendly wave and hurried to their table. "Hello, Mrs. Hampton. Sarah. Isn't this glorious?"

"It is, Lady Hughes. Would you and Penelope care to join us?"

"That would be so kind," the woman said. "Will we inconvenience you?"

"No, Lady Hughes, please accept my chair." Sarah rose, taking advantage of the opportunity. With her plan in motion, she touched her mother's shoulder. "Perhaps, Penelope and I could view the displays nearby. Do you mind, Mama?" Would her mother refuse with Lady Hughes in her presence?

"Two young ladies without an escort?" her mother responded. "I think not."

Eyeing Lady Hughes, Sarah was unable to read her thoughts. "Please, Mama. We'll stay nearby, I promise."

Her mother's arched brow silenced her pleading.

Chapter 5

Disappointed, Sarah conversed quietly with Penelope about the displays, while her mother and Lady Hughes prattled about something called McCormick's reaper and the giant cannon; eventually, her mother turned the discourse to Sarah's coming out.

When the tea had vanished and only crumbs lay on their plates, Lady Hughes and Penelope made their goodbyes and wended their way through the crowd.

"Before we had tea, I noticed the most amazing spinning machine, Mama." She beckoned her mother to follow and led the way back.

Pausing to view the automated spinning machine, Sarah scanned the crowd, praying that John had not vanished. Her heart lifted when she saw him. He stood deep in the assemblage, his height jutting above the others.

"I see Mr. Banning, Mama. May I move forward? I'm unable to see well." Without waiting for an answer, she shouldered her way between two patrons, leaving her mother behind.

"Mr. Banning," Sarah said, breathless with excitement.

His gaze darted in every direction. "Where is your mother?"

"In the crowd," Sarah said, motioning behind her.

"You should not leave her alone."

"I longed for a moment with you, Mr. Banning." She grasped his forearm, and he brushed his fingers against hers for a heartbeat before moving his hand.

Sarah's heart fluttered beneath her bodice. Frightened of her emotion, she focused on the exhibit. "What displays have you enjoyed?"

"The new machinery. My mind flies from one idea to the next." Excitement rose in his voice.

"Sarah."

She jumped at her mother's voice. "Here, Mama."

Her mother's eyebrow arched. "I see. Please don't force your way through a crowd, Sarah. You must mind your manners."

"I'm sorry, but I find the displays exciting. See there." She pointed to an unfamiliar apparatus. "What is the strange device, Mr. Banning?"

"It's a press."

She raised on tiptoe, unable to see over the tall man blocking her view. "I can't see well. Can you see, Mama?"

"Let me assist you," he said, shifting to the side and allowing Sarah and her mother to have a clearer view. He stepped behind them. "It's called a hydraulic press."

Sarah's concentration blurred. Standing so close, she could almost feel the beating of his heart. He smelled of peppermint and body-warmed wool, and she longed to turn to face him and feel the prickle of whiskers beginning to show after the lengthy day.

"What is it called again, Mr. Banning?" her mother asked.

"A hydraulic press," he said, hunching over to lean closer so her mother could hear. "It's an amazing invention. Wonderful prospects."

His breath brushed against Sarah's ear and ruffled wisps of curls around her face. She tried to ignore the lovely feeling and ask a sensible question. "What is its purpose?"

His voice animated, John explained the use in simple terms. A flush of excitement rose on his face as he described how running water could be halted by a valve so the flow was forced upward, making a press function with little effort. Sarah made little sense of it, but she knew from his demeanor that this invention would be something important.

He had piqued her mother's interest. She listened intently to his explanation.

"We will be able to press apples with less manual labor," he said. "Less labor with greater speed, less monetary investment with more efficiency. It will work exceedingly well for your family's cyder business."

"An interesting concept, Mr. Banning. I'm sure Mr. Hampton will be most interested in your thoughts."

"The press will help your own family, also," Sarah added.

"The cost is too great for a farmer." He turned to her mother. "But for a man of Mr. Hampton's stature, it will make all the difference."

"Thank you, Mr. Banning," her mother said. "Sarah, let's move along. We'll leave you to enjoy the exhibit on your own."

He bowed to her mother and Sarah. "Mrs. Hampton. Miss Hampton."

Capturing Sarah's arm, her mother moved her through the crowd, while Sarah struggled for composure. She expected her mother's rancor for her improper behavior. But when she saw John she'd been stirred to forget propriety and station. In time, her mother would forgive her. Yet Sarah realized she treaded on unsafe ground. Not only could her disobedience bring retribution to herself, but her actions could cause untold distress for John.

Tonight in the quiet of her bed, she would ask God to give her wisdom to amend her improper behavior and guide her in the Lord's direction.

"The exhibit was amazing, Sir," John said, sitting in Edward Hampton's study. "You must go to London before the closing and see the hydraulic press. The invention will do wonders for the cyder business, and you could be one of the first to use it."

"You astound me, Big John. You have a creative eye. No one has thought to use the press for cyder?"

"No, not that I've heard," John said.

"You are brilliant."

John squirmed in the chair, uncomfortable with the man's compliments. "Thank you, Sir, but I think others will envision the idea soon. If you approach a machine builder first, you will be ahead of your time."

"I will," Hampton said. "My lad, I will reward you for this. Once Sarah's ball is ended, I will leave for London. I cannot thank you enough for your resourceful thinking. Clever, that's what you are, Big John."

John lowered his eyes and nodded. He only wished he could share the knowledge with his father, but a project of this magnitude needed financing to make the presses, and for his family, the concept would be an impossible dream.

Sarah's comment rose in John's thought. *With God all things are possible.* Could Sarah be correct? Did God help farmers or only the lords and ladies of the world?

Hampton leaned forward over his desk. "Mrs. Hampton enjoyed the trip immensely. She has talked about nothing else since she returned—Belgian chocolates, majolica earthenware, French perfume." He arched a bushy brow and gave a chuckle. "But could you imagine what my Sarah has talked about?"

Fear rifled through John. Could her father suspect his fondness for his lovely daughter? John shook his head. "No, Sir, I have no idea."

Hampton's chuckle turned to a full-bodied laugh. "Gummed envelopes. My practical daughter talked about daguerreotypes and gummed envelopes. She is amazing." His face glowed.

"She is amazing," John said, wishing he could open his heart and confess how Sarah had changed his tiresome life. Each day he filled with excitement hoping to see her for a fleeting moment. Her candid responses, her open mind, her intelligence completed the man he wanted to be.

"I thank you, John, for the care you extended my family and your stimulating information. My visit to the exhibition months ago had been so brief that—" He halted, hearing a tap on the door. "Come in."

The door swung open, and Sarah stood in the threshold. Her focus swung from her father to John, while a flush ignited her face.

"Don't be disconcerted, Sarah," Hampton said. "Mr. Banning and I are nearly finished. Come join us."

Sarah hesitated, then crept into the room, her hands folded in front of her.

"Come here, my girl," Edward said. "I have only now thanked Mr. Banning for escorting you and your mother to London."

"It was very kind," Sarah said, her gaze evading John's.

"Is this a private matter, Sarah?" Hampton asked.

At his question, John rose and backed from the desk. "I can excuse myself, Sir."

Giving John a sidelong glance, Sarah paled. "No, Father, my gowns have arrived from London and mother thought you would like to see them." Her timid gaze shifted to John.

"The pleasure of being a father, Big John. A man must look at fabric with ribbons, ruffles, and lace that has cost a small fortune." He patted Sarah's arm. "But admiring my daughter brings me much joy. One day you will know such joy."

John quaked at his direct gaze, fearing an inference in the man's comment.

"One day," Hampton continued, "you will have a daughter of your own."

Relief bathed John's fearful guilt. "One day in the distant future, Sir."

Hampton smiled. "I must follow this lovely young lady and view the trappings that will capture some young man's heart."

"I'll be on my way then, Sir." John backed away, his emotions whirling like a dervish. Futile, but true: he longed to be the young man who could offer his heart to Sarah and proclaim it to the world.

John returned from the orchard on foot. The morning had been cool, hinting rain, and he wanted the exercise. On hot days, he road his horse, but the overcast sky and invigorating breeze urged him to go on foot. In the distance, he spied a tumble of skirt and parasol sitting on a stone outcropping. His stomach knotted, seeing Sarah waiting for him.

The four days he had accompanied her and her mother to London had been a paradox—a rapturous torment. Despite Mrs. Hampton's obvious scorn at learning he would be their escort, she had acquiesced and appeared impressed with his knowledge and fortitude. Though Edward Hampton admired his faithfulness, he could never presume to be accepted as an equal.

"Mr. Banning," Sarah's voice called as he neared.

John tipped his cap. "Good morning."

She eyed him from beneath her white wispy parasol. "I had a lovely holiday in London. Thank you for your gracious company." She sent him a beautiful smile.

His strong legs staggered, trembling beneath him as unstable as apple pomace.

She lifted her hand upward for assistance to rise. John inspected her soft, slender fingers extended toward him and longed to press them to his lips, to taste the sweet rose attar she rubbed on her skin to keep them soft. He'd smelled the aroma on days she had followed him to the garden, and he could no longer separate the flower's fragrance from the blossoming woman who lingered in his sight so often. He could not forget the moment in London when she clung to his arm and he dared to brush his hand against hers. Again, with caution, he propelled his arm forward and grasped her tiny fingers in his giant palm.

She rose, and her gaze dwelt on the incongruity of her hand swallowed in his. Then she focused on his face. "You are a Titan, Mr. Banning. A giant. . .in heart as well as size."

Her flattery caught him unaware, and he faltered before making light of her comment. "Do not say such things, Miss."

She withdrew her hand, clasped it to her parasol, and took one step forward, then stopped to gaze at him. Time ceased as he basked in her admiring eyes.

"You are a handsome man, Mr. Banning. I must share a secret. In my mind I speak your name. John."

The sound of his name on her lips sent joyous shivers

down his sun-warmed back. *I am a daring fool,* he thought, knowing he should not allow the remarkable sensations to remain in his thoughts. "You should not think of my name."

"But it pleases me," she said. "Would you speak my name, John?"

Her question stopped him like a man who has spied a coiled viper. He desired to bolt from the charming woman. "That is impossible. Totally improper. Please, don't ask."

"But—"

"Your father would discharge me. You are the daughter of gentry. I am little better than a servant."

Her eyes lowered, and he could barely hear the whisper of her voice. "Please let me hear you say Sarah."

Longing swelled in his chest, and he closed his eyes to control the sweet feelings that rambled through him. "I. . .I cannot."

"Only once, John. Please." She rested her hand against his forearm. "John."

He struggled to sound the name against his tongue. The sweetness of the tone filled his breath, and he could only murmur. "S. . .Sarah."

Their gazes met, and he clung to the moment like a baby bird ready to leap with faith into the air.

"Thank you," she whispered. She stepped back and appeared suddenly shy. "Please return alone, John. I'll be along shortly. I know you have work to do. . .and you would rather reach the garden without me at your side."

He could only nod, for his lungs had disregarded his

command to breathe. Pulling his gaze from her fair face, he moved off, his long strides creating distance between them. He could not look back for fear he would turn around and run back to her, lifting her in his arms and carrying her away. She had captured his mind and heart.

In the lamplight, Sarah gazed at her elegant ball gown. She eyed herself in the glass, admiring the delicate pink silk frock fashioned with balloon sleeves graced with deep lace epaulets. Her gaze swept along the demure rounded neckline, and she caressed the darker pink ribbon serving as a sash and admired the same shade bows along the lacy hem. The gown was exquisite.

She had pulled back her hair with a satin bow, and Dulcie had combed it into banana curls that brushed against her bare neck. Her only jewelry was pearls at her throat and small pearl earrings, a gift from her father.

Carriages had been arriving, and music drifted up from the parlor adjoining the small ballroom. Beyond, the conservatory had been readied where the dancers could retire and sit on benches among the palms.

She slid into her white satin evening slippers and lifted the delicate ivory fan trimmed with pink lace. She fluttered it in front of her face, reviewing her mother's prodding to display the fan properly. Without her mother's knowledge, she had practiced twirling it in her left hand. A young man knew it meant *I love another.*

If only John were one of the eligible young men of the village, the evening would be perfect. Instead, he had spent the day toting in bouquets of flowers from the garden and adding palms and fern along the terrace. In the frenzy of her ball, Sarah had only seen him through her window and caught a glimpse of him in the conservatory. Her knees weakened as she remembered the afternoon he'd whispered her name. *Sarah.* The word filled her heart like a glorious symphony.

Calming her thoughts, Sarah took a deep breath and opened her door. If she didn't make her entrance soon, her mother would appear to escort her down the staircase.

Laughter and voices drifted from the ground floor, and she crept forward, forcing her legs to carry her to the wide steps. She hesitated at the top, as her mother had insisted, until enough eyes were drawn to her entrance. Then in the growing hush, she made her way down the staircase.

A young man she had seen on other social occasions waited for her, taking her hand as she neared the bottom. Applause rang through the entrance hall, and joining her parents, she stood in the receiving line until her legs trembled and her face grew weary from her forced smile.

The music livened, and when the first reel began, another gentleman led her to the dance floor. One by one, the possible suitors took turns asking her to dance, bowing and scraping with an attempt to leave her with a lasting impression. All failed miserably. Sarah could only envision the chestnut-haired orchard keeper with his tender, dark eyes.

The meal seemed an endless series of tiresome conversations while Sarah nibbled from each course—julienne soup to boiled salmon followed by lamb cutlets and spring chicken served with her father's best cyder. Desserts were on a sideboard to be enjoyed later by those who wished. Sarah had eyed the fresh fruit, cherry tarts, custard, and her favorite charlotte russe, but her stomach had no interest in the food nor her heart in discourse.

At the appropriate time, Sarah invited the guests to return to the ballroom. The older guests settled in the parlor, leaving the young men and women to dance. Her face flushed from the heat, Sarah excused herself and hurried through the conservatory, then slid through the door into the moon-filled night.

Strolling away from the conservatory's glow, Sarah drew in the fragrance of the night air and looked into the sky. The lilting music filled the soft night, and her long-ing tugged at her heart.

"Why have you left your guests?"

Sarah gasped, then recognized John's voice emanat-ing from the shadow of the privet fence. She rushed toward his voice as he stepped away from the shrubs into the moonlight.

Without hesitation, Sarah fell into John's wide opened arms. He clasped her to him, her head pressing against his heart. "John, I am so glad you are here." She clung to him, her pulse racing at the delight of his pres-ence more than the fear of discovery.

"Sarah," he murmured, his heart thundering against his chest, "my sweet, dearest Sarah. I am wrong to hold you in my arms, but I can no longer contain my joy at seeing you. You are an angel in the moonlight."

"You have acted with honor," she whispered into the

linen of his shirt. As if providence decreed, a slow waltz drifted across the grass, and she swayed to the music.

John joined her, gliding and swaying together with only the stars as their witness. She spun away, and he brought her back into the fold of his arms. Together they spun in three-quarter time, their darker silhouettes melting into the night's shadows.

Washed with wisdom, John slowed and eased her deeper into the darkness, his eyes drinking in her ethereal loveliness. "You are the lovely dreams that fill my nights, the sun that warms my days, the stars that light the heavens. I do not deserve to even speak your name, dearest Sarah, but I cannot stop myself from the delight."

Her voice muffled against his chest. "I aspire for no other man to come courting, John. I desire only you." She lifted her hand and pressed it against his cheek. "Your hair as black as the night sky, your eyes as deep and mysterious as the ocean, your heart and soul as tender as a babe's."

Cautioned by reality, John faltered. "I fear God does not approve of my feelings. You know the Lord so much better than I, Sarah. I remember you said with God all things are possible. I yearn to believe it is true."

"It is true, John. God has guided me to you, and I believe the Almighty Father approves. Now we must convince my earthly parents. . .and that is the more difficult task."

Her words struck a chord of truth in John's heart. When he had attended church, he'd heard the vicar proclaim God as good and merciful, and if that were so, God would truly perceive the purity of his heart and his intentions. John cherished Sarah, and if God approved, he would swim oceans to take Sarah as his own. "I long to say the words that lay on my tongue, Dearest.

She looked into his eyes. "Say the words, John, for I long to hear them."

"I love you," he whispered. "My life is incomplete without your gentle spirit in my care."

"I must speak what my heart has known forever. I love you, John, and God willing, one day we will proclaim it to the world."

In his peripheral vision, John saw movement near the conservatory door. He stepped deeper into the shadow. "Go, Sarah, before we are discovered."

She reached toward him as he slid through the privet.

"What inappropriate behavior has urged you to leave your guests, Sarah?" Her mother's voice pierced the night.

Sarah swung around and approached her mother. "I am enjoying the fresh air, Mama."

Her mother looked beyond her toward the privets.

Sarah's heart sank to her feet.

Chapter 6

Riddled with guilt, Sarah stood before her mother. "Isn't the night beautiful, Mama? I am mesmerized by the full moon and the scent of roses drifting from the garden. The ballroom is stuffy. Could we bring the music outside?"

"Don't be foolish. No one has a ball on the terrace. Now come inside with your guests. You'll catch a chill and catch your death."

Relief washed over her as she took her mother's arm and entered the glass door into the conservatory. With a sigh, she slipped from her mother's grasp and paused to speak to a friend and her beau. The distraction gave her a reprieve, and Sarah's mother wandered back to the ballroom, away from Sarah's fear-filled eyes.

If her mother knew the truth, she would send her away. . .to India or worse. Turning back to the glass walls, Sarah could not see into the garden. The reflection of light from the oil lamps painted images of ferns and palms mingled with a wash of color from the young ladies' gowns.

Still, she knew beyond the hedge John stood in the shadows, loving her.

John waited for three days, praying Sarah would find him to relate whether or not they had been discovered. The longer he waited for her to appear the more he feared she had been locked in her room or sent away. His gaze lingered on the empty garden bench, and he forced himself to turn and tend to the plants. His mind, however, tangled around a dainty woman who had declared her love for him.

With his back to the gate, John heard footsteps and spun around to face Edward Hamilton. His stomach knotted, fearing why his employer had come to find him.

"Good day," Hampton said, approaching him.

"Good day, Sir." He averted his eyes, imagining he could read his guilt in the man's gaze. But the man's friendly face did not fit John's speculation.

"We are on our way to London, my lad. I pray when I see you again the news will be good." He extended his hand toward John.

Looking at his soiled fingers, John drew them across his trousers and grasped Hampton's hand in a firm shake. "I pray your trip is successful, Sir." But his mind whirred. His employer had said *we* are leaving, and John's heart twitched. Would Sarah accompany them to London?

"My wife is waiting for me, so I must be off." he said. As he stepped away, Hampton called over his shoulder. "We'll return on Monday, John. I'll speak with you then."

My wife. Had he meant only Mrs. Hampton would travel with him? John observed the man until he vanished beyond the gate. His curiosity piqued, John edged forward and neared the garden wall, hoping to see who would pass in the carriage, but only a blur flashed past through the carriage windows.

He wiped his brow with the back of his hand. Five days he would wait for the news of Hampton's success. . . and perhaps to see Sarah again. He returned to the beds beyond the garden shed, his mind twisted in thought. While he bent over the plants, a shadow fell across his hand. Startled, he bolted upright.

Sarah stood before him, a look of shyness on her face. His mind propelled forward, but he demanded his feet to remain still. "You didn't journey to London?"

She shook her head. "I remained behind. We have five days, John. Five days that we may become friends. Tomorrow I will inform the cook I desire a picnic in the meadow." She drew nearer. "Will you meet me there?"

Five days. Confusion rattled his brain. Good judgment restrained him, but opportunity nudged him forward. Casting wisdom aside, he answered. "I will, Sarah."

"May we walk a moment?" she asked.

He rose, and they followed the lane to the meadow. John held her securely, lest she stumble in the long grasses. When they reached the edge of the woods in the speckled shade, he bade her rest on a fallen tree trunk.

Facing her, John's gaze lingered on her dainty hand, her long tapered fingers resting against the folds of her skirt, as delicate and white as angel wings.

"May I touch your hand, Sarah?" Anxiety sparked with his question.

She extended her right arm toward him. "I have dreamed of your touch."

With caution, he wrapped her hand in his, reveling in the softness of her silken skin. She raised a finger of her left hand and laid it against his cheek, and he captured it beneath his free palm.

A shudder ran through him, but caution rose in his consciousness and he withdrew his hand. "Sarah, I must guard against my emotions. You are a lady. A Christian woman, and I respect you."

"No man has held my hand or been so near. . .except my father." She sent him a shy smile. "I have only imagined such joy."

John grappled with good sense. "I cannot be in your presence without longing to kiss your lips, but propriety and station restrain me."

"You may kiss my hand if you will. I would delight in it."

Overcome by her tenderness, he lifted her satiny hand and pressed it to his lips, feeling as if his heart would burst.

"Your lips are soft, John. One day I pray they shall touch mine."

"If God blesses us." He rose and walked away to calm his rising pulse. But a new request rose in his thoughts— one more pleasing to God. Sarah's love for the Lord had grown in John's thoughts and fired his heart. Eagerness rose to understand her faith.

"Tell me about God, Sarah. I believe, but I'm afraid my faith is not as strong or unfailing as yours. You're like a mountain. Your voice is filled with trust when you speak of the Lord."

He studied her profile as she looked across the meadow.

Her voice rang like the bells on Sunday as she spoke about her relationship with God. "He is my friend. Jesus walks with me daily and guides my feet. Though I feel secure and safe with you, I am more than sheltered in God's presence. The Lord promises His children eternal life if we believe. You stated you believe, John."

"Yes, I believe, but now I want to know the personal relationship you do, Sarah. I yearn to have a confident faith and to trust that God cares about someone as unimportant as an orchard keeper."

She shifted to face him. "John, don't say such things. Remember where Jesus was born?" Her gaze penetrated his.

"In Bethlehem."

"But *where* in Bethlehem?"

"A stable."

"Yes," she said, a smile lighting her face. "And to whom did the angel's first announce Jesus' birth?"

"Shepherds." His heart tripped at his answer. "Shepherds," John repeated, the meaning of her questions becoming clear. "Christ was born in a humble stable and welcomed first by lowly shepherds."

"Yes. Yes." She leaned forward and pressed her cheek to his. "God does not create one person more important or precious than another. We are equal in God's sight. . . and in my sight, John."

His heart lifted at her words. "I don't know why the Lord has so wonderfully blessed me, Sarah." Turning his eyes heavenward, he noted the sun dropping to the west. "The time grows late. You must return before the servants come looking."

He slid from the wooden perch and helped her rise. With a watchful eye, John guided her across the meadow. When they reached the path to the garden, he halted. Benefited by his height, in the distance he witnessed a man walking their way. He hurried Sarah to the side of the barrel shed, his body trembling. "Someone is coming, Sarah."

Concern filled her face. "What shall we do?"

Their solution stood beside him. He dug into his pocket, extracted the key, and yanked the lock from the shed latch. "Inside, quickly."

Sarah scurried through the doorway as John followed and slid the door closed. "Withdraw behind the kegs, Sarah, and I pray whoever comes will not notice the unlocked shed."

In silence, he inched his large frame backward. When he reached Sarah cowering in the corner, he filled with shame. What man would endanger the reputation of an innocent woman as he had done? Only a fool.

He retreated into the darkness and waited.

The door swung open and a long dark shadow haloed by sunlight extended along the floor. "Now what fool left this shed unlocked?" a voice mumbled. Instead of leaving to find a key, the man lumbered into the shed, while Sarah's body trembled behind John.

Responding with haste, John stepped into the light. "What are you doing, Devon?"

The man stumbled backward, as if a ghost had risen from the shadows. "Big John, is it you?"

"You can see, it is." John strode forward, deterring the man from entering farther.

"But what are you doing in the barrel shed?"

John lifted a large cask and shook it, a faint slosh of water moved inside the barrel. "What does it look like, Devon? Soon we'll harvest the apples and press them into cyder. Where do you think we will store the cyder?" He frowned down at the smaller man.

Devon edged backward. "I'm not challenging you, Big John. I only feared—"

"Where do we store the cyder, Devon?" He repeated the question, mustering his confidence.

Devon clutched the doorjamb. "In the barrels. You know that, Big John."

"And what if our barrels dried out and cracked? What then?" He moved forward as Devon stepped outside into the sunlight.

"I only asked," Devon said, turning on his heel and continuing his march down the lane.

Ashamed of his bullying, John remained in the doorway until the man vanished from sight. With haste, he beckoned to Sarah.

She hurried forward and clasped John's arm. "Thank you, my dearest."

"You are safe now. Return to the manor. I shall linger behind before returning." He lifted her hand and pressed it to his cheek. "I will await you tomorrow at the edge of the woods."

"For our picnic?" she asked, stepping into the light.

"Yes. It is safer than the meadow."

"Until tomorrow, dear John." She hurried away down the path.

John braced his back against the wall, staring into the shadows. Tomorrow he would tell her he could no longer endanger her reputation. He cherished Sarah and would do nothing to lessen her purity in the eyes of man or God.

Chapter 7

Sarah lifted her basket higher above the long grass, her eyes directed on the woods. She didn't see John and wondered if he had been delayed or feared discovery. The servants, she sensed, kept a close eye on her.

Reaching the woods, Sarah paused. To her joy, John appeared from behind a broad tree trunk and hurried to meet her. He grasped the basket and guided her along the root-filled pathway.

"I've found a secluded spot," he said, leading her deeper into the shelter of the trees.

Before her, sunlight broke through the trees, and in moments, they stepped into a private glade speckled with wildflowers. The beauty prompted her to break from John's arm and bound into their private sanctuary. Her legs tangled in the cross-leaf heather, and her skirt brushed against the fading purple thistle and goldenrod. Breathless, she stopped and beckoned him to follow.

Joining her, John rested the basket on the ground wherein Sarah opened the lid and pulled out a cloth. Tossing it on the shorter grass, she sank to the earth, spreading her skirts over her ankles. John joined her.

Delving inside the wicker, Sarah eyed the picnic fare. "I hope the meal meets your pleasure, John. We have cold meat and bread. Fruit," she said lifting the items from the basket. "And cyder."

As she gazed at John, a magpie moth settled on his shoulder. She gasped in delight. "Don't move, John. You've been visited by a butterfly."

John shifted his head to view his winged friend and chuckled. "It's only a moth," he whispered.

"But it's a lovely moth."

He grinned as the moth fluttered away.

Relieved by his less strained face, she returned to the cold meat, and John grasped a hunk of bread and wrapped it around a morsel of chicken. The picnic fare vanished, and while Sarah sipped cyder from the drinking glass, John swigged from the jug.

The sun spilled warmth over their backs, and Sarah looked into the bright sky, admiring the clouds floating overhead. With pleasure, she pointed to shapes of sea creatures and ladies with long tresses.

"I'm overwhelmed by your vivid imagination," John said, "but life cannot always abound in fantasy."

"Look there. That is not fantasy," she said, pointing to a thrush feeding on the rowanberries.

"No, the bird is real, my sweetest."

"It's lovely, John. A glorious day. Would you help me rise?" The wildflowers had captured her attention, and Sarah yearned to gather a bouquet. When her feet touched the grass, she darted away, filling her arms with blossoms—heather, lavender, harebells, and Mayweed. Then to her delight, she came upon a cluster of wild red poppies. Without a word, John waited in the distance, observing her.

With her arms overflowing with flowers, she ambled back, filling her lungs with the scent of sun-warmed meadow grass and watching the white moths flit across the blooms.

"I should return before the flowers wilt," she said, yearning for the day to last forever.

"Yes," he said, his face weighted with concern.

Fear rifled through her. "What troubles you, John?"

"Before you return home, I must speak with you, Sarah."

Her hand trembled as she nestled the flowers against her bodice. "What is it?"

"Us."

"What do you mean?" Sarah's chest constricted and she struggled to breathe. "You declared your love for me, and I, for you. What could be wrong?"

"I do love you, Sarah, but our love is as much a fantasy as the cloud pictures."

His words stabbed her heart, and her thoughts flew back to the comment she'd ignored earlier. A comment wrought with nostalgia she'd been afraid to understand. *Life cannot always abound in fantasy.*

"I have made a decision," he said. "Our friendship must cease. If God wills it, then it shall be. My heart breaks with my resolve, but I see no other way."

"I believe God wills us to be together," Sarah whispered. "I have prayed, and the Lord has moved me to love you."

"I believe our relationship is insurmountable, Sarah. But God is the ruler of all things, and His will makes the impossible become possible. You said those very words." John brushed her cheek with his fingers.

The flowers tumbled to the ground, and Sarah crumpled against his chest, tears streaming from her eyes and dripping to her bodice.

"Don't cry, Sarah. You have led me to understand the Lord. Now where is your faith? With God all things are possible. Say it over and over." He tilted her chin upward with his knuckle. "Say it, my dearest."

"With God all things are possible. With God all things are possible." She murmured the words, while John gathered her bouquet and returned them to her arms. Her eyes blurred with tears, and she gazed at the bright blossoms against her chest, their colors merging shades of a rainbow. Without the man whom she perceived God had given her, life would be like the fading flowers—joy obscured by sadness.

"But Mama, please," Sarah begged, "I've no desire to entertain these gentleman. I shall send them my regrets."

"Stop sniveling, Sarah. I must insist you accept an occasional gentleman caller. Let us examine their calling cards again. You may choose the ones you favor, Dear."

Sarah curled on her bed, unwilling to look at even one card but to dishonor her parents hurt more deeply. Without proper escort, she'd held conversation with John and allowed him to kiss her hand. By loving a man beneath her social standing, she had already erred gravely, dishonoring her parents, thus dishonoring God. Her remorse had become unsettling.

Yet she loved John. How could she tell her mother

where her heart lay? "Are you so anxious for me to depart my girlhood home?"

Her mother wagged her head. "I do not understand you, Daughter. Young women await the day they reach adulthood—to be courted and wed. But you. . .you are impossible. I must consult your father on this matter." Marching from the bedroom, she closed the door.

Sarah longed to vanish, to hide, anything to stop her mother's insistence. Thoughts tumbled in her head as she slid her feet to the floor and sat on the edge of her quilt. She would select one young man and make him so miserable that all the eligible gentleman of the village would withdraw their cards. Shame filled her at the vile thought. What had become of her good sense?

Why had she given her heart to John? A farmer, yes, but a man of honesty, a man with vision, a man of simple pleasure who loved the earth and laughed at her delight in a butterfly. Sarah recalled the hours she'd wearied with the eligible bachelors she found pretentious and tiresome. Would God have her marry a man she didn't love because of social breeding?

Falling to her knees, Sarah pressed her face against the quilt and wept. She had dishonored her parents with her clandestine meetings and endangered John's character. She regarded him blameless. He had captured her heart, but she had pursued him. Utterly improper for a young woman of her standing. Yet in her heart, she perceived the Heavenly Father understood and approved. Could she have misjudged the Lord's bidding?

Everything had changed since the picnic weeks earlier. The lovely afternoon lingered in her thoughts—the sky painted with cloud-creatures and her arms weighted with wildflowers. She pictured John's pensive face, and loneliness blanketed her.

Since that day, John had kept his word. She had not seen him alone. Sarah dried her tears and bowed her head. If a solution to her problem existed, God would have the answer.

John strode toward the cyder house. The apples hung ripe on the branches, nearly ready for harvest, and the presses required inspection. Gratitude filled him as he thought of his conversation with Edward Hampton. His employer had ordered a new apple press, and as a gift to John's family, he had purchased another for the Bannings' farm. Smaller in size, but a hydraulic apple press just the same. The gift reached beyond John's expectation and served as his only bright moment since Sarah's picnic.

John unlocked the cyder house door and entered. In another week, workers would arrive to harvest the apples, and with Mr. Hampton's encouragement, John had already selected maiden trees—the new varieties—to be planted in the early spring. One day, Hampton cyder would be proclaimed the best in the country.

Working in shadows, John unlatched a shutter to chase away the gloom. He inspected the wooden hopper, then examined the bladed cylinder attached to the handle. Before he reached the gears, the room brightened as a gust of wind caught the door and flung it open.

John hastened to the door and looked outside. A wind tossed the branches, then subsided as quickly as it had appeared. The intoxicating scent of apples drifted on the breeze, and John felt drawn away from the cyder house toward the orchard. What prompted him he didn't know, but a deep sense of purpose sped his feet along the path.

The cyder apples hung deep red on the branches awaiting the harvest, and he plucked one from the branch. He breathed in the rich, ripe scent, but the puzzling urge compelled him deeper into the orchard. Reaching the Morris apples, he faltered, his heart thundering.

"Sarah."

She stood beneath the tree, gazing into the branches.

"What are you doing here?" he asked, amazed he'd been drawn here.

"John." Her foot moved forward as if to run to him, but she stopped. "Something has. . . I–I have been longing for an apple."

"Here," he said, handing her the fruit he had picked.

She eyed it and shook her head. "That one is for cyder. The Morris apples are good for cyder and eating."

Surprised at her knowledge, John agreed. "Then I shall pick you one of these."

"I desire one in particular, John. Please, lift me so I may reach it."

His chest ached against his hammering heart. He gazed at the delicate woman for whom he would give his life. Would he not grant her an apple?

His caution vanishing on the breeze, he bent down and boosted her to the branches. The rustle of her skirts, her petite frame beneath the layers of cloth, the nearness of her overwhelmed him.

She plucked the apple, shined it on her bodice, and bit into it. The snap of the pulp sprayed, and the juice rolled down her chin.

John marveled at the dear woman in his arms and lowered her to the ground. Should he be deemed a coward? Should he march into her father's study and demand Hampton's precious daughter? Foolishness.

With downcast eyes, Sarah fingered the half-eaten apple. "I have missed you, John. But I have prayed."

Unable to resist, he caressed her soft hair fragrant with lavender. "We must both be steadfast with our prayers."

"You have acted with good judgment, I know. We must await God's bidding."

"Sweet Sarah, you are truly the apple of my eye. We shall continue to pray. . .and God will provide. The Lord has already answered one prayer."

Her sad eyes brightened. "Which prayer, John?"

"For my family. Your father has requisitioned a cyder press for the Banning cyder mill. His generosity is beyond expectation."

With hesitation, she rested her hand on his arm. "My father finds you worthy of good things. He has spoken highly of you. . .even at our dinner table."

"You're dinner table? In your mother's presence?" The thought left John unsettled.

Sarah paused, her eyes flashing. "John, do you think. . . could it be?" She clutched the neck of her bodice. "No, I cannot believe it, but perhaps. . ."

"What, Sarah?" He drew her closer, his eyes basking in the bloom of excitement lighting her face. "You have not spoken a full sentence."

"You must wait, John. If I speak it, my dream may be only a dream."

Chapter 8

Sarah stood in her father's study like a criminal standing in a court dock with her father the judge. Her mother, the prosecuting attorney, paced the carpet in front of the desk, her arms fluttering like a frightened bird.

"It is mid-November, and she's refused every suitor." Mary stopped and sent a disparaging look toward Sarah. "Now the holiday parties begin. . .and what will she do?"

Edward hadn't uttered a sound since the evidence against Sarah had been laid before him.

"You must speak with her, Edward," Mary said.

Edward peered at Sarah over his spectacles.

The desire to defend herself charged through Sarah, but in her parents' eyes, she knew she had no defense. She sat like a condemned prisoner, unable to speak.

Two pairs of eyes condemned her, but her father's held a look of tenderness.

"Mary," Edward said, "would you leave Sarah with me?"

Her mother's gaze shifted like a searchlight before she answered. "Whatever you say, Edward. You know what is proper and expected."

He only nodded.

With a last look, Mary headed toward the exit.

He rose and waited for her mother to close the door before he turned to Sarah. "Come, Sarah," he said, sinking into an armchair, then gestured to one across from him. "Sit with me. We must talk."

Sarah crept to the chair and lowered herself, expelling a deep sigh.

"Why do you struggle with your social responsibilities, Daughter? Your mother does not understand. . .and, frankly, neither do I."

Looking into her father's sincere eyes, Sarah felt tears pool in hers.

Her father leaned forward and patted her hand. "Do not weep, Child. Tell me why you cry."

Searching for the appropriate words, Sarah toiled to form the sentence.

Her father's face grew heavy with concern.

"It is my heart, Papa," she said finally.

"Your heart? I don't understand." His countenance darkened. "Has someone. . .wronged you, Sarah?"

"No, Papa, never." If she confessed the truth, how would her father respond? His disconcerted tenderness assured her he would listen and understand.

"I don't have a heart to give another, Papa. Without my bidding, I love an honorable man."

"You what?" He drew back, his face pale and contorted.

Seeing his despair, Sarah could no longer look into her father's eyes.

"Tell me who he is Sarah? Did this man. . .behave improperly?"

"Oh, no, not he. He has done nothing but endeavored to protect my reputation and to encourage propriety." Tears spilled from her eyes and dripped to her knotted fingers.

"This man is concerned with propriety?" Edward asked, his voice calming.

"Oh, yes, Papa." Sarah rose and dropped at her father's feet. She prayed, asking God to grant her a solution, and she found it in her father's eyes.

"Daughter, don't cry. Is he a young man of the village? Where did you meet him? At church? Tell me his name."

Her mouth opened to answer, but the words stuck in her throat. "You will be angry," she murmured.

"Not angry, but startled. Bewildered. It is improper to be alone with a young man before you have a commitment."

Sarah brushed at her tears. "He expressed the same, Papa. But God was our chaperone."

His face flickered with concern. "Society asks for more, Daughter."

"More. . .than God?" she questioned.

He shook his head. "You amaze me, Sarah." He rested his hand on her head. "Now, tell me the name of the young man who has captured your heart?"

"I love John, Papa."

"John?" His voice softened to a whisper. "I recall no young man named John."

She lowered her head. "The orchard keeper. You have spoken highly of him, Father. You have said he is clever, and he will be a success one day." Slowly, she turned her head, and seeing her father's expression, her heart ached.

The room hung with silence until her father spoke. "Yes, I did say that. He is a man of virtue and intelligence. One day he may find success, but. . ."

Rising, he took Sarah's hand and drew her to her feet. "You are my most precious daughter, but. . .I must contemplate this, Sarah. Your mother will be distressed." His piercing gaze caught hers. "Are you certain? Have you considered a lifetime with this farmer?"

"I am sure, Papa."

"Then I will do what I can." His face ashen, he sank into his desk chair and buried his face in this hands. "Leave me, Sarah, and let your papa decide what is best."

❦

The choir and clergy filed past the worshipers, and when the pomp ended, Sarah followed others down the aisle and into the brisk autumn air.

The family carriage waited nearby, but Sarah hesitated. With her father away on business and her mother indisposed with a headache, Sarah had a rare opportunity to be alone in the village. Though the wind nipped beneath her cloak, she asked the driver to wait and hurried away on foot.

At the far end of the street stood a small country church. Its white clapboard siding and pointed steeple made direct contrast the gray stone of the Anglican church graced by an elegant bell tower. As she neared the smaller church, she prayed John had attended worship that morning. Weeks earlier, she'd learned he'd begun to attend the small church. The conversation with her father necessitated her desire to speak with him. It seemed imperative he be aware of their discourse.

In the park square across from the clapboard building, Sarah waited. When the doors opened, parishioners exited and made their way on foot toward their homes. Trembling with cold and her purpose, Sarah waited until John stepped into the sunlight. Pulling the cloak's hood over her head, she followed him along the opposite side of the street. When she felt assured no one would hear, Sarah called his name.

John's head swiveled, and he faltered before crossing the street to meet her. "Sarah. Where are your par—"

"I'm alone. I must speak with you a moment." The wind sent a shiver through her.

"It's cold in the street. Please return to the carriage."

Sarah grasped his arm and drew him under the shelter of a large oak, it's wide trunk minimal protection from the breeze. "I have spoken with my father. . .about us."

His face paled. "I was wrong to allow our indiscretion to continue so long."

"Indiscretion? Please, John—" His words pierced her heart.

"After I complete the final inventory tomorrow, I will speak with your father. I must leave his employ."

Tears welled in Sarah's eyes before her faith caused them to subside. "Do you not trust God, John?"

He shifted and tucked his hands deeper in his pockets. "Why do you ask me now?"

"You told me God's Word has touched your heart.

Yet, you do not have faith in the Lord's promise." She clutched the cloak around her, the damp cold shivering through her body.

"I am trying to rely on God, but I'm not foolish. God provides for our needs. . .not our fantasies." He drew her cloak more firmly around her. "You are chilled, Sarah. You must go."

"God makes all things possible, John. No matter what you say, the Lord can move mountains. If it is the Lord's will, we can be together."

She stepped back, and he caught her hand and pressed it to his lips. "My dearest, Sarah, I pray you are correct."

She backed away. Turning, she hurried toward the carriage, feeling John's gaze on her back and his love in her heart.

John strode through the cyder house, checking his figures and taking stock of the barrels. The apple harvest had been outstanding, and Hampton cyder had been carried on large wagons to the markets while John rotated barrels, allowing the new cyder to age or become vinegar.

His days at Hampton Manor were over. If Sarah had not spoken to her father, John would have returned to the manor on occasion to siphon the cyder into large crockery jugs and clean the kegs. His chest weighted with the memory of the trees he had ordered to be planted in the spring. . .and the new hydraulic press. But now, he would have to leave forever. The gardener, Charles Benson, had returned to mulch the plants for winter, and the older man would be there to plant and prune in the spring.

Still, life would go on. . .at the manor and for John. He knew vanishing from Sarah's life would be for the best—the only way, but a hole the size of heaven tore through his heart. His life, which had become a joyful adventure, would now return to drab, plodding hours.

Finishing his inventory, John closed the ledger and turned toward the doorway. When he stepped into the clouded daylight, a house servant hailed him at the threshold.

"Mr. Hampton requests your presence before you leave today."

"Thank you," John said, turning and locking the door.

"He is in his study," the servant added over his shoulder as he strode away.

John raised the collar of his lamb's wool coat and mounted his horse, his spirit weighted by the messenger's words. He would be discharged before he could offer to leave the Hamptons' employ. The concern affected only his pride, he realized and shook his head at his vanity.

The horse whinnied and stomped his hoof; John pulled the reins and trotted up the path. He passed the servant and, in a few moments, reached the house. Climbing from the mare, he dismounted and tethered it. Heavy-hearted, he paused before trudging up the steps.

Inside, he knew Sarah sat somewhere filling her time with womanly tasks, learning to be a good wife and mother for some lucky gentleman. The thought tore at him. Already, he missed Sarah's smile and determined ways. At twenty-five, John knew he should think of taking a wife, but his mind could not erase Sarah's glowing countenance.

He rang the bell and waited. When the servant arrived, he led John to Hampton's study. He viewed the familiar scene, knowing after his meeting he would walk out the manor door for the last time.

Standing in the middle of the room, Hampton motioned to a chair. "Sit, John."

John sank into the seat and rested a hand on each knee, eyeing his employer's steady gaze.

Hampton clamped his hands behind his back and paced. "Have you completed the accounting?"

"Yes, Sir. Here are the figures." Pulling the ledger from his pocket, he held his notations toward Hampton. "Cyder barrels, vinegar barrels, jugs ready for the market."

He grasped the ledger and scanned it. "You've done well."

John's head shot upward. *Done well?* Tension knotted in John's shoulders. Why did the man not state his purpose and end it? "Thank you," he mumbled, waiting for the condemning finger to point the way toward the door.

Placing the book on his desk, Hampton focused on John. "You've done well," he repeated, sinking to his chair. "Months ago, I promised you a reward, John and—"

"Please, Sir, you have been most generous providing my family with a new cyder press. I expect nothing more." With downcast eyes, John waited for a response.

"But you've already accepted more, John. You've stolen something precious," Hampton said, his voice rising.

"Stolen? No sir, I am a poor but honest man."

"I know you are honest, John, but no matter, you have stolen my daughter's heart." Sadness reverberated in the man's voice.

Fear and sorrow seeped through John's veins like ice water. "I have tried to contain my feelings, Sir, but Miss Hampton is. . .she did not heed my warning. . .and my own heart would not obey my good counsel."

Hampton shook his head and rose. "My daughter is a stubborn young woman, John. When she desires something, she is not easily dissuaded." He rounded the desk and stood before him. "I am as guilty as any for giving her all for which she longs."

With no need to respond, John held his breath and waited, confused as to where the discourse might be headed.

"My daughter told me of your concern for social proprieties, and I thank you."

John rose and stepped toward Hampton. "I would do nothing to harm your daughter or her reputation, Sir. I have her best interest at heart."

"I have no doubt. . .but my daughter says she loves you." Hampton's gaze riveted to John's.

As if shrinking, John's large body seemed no bigger or worthy than a pesky mouse as he spoke from his heart. "I love her. . .with all my being." His words sounded frail and meaningless. "Yet I know it is impossible except if God wills it."

"You are a Christian man?" Hampton asked, his eyes narrowing.

"A new one, Sir, but Sarah has helped me to know

God in a more personal way. I believe in God's sovereignty and in Christ's saving grace."

"That is a blessed understanding, John. Do you know how difficult earthly life would be if I grant you my daughter's hand?"

"I do." His stomach churned as he saw the pain in Hampton's eyes.

"I cannot make things right, John, but I can give my daughter a secure life if nothing else."

John's heart stopped, then lurched while he waited for his dismissal papers.

Hampton walked behind his desk, opened a draw, and pulled out a document. "I will give you this." He extended it to him.

John grasped the paper, his pulse coursing through him as he eyed the certificate. Confusion spiraled in his mind. "What is this, Sir?"

"It is a deed to the apple orchard, John. It is yours. I have made a public notice to appear on the Barnham and Norwich Post. You may read it here." He slipped another paper into John's hands and tapped his finger on the spot.

John scanned the text.

Whereas an advertisement appeared in this paper informing the public that the Hampton apple orchards have been granted to Edward Hampton's future son-in-law, John Banning of Barnham, Norfolk, declaring that following the wedding of Sarah Hampton and John Banning, the Cydermaking Business will be carried on by

John Banning aforesaid by whom all orders will
be thankfully received and readily executed.

The words ran together in tears of gratitude and disbelief. John opened his mouth to express his thanks, but Hampton detained him with his hand.

"No need to say a word, John. I have witnessed your labor. I have admired your creativity and fortitude. I proclaimed one day you would be a successful businessman. If my daughter loves you and you cherish her, I will not let society stand in your way. But you must be a good husband to my daughter."

John's hand trembled as he clutched the deed. "I could be nothing less if she will have me."

Chapter 9

Sarah looked across the table during the Christmas Day meal, unable to believe John sat across from her. Once her mother had accepted the inevitable, she had been quiet but cooperative.

Sarah loathed hurting her parents, but she had put her life in God's hands and God had led her to John—a farmer, a man of lower station. Though she did not consider herself an intellect, Sarah could not but wonder if God were proclaiming a statement to the world about inequities. John Banning had been born as worthy as any man. . .and far more worthy of Sarah's love than any other.

"We must plan the guest list," her mother said, eyeing Sarah as if waiting for her to reject the idea.

"Yes, as soon as possible," Sarah agreed. "But the list will be smaller than my coming out, don't you think?"

Her mother nodded, a look of distant sadness in her eyes. "But it will be as lovely."

Sarah yearned to rise and kiss her mother for her rallied thought. Though Sarah's marriage would not be without obstacles, with God it would be possible and blessed.

John listened to the discourse of his future mother-in-law and his betrothed. He'd been astounded when Sarah revealed her dowry would be a small house at the edge of the orchard. Small now, but one day, with the Lord's continued blessing, he would acquire a larger home for his wife and children. An abundance of children, he prayed. . .if it were God's will.

His own family had been startled by his announcement, but being kind and honest people, they were delighted for John and prayed only the best for each family member.

John rejoiced in the blessings God had sent him—intelligence, ingenuity, and a good business sense. But the greatest gift was Sarah's unquestioning love and her parents' acceptance. His life had been filled with the unexpected. Having eaten the holiday meal of goose and a joint of roast beef, John moved aside his plate and enjoyed a dish of delicious Christmas pudding.

Hampton smiled and drained the last of his cyder. "I shall offer a toast to my daughter, to John, and to their happiness." He tilted the decanter and poured a splash of cyder into each glass.

"Before our toast," he said to John, "share what further wish would bring you joy."

"I have dreamed, Sir, that Hampton. . .Banning cyder would receive a Royal Warrant one day. That would honor you, Sir, as well as your daughter."

"To happiness and a Royal Warrant," Hampton said.

They lifted their glasses and sipped the sweet cyder.

"And now," Hampton said, "I'm certain you young people would enjoy time alone."

While Sarah sent her father a grateful smile, John's spirit lifted with his offer.

"Thank you, Father," she said. "May we be excused? We will join you later in the parlor."

With Sarah's parents' blessing. John rose, clasped Sarah's hand, and escorted her from the table. Sarah urged him forward until they wended their way into the conservatory where ribbons and ivy adorned the circumference of the glass room. Looking into the moonlit garden, John's thoughts flew back to the August evening Sarah danced with him in the moonlight.

He drew Sarah into his arms, engulfed in new emotion. "Sarah, I love you more than life itself. You are my sun and moon. Stars glow in your eyes." He cherished every look and touch of the angel who would soon be his wife. "Tell me the day you'll be mine."

"Do you agree April is a good month for our wedding, John?"

"Tomorrow would not be too soon, dearest Sarah."

She laughed. "But we must appease my mother. The wedding will be small. . .not the social event she envisioned, but I will be happier and more content."

Happier and more content. Those words filled his heart. Gazing at his future wife, John surged with joy. Looking toward the entrance, he spied the green sprig pinned above the door.

"Come with me," he said, guiding her to the greenery.

"Are we joining my parents already?" Sarah asked beneath the doorway.

He smiled and pointed upward. "No, sweet Sarah, I am only claiming the last berry on this sprig of mistletoe. One kiss is left."

"Only one?"

Plucking the white berry from the leaves, John looked down at the demure woman at his side, her chin tilted upward, her lips soft and waiting. Cautiously, he lowered his mouth and brushed his lips against hers, feeling his heart melt and his knees grow weak.

"I love you, my dearest," she said, placing her fingertip against her lips as if holding onto his kiss.

"I'll love you forever, Sarah."

Though he had spoken, no words could truly express John's devotion and deep adoration for the woman who would soon be his wife. He had once said Sarah was the apple of his eye, but today he remembered the same phrase in God's Word. *"Keep my commandments, and live; And my law as the apple of thine eye. Bind them upon thy fingers, write them upon the tablet of thine heart."*

Sarah had not only brought contentment and happiness to his uneventful earthly life, but through her example and love, she had led him to realize that in Jesus, he had life eternal. No one could have given him more peace and joy than the unlikely woman God had chosen to be his.

John drew Sarah against his chest feeling her heart beat in rhythm to his own. God willing, he would hold her in his arms forever.

Epilogue

England, 1988

Williiam Banning stood in his office at Attleborough Station, staring at the document clutched in his hand. He'd been the managing director of the Banning Cyder Company since his father's passing in 1952. The business had been in his family since the middle of the nineteenth century when his great, great grandfather John Banning married Sarah Hampton and received the apple orchard and cyder business as a wedding gift.

After John and Sarah married, they continued to make their home in Banham, perfecting the cyder and raising seven children—six sons and one daughter. The hydraulic cyder press had made all the difference. The business grew and prospered, and when John died, the business was handed down from father to son. The pattern of ownership—from father to son—continued for four generations.

As the business grew and transporting the cyder

became expensive, William's grandfather Richard Banning moved the cyder business in 1906 from Barnham to its present location nearer London.

William had heard the story many times from his grandfather and his father how Big John Banning had made a daring proclamation—an admission of his bold dream—on Christmas Day 1851, the day John, a farmer, and Sarah, a woman of position, were officially engaged.

Adjusting his spectacles, William studied the document again, both amazed and satisfied. If only his great, great grandfather were here, he thought as he gazed at the official document bestowed by Her Majesty, Queen Elizabeth II.

Banning Cyder had been granted a Royal Warrant.

GAIL GAYMER MARTIN

Gail loves nothing more than to write, talk, and sing—especially if it's about her Lord. With hundreds of articles and stories as a freelance writer and numerous church resource books, she sold her first novel to Barbour in 1998. Now, she has been blessed as an award-winning, multi-published romance author with seventeen contracted novels or novellas. "If God blessed me with a 'bestseller,' I'd continue writing worship materials. It's a direct way I can share my faith with worshiping Christians." Gail has three **Heartsong Presents** novels and three previous novellas published with Barbour fiction. She is also a contributing editor and columnist for *The Christian Communicator.*

Besides being active in her home church, Gail has worked as an adjunct English instructor for Davenport University and maintains her professional counselor license in the state of Michigan. She is involved in numerous writers' organizations and especially enjoys public speaking and presenting workshops for writers. Gail loves traveling, as well as singing with the Detroit Lutheran Singers. She lives in Lathrup Village, Michigan, with her husband and real-life hero, Bob, who proofreads all her work. "Praise God from whom all blessings flow."

A Flower
Amidst the Ashes

by DiAnn Mills

Dedication

To Margaret Harry who served England
as a member of the Women's Auxiliary Air Force
during World War II. May God Bless.

"He giveth power to the faint;
and to them that have no might He increaseth strength.
Even the youths shall faint and be weary,
and the young men shall utterly fall.
But they that wait upon the Lord shall renew their strength;
they shall mount up with wings as eagles; they shall run,
and not be weary; and they shall walk, and not faint."
ISAIAH 40: 29-31

Chapter 1

November 1940

I n the twilight between sleep and consciousness, Corporal Margaret Walker of Britain's Women's Auxiliary Air Force suddenly woke to the familiar call of air raid sirens alerting London to another round of German bombings.

"Oh, no." She moaned and covered her head with the pillow. *I'm not moving. I'm not going anywhere. I'm staying right here in this bed. I spent the entire day transporting pilots back and forth from the barracks to the hangars, and I'm exhausted.*

Margaret closed her eyes as her body relaxed, despite

the death-screech echoing around her. The day had been too long. . .too exhausting. . .with too many Royal Air Force pilots not returning from their combat missions. She didn't want to consider the ongoing nightmare since September seventh when German bomber and fighter planes first razed London. In August the enemy hadn't been successful in forcing the island to surrender when they bombed the navy and later the coastal factories involved in airplane assembly. Now, the Luftwaffe attempted to level the capital, hailing the city with bombs and leaving destruction in its wake. Although Britons young and old, men and women, had prepared for the ordeal, no one really anticipated the decimation of property and the loss of lives in their city. At least she hadn't.

Someone shook her. "Margaret, are you awake? Come on, we have to hurry."

She recognized the voice and lifted the pillow from her head. "I'm not going, Beryl. I'm tired and I want to sleep."

Her friend continued to shake her. "If you don't get up, I'm going after the lieutenant. She'll get you moving."

Margaret threw back the thin coverlet and scurried to her feet. "All right," she grumbled. "I'm up and going. Be glad I hadn't run the bath before the sirens."

Beryl laughed. "You'd have worn your blanket, I'm afraid."

Margaret smiled in spite of her interrupted sleep. How long had it been since she enjoyed a long leisurely bath instead of the brisk showers housed beyond their quarters? She adjusted her trousers and quickly buttoned the shirt of her blue-gray work uniform. Her desire to sleep quickly fled in light of the servitude she owed her beloved England. To ignore the warning sirens would be folly; she'd do her country no good dead. Without another word, they raced with the other WAAFs from their barracks to their designated shelter.

Pulling back the tarp to the entrance, Margaret ushered the way for Beryl. Downward they trod to the damp, dimly lit underground shelter protecting them from bombs. They found an empty spot near the back on one of the long benches and waited.

"I thought you had night duty," Beryl said. "I was surprised to see you on your cot."

"No, that's tomorrow night," Margaret replied, closing her eyes for a minute's respite. "Perhaps the Germans will cease their bombing, and all will be quiet. The last time I drove an ambulance during an air raid, the cries of the injured kept me awake for nights."

"When will it end?" Beryl whispered. "My Patrick risked his life every time he flew against the Germans until the day they shot him down." She took a deep breath. "My heart longs for him and my dear boy, Christopher."

Margaret knew how Beryl grieved her husband's death and how she missed her young son tucked away safely in an Irish country home. "God will protect Christopher and save England from invasion. We must have faith and trust that not one Nazi will set foot on British soil."

"Faith is all I have left." Beryl released a faint sob. "One day I'm going to ask for a long pass, and then I'll go see my precious son. Holding him will help ease the pain. Oh, he looks like his father, you know."

Margaret smiled in the darkness and gently took Beryl's hand. Her friend held a secret, one of bittersweet memories. New life nestled within Beryl's womb, but Margaret had promised not to disclose the information until Beryl could talk to their lieutenant. "We knew this war would be difficult, and we'd have to make sacrifices, but it's so hard to keep our minds centered on our duties when we hurt."

"I need your strength." Beryl patted the hand over hers. "I thought others would be killed, nameless faces who might never touch my life. I never thought the war would affect me or take my beloved Patrick, just like you never thought your brother would be shot down."

Margaret swallowed her own pain. She welcomed the darkness to hide the tears coursing down her cheeks. Sometimes she believed her heart held visible scars of the war's carnage. How did one live without the reassurance of God's provision?

The low timbre of men's voices captured Margaret's attention. Why did men sit among them in a women's shelter? Straining her ears to listen and not concentrate on the roaring challenger above them, she heard a distinctly male laugh.

"Ladies, there's only two of us and even though none of you are our mums or sisters, have mercy on these two poor pilots," a man said, his voice laden with merriment.

She heard the women giggle, and for a moment she welcomed the man's humor in the dismal place, but the question still plagued her as to why they were there at all.

Irritated, Margaret shook her head. The men had

obviously strayed beyond their own barracks and were caught by the sirens. She glanced about in the darkness and didn't see the profile of her lieutenant. In fact, she could barely make out Beryl beside her.

"What rank are you men?" Margaret asked.

"I'm Lieutenant Stuart, and my companion is Corporal Harris of the Royal Air Force," came a different, quieter voice. "We're in the area on business."

I dare say you had RAF business among the women's barracks. "I see," Margaret replied. Gentleman officers among the women's quarters infuriated her.

"And your rank?" the lieutenant asked.

"Corporal Margaret Walker."

"Kindly forgive us, Corporal, for invading this shelter. We had no choice."

At least the lieutenant possessed the courtesy to address her properly.

She said nothing in response. Tomorrow she'd investigate the matter, but right now she wanted the all-clear signal before sleep overcame her.

For the next thirty minutes, Margaret leaned her head back against the cold, moist wall and dozed until the familiar wail broke the air.

"Moaning Minnie is telling us it's over for the moment," Beryl said. "I wonder how bad the damage."

Margaret shrugged. A lot of wounded meant she'd be robbed of sleep to drive an ambulance. She'd been caught out in the open in enough air raids during work hours to appreciate the shelter's safety. In those times when she had to remain aboveground, her work went on: dodging bombs and tending to the needs of the injured. Immediately she regretted her selfish thoughts. The wounded always took precedence, as it should.

Margaret longed for sleep and a reprieve from her responsibilities. Rarely did she feel melancholy, but rather she took it upon herself to boost the morale of the other women. Light-heartedness gained her respect among the WAAFs along with a keen sense of love and commitment to the women in her barracks. Her current mood must be caused by exhaustion and by thinking about poor Beryl's sad circumstances.

At least I have no one to worry about. How distressing to be among the parents who had to send their children away from the cities.

Numbly, Margaret stood in line to leave the shelter. Tomorrow she'd feel better. Tomorrow she'd find her wit and humor.

"Excuse me, Corporal," a male voice said once they stepped above ground. She recognized the voice of the reserved Lieutenant Stuart.

Margaret stiffened and turned in the darkness to face the officer. "Yes sir." His face was silhouetted in front of her, but she could make out nothing more.

"In defense of Corporal Harris and myself, we were here in search of a couple of our pilots who may have been wandering among the women's barracks."

"I appreciate your clarification," she replied. "In all due respect, Sir, I hope you understand how suspicious your presence sounded."

"Yes, I do, but it's the truth."

She knew he didn't have to clarify his motives since he held the higher rank, and the fact he offered an explanation impressed her. "Thank you, Sir. If I observe anything out of protocol, I'll notify you."

"Thank you for your cooperation and dedication to those in your charge. Have a good night, Corporal."

Margaret saluted and stepped beyond the shelter without taking a look back. She trudged back to the barracks with Beryl, too tired to speak. The acid smell of destruction alerted her to fires in the distance. She heard the cries of ambulances rushing to the aid of victims and felt the flow of adrenaline through her veins. In a strange way, she wished they did need her to drive. At least then she'd feel like she'd accomplished something instead of only bemoaning her lack of sleep. This was reality: Another war-torn night on the edges of London.

Two weeks passed, each day the same as before. Margaret pursued her optimism, encouraging those around her and always finding victory in the bleakest of defeats. She took pride in her job, operating whatever vehicle the Royal Air Force needed. Sometimes her assignment led her to drive pilots in tarp-covered lorries to the hangars, move the injured to hospitals, pick up mail, deliver food and medical supplies, or simply chauffeur an officer to his or her destination. After all, she had trained for six weeks to learn how to drive, and it didn't matter what manner of vehicle.

On a mid-November afternoon, Lieutenant Elizabeth Fitzgerald issued Margaret an order. "I need for you to transport two pilots from the hangars to an officers' meeting immediately. I've been told you'll need petrol before you leave."

Margaret grasped the keys to the government vehicle and saluted the lieutenant. She'd taken pilots earlier that morning and wondered why these two fliers returned alone. After missions, the men normally tarried at the hangars until radar determined hostile airplanes en route over the English Channel. Praise God for this system of warning, for it hastened bombers and fighters to the skies.

Her stomach curdled. Surely nothing had happened to the other men. Generally, downed pilots parachuted into the water where sea vessels rescued them.

Another possibility occurred to Margaret. The two officers could have taken pictures over enemy territory and now needed to report their findings. For certain, though, it had nothing to do with her duties.

Winding the officer's car through the outskirts of London could have been a rough assignment if Margaret had not known the way. Road signs had been removed in the event invaders prowled over their land. Let the enemy stumble about; Britons valued vigilance.

The government had initiated various protective measures for its people. The air-raid alerts and under-ground shelters saved many lives. Blackout shields covered the headlights of what few vehicles were permitted to roam the streets. Lampposts were painted white so drivers could find their way during the night. All children ages fifteen and under had been removed from the larger cities to safety in the country. Rationing and training the citizens of England to protect their lives and property became an integral part of life. This and so much more kept the enemy at bay.

Women did more than their share by filling men's jobs. They delivered the mail, trained for the home guard, joined a branch of the military, and worked in factories. Everyone had a job. Everyone had a purpose.

At the hangars, Margaret parked the car where two pilots stood talking with the mechanics. She rounded the front of the lorry and saluted two RAF officers, one a lieutenant and the other a corporal. Perhaps their rank supported special treatment or an undisclosed mission. She opened the passenger side of the backseat for them.

"To the colonel's office," the lieutenant said, his voice oddly familiar.

"Yes sir." Her mind spun as she searched her memory for the officer's identity, but nothing came to mind.

As soon as Margaret started the engine, the corporal began to talk endlessly about nothing important. She recognized his voice as one of the two officers in the air-raid shelter. Glancing in the rearview mirror, she instantly met the most incredible brown eyes she'd ever seen. They belonged to the quiet lieutenant. He smiled at her, a shy smile, almost innocent looking.

A moment later, she swerved to keep from hitting a huge rut in the road, but the maneuver proved too late. She tore her gaze away from the mirror while warmth rose from her neck to her cheeks. Had she gone daft? Embarrassment continued to flow through her veins, and she wondered how she could avoid facing the lieutenant, but she must. Once they did reach their barracks, she must open his door and salute him. What fun he must be making of her.

Stiffening, Margaret vowed to regain her composure and will away the redness she knew colored her cheeks. She tightened her fingers around the steering wheel and focused her attention on the road ahead, but her mind could not shut out the endless chatter of the corporal. He could hold his own in a host of women.

Once they reached the officers' area, Margaret summoned the strength to complete her assignment. After all, she was a WAAF and certainly above petty nonsense about a man's eyes. Yet she had driven poorly by hitting the hole in the road.

Lieutenant Stuart waited beside the car, while Corporal Harris, the more muscular of the two, exited. "Go on ahead. I'll be there in a moment," he said.

She watched the chatty corporal walk toward the colonel's office, all the while expecting a reprimand for her driving.

"Corporal Walker?"

"Yes sir." She lifted her chin.

He smiled, the half grin she'd seen before, the kind that could easily melt a woman's heart. But not hers. "What time do you get off duty today?"

"Seventeen hundred hours, Sir."

"Would you consider a stroll?"

Her pulse quickened. "Well. . .have I violated a procedure? I mean I apologize for not minding the bumpy road."

His pleasant demeanor remained intact. "No, Ma'am,

I'm not concerned with your driving expertise. I'd simply like your company."

Her emotions bounced between relief and caution, and she wavered. This could be official RAF business. "Yes sir. I mean that would be fine with me."

He touched the brim of his cap where a tousle of sandy-colored hair slipped onto his forehead. "Thank you. I'll be at your barracks around eighteen hundred?"

"Do you know which one, Sir?"

A hint of amusement glistened in his eyes, and she felt her color mount. "Yes, Corporal, I do."

The rest of the day sped by, and in those moments of idleness Margaret questioned the lieutenant's motives. If this had nothing to do with the defense of Britain, then he must be interested in her as a woman, and she had no intention of becoming involved with any man until the British won the war.

Visions of the young pilots who never returned flashed across her mind. Her brother's demise had caused her to avoid all men. Shaking her head in denial of the pain, her thoughts turned to Beryl and how she mourned the death of her husband. With four-year-old Christopher and another babe yet to be born, Beryl's future looked frightening, even without considering the events of the war.

Margaret had only one love—the Lord—and when the fighting ceased He'd be the one to initiate any kind of a relationship between her and a man.

Promptly at seventeen hundred hours, Margaret raced to the showers, hoping a quick spray of water would soothe her rattled nerves. Moments later, she slipped into clean work trousers and shirt. She huffed. If Lieutenant Stuart had stated the purpose of their time together—professional or personal—she would have known whether to wear her dress uniform.

Beryl met her back at the barracks. "Where are you going?"

Margaret fluffed at her hair, then held up a mirror to make sure the curls fell just so on her shoulders. She noticed a thickening around Beryl's middle but refused to mention it. "Business, I think," she replied, avoiding her friend's scrutiny.

"You don't know?"

Dare she tell Beryl what occurred this morning? "I'm supposed to meet Lieutenant Stuart at eighteen hundred."

Beryl touched her finger to her lips. She reminded Margaret of a mere girl with her oval face encircled in blond curls. "The name is familiar. Female or male?"

"Male," Margaret whispered, glancing about to make sure no one listened.

"Weren't you briefed on your assignment?" Beryl asked, her forehead crinkling.

"Not exactly." Margaret slipped the mirror back into her personal belongings. "Oh, Beryl, you remember him. The night in the shelter when those two pilots joined us?"

"Which one—the chatty or reserved one?"

"The reserved lieutenant."

Beryl smiled and nodded. "Is this something special?"

Margaret felt the color rise in her cheeks. "I have no idea. He invited me for a stroll, but I don't know why."

Her friend giggled and positioned her hands on her

hips. "I say he's a man who has taken a fancy to a lovely young woman, and you're fancying him as well, or you wouldn't be so flushed."

"Nonsense. I'm sure this is RAF related."

"Your lip is quivering."

Margaret cringed. "Is it? Oh, dear, what am I to do?"

A woman's voice from the door of the barracks diverted Margaret's attention. "Corporal Walker, there's a Lieutenant Stuart waiting outside for you."

Chapter 2

"It is to wage war, by sea, land, and air, with all our might
and with all the strength that God can give us;
to wage war against a monstrous tyranny, never surpassed
in the dark, lamentable catalogue of human crime.
That is our policy. You ask, what is our aim?
I can answer in one word: It is victory, victory at all costs,
victory in spite of all terror, victory, however long and hard
the road may be; for without victory, there is no survival."
WINSTON CHURCHILL

Lieutenant Andrew Stuart toyed with the crease of his cap. He flecked imaginary dust from his alba-tross insignia and shifted from one foot to the other. What had gotten into him to invite the lady for a stroll? He didn't have time for such nonsense when he had a job to do. Hadn't he and the other men been warned by a superior about allowing women to interfere with duty? He'd been better off to spend his time in a dart tournament. The war effort was the utmost priority;

victory outweighed every selfish desire.

Unfortunately, once he'd met Corporal Margaret Walker in the shelter, she'd haunted him until he found out all he could about her. Only curious, mind you. He couldn't see her face in the blackness of night, but something about her intrigued him.

This morning he saw the sun's rays pick up reddish highlights in her thick, rich brown hair. Those tresses were the kind a man could weave through his fingers. When she spoke, a sparkle lit up her arresting eyes and drew him even closer. In the past, he held little regard for men who lost themselves in a woman's beauty, and now he threatened to do the same.

All he ever hoped to find in these dark days was friendship. He wanted a woman friend to talk to when the day ended, when he wanted to put behind him the peril of his beloved country and the terror raging over Europe.

What he'd learned about Margaret also saddened him: She'd lost a brother in '39. Her brother had flown a Wellington on a mission to destroy a German naval ship and met up with the Messerschmitt 109 bombers. Andrew's source said he doubted if any pilot could convince the lovely Corporal Margaret Walker to do anything other than transport fliers back and forth to the hangars, much less befriend a chap. Couldn't blame the lady for her apprehension. Britons were noted for their sense of humor and hopefulness in the midst of bleak times, but that attitude didn't stop the pain of losing someone they loved.

Although his chums refused to believe it, Margaret had agreed to accompany him on a stroll, and no matter the outcome he planned to enjoy the company of a beautiful woman.

No sooner had his thoughts scattered about in his head, than the subject of his musings appeared in the doorway. She looked a bit flustered with her reddened cheeks and crinkled brow, reminding him of earlier when he caught her observing him through the rearview mirror. To his amusement, she hit a rather large bump in the road. The force jolted him up off the seat. She'd been embarrassed; he'd found it delightful.

"Good evening, Lieutenant," she greeted, smoothing her trousers.

He grinned like an awkward schoolboy. "Hello, and my name's Andrew." He noted his sweaty palms gripping the crease of his cap. How many missions had he flown with less turmoil waging his insides? "You look lovely."

"Thank you, and I'm Margaret."

She returned a measure of congeniality, while he battled his increasing nervousness. He hooked his arm, and she linked hers into his. Margaret's touch unnerved him, leaving him stumbling for words. They walked for several minutes while he searched for something clever to say— he so wanted a topic aside from the war.

"I'm not good at conversation," he finally admitted.

"Unlike your friend, Corporal Harris?"

"Perhaps I should have taken a few notes the night we invaded the women's shelter."

Margaret appeared amused. "Quite the talker, isn't he? Does he ever run out of subjects?"

"Only the queen has more subjects than James

Harris. I once saw him make friends with a lamppost. He's a fine chap, though, an excellent fighter pilot."

"Ah, so you're the witty one," she said.

For the first time, he relaxed slightly. "Not exactly. More like the quiet one. I prefer watching and listening."

"I prefer quiet," she said softly.

He felt his heart do an upward climb, level off, spin, and soar even higher.

"Why don't you tell me about yourself, Lieutenant?"

He'd rather be outnumbered by Nazi aircraft ten-to-one than talk about himself, but he didn't have a choice. "I attended Cambridge before the war and plan to finish there when it's over. My family lives outside of Northamptonshire, and I fly Spitfires for the RAF." He managed to say it all in one breath.

She laughed. He liked the sound of it, light and cheery as if inviting him to join along.

"Andrew, must I ask more questions to find out about you? What did you study at Cambridge?"

His heart hammered louder than gunfire riddling his Spitfire. "Philosophy. I almost have my masters."

"Then what?"

"Oh, I imagine myself as a professor someday, once I receive my doctorate." Andrew felt decidedly uncomfortable. Blood rushed through his veins and heated him despite the chilly temperatures of the November day.

"Splendid." Her eyes seemed to dance. "And do you have brothers and sisters?"

"Ah, yes I do. Three older brothers and two younger sisters." His voice faltered.

Margaret tilted her head. "I see I've touched on something sad. I'm sorry."

Andrew thought he masked his sorrow. "I'm the one who must apologize. It's my sister. She died in childbirth about five months ago. Hard on my family, you know. Luckily they live in the country and the babe is with them, while his father commands an army post."

"I'm so sorry. Times are hard for England. Everywhere you look is some type of devastation, but we have to go on."

She offered kind words and no false expectations. He liked that.

"Are you Christian?" Margaret asked.

Startled, he nodded. "My faith is what helps me climb into my cockpit. Either in this life or the next, God will give England peace, but until then I will fight for those things He declares important. I firmly believe He will see the free world reign over the atrocities of the Germans."

"I do as well. God guards the way of those who fight for His principles, and He will not allow this to continue forever." She stopped and turned to him. "I lost a brother to the cause. It grieves me, but like your sister, he is in a better place."

Andrew stared into the young woman's face, realizing her empathy was sincere and not a mixing of words to gain his attention. "Thank you, Margaret." He didn't know what else to say, especially when he'd already spoken more than usual.

They walked a bit farther in silence, and he felt his spirit strangely exhilarated with her arm coupled in his.

He grappled for another topic and forged on. "Enough nonsense about me, tell me about yourself."

"Oh, I'm a country girl, Andrew, and I long to one day return. Strange as it sounds, I'd never been in a large city until joining the WAAF. Before then I had plans to become a teacher, and I'll finish my degree once the war is over."

She didn't dwell on herself, either. "Whereabouts?" he asked.

"Northwest of Manchester." She sighed as if remembering another place in time. "A beautiful piece of land: tranquil, lush green, and full of unusual gardens. It's my own promised land."

"How commendable to know what you want. I've met people who strive to merely end the war and don't know what they will do afterwards. We need dreams of a future to keep us alive." He hesitated, a bit self-conscious for speaking his mind and mentioning the war. "Do you have a large family?"

"Just my parents now. We're all doing what we can. My mum took in six children without consulting my father. When he found out, he added two more."

Andrew allowed his laughter to roll about them. "I neglected to mention my family is housing several children as well. How are your parents faring with the additions to their home?"

"Quite well. They both insist having little ones about keeps them young."

He took a gander about them and realized they'd walked farther than he anticipated. Evening shadows danced about, and with the promise of night also came the reality of bombing.

"We should make our way back before the Germans bestow us with their gifts," he said.

"Yes, I suppose you're right," she replied, glancing upward.

For a moment he permitted himself to think she didn't want the evening to end any more than he. They stopped at a crossroad. One building stood, while another lay in shambles beside it. The philosophical side of him compared the sight to all affected by the war. He knew where he stood; he'd stepped across the line separating the weak from the strong, the resolute from the defeated. God held his destiny in the palm of His hands as well as all Britons who'd willingly give their lives.

"What are you thinking?" Margaret asked. "Or is it none of my concern? You look hundreds of miles away."

"Simply thinking about the war—a topic I vowed not to discuss this evening." They slowly walked back toward the barracks.

She nodded. "I understand, but it's quite all right, you know. It consumes us but will not overtake us."

"Good show, fair lady. I admire your spunk, but I'd rather speak of dearer things." He stared into her flawless face. "Thank you for agreeing to meet me."

"You're welcome, Andrew. I have enjoyed our time together." She glanced up at the sky with its pressing shadows. He saw a frown, and they increased their pace. "Now tell me about your boyhood. What was your most favorite thing to do?"

They chatted all the way back, and much too soon they stood in front of the round-roofed wooden building she referred to as home.

"Sometimes I think I'd like to plant flowers around these barracks," she said. "My friends think the idea foolish."

He attempted to envision a spot of color around the drab quarters. "What kind would you plant?"

For a moment, she closed her eyes, and he marveled at the serene smile gracing her face. "Oh, roses. I can only imagine how lovely they'd look, and their sweet fragrance would make the days brighter."

Suddenly Andrew remembered a matter of importance. He shuddered at his actions in complete disregard for his careful upbringing. "Margaret, I never asked. You missed the evening meal, didn't you?"

"Yes, but it's perfectly fine. Did you not eat as well?"

He refused to confess his thoughts had been on her and not his stomach. "I'm sorry. So much for my being a gentleman."

She laughed. "If I'd been hungry, I'd have stated so."

A strange silence enveloped them, and she slipped her hand from the crook of his arm. "I best be going inside."

"Of course. Thank you again for joining me. I had a grand time."

"You're a fine man, Lieutenant Stuart." Her eyes fairly glistened.

"May. . .may we do this another time? I'd like to see you at another time."

Margaret took a deep breath and hesitated. She appeared to carefully form her words. "I don't think so, Andrew. It wouldn't be a good idea."

With her decision made, she hurried inside the barracks, leaving a whipping blast of chilling air behind her.

Margaret braced herself and slowly made her way down the narrow row of iron cots to hers. She smiled at the women who greeted her, hearing them but not truly seeing them. Some would want to talk. They always did. She had the gift of listening to their problems and offering prayer and encouragement. Beryl said Margaret reminded her of a mother hen with her chicks—always drawing them close and fussing over each one.

Tonight, Margaret's heart felt heavy. She'd find it hard to cover her burden and take care of these precious ladies. The truth lay before her plain and simple. She couldn't see Andrew again, in fact not ever. He reminded her too much of the dreams she'd put aside until after the war. Someday she wanted to build her life around a man like Andrew, have his children, and grow old with him according to the plan God designed for a man and a woman. But not until the free world won the war. Worrying over a man flying missions against the enemy didn't fall into her plans.

Andrew held the same ideals as Ross, her sweet brother, and she didn't dare let her heart feel such intense grief over a man again. Some scars bled easier than others, and caring for men who knew the probability of their destiny made them easier to love—if not for the man, for the integrity of their values. All she needed to do was consider Beryl: a widow with one small child and expecting another.

Every time Margaret transported a lorry full of pilots to the hangars, she couldn't help but count them and calculate how many would not return. That's why she declined invitations to dances, the theater, and social events sponsored by the churches and the air force. No relationships for her, not even friendships. She couldn't involve herself casually and learn later they'd been shot down.

"Margaret, you look a fright," Beryl said. She rose from her cot and tossed aside a newspaper. "What happened?" A fierce look passed over Beryl's round face, and she whispered, "Did the lieutenant have dishonorable intentions?"

Margaret pretended to smooth her blanket. "Oh, no. He acted quite the gentleman."

"What happened?"

"I liked him."

Tears pooled her friend's eyes. "Then why are you so sad?"

Margaret eased down onto her cot, unable to gaze into her friend's eyes. "Because I don't dare see him after tonight. It makes losing him harder to bear. Oh, Beryl, I know we only had a brief walk together, but he's a good man, a Christian who puts others before him."

"Maybe God means for you to know a man like him—like a gift from heaven." She sat beside Margaret and lightly squeezed her shoulders. "For all the hardships and sorrow, I don't regret ever loving my Patrick." She muffled a sob. "And now I'll have two wonderful pieces of him to cherish forever."

Margaret choked back her own emotion. Sweet Beryl, she always saw past the storm to the rainbow. "I don't think I can be like you. Right now the only thing consuming me is my desire for victory, but if I can avoid some of the costs I must."

Much later, long after the sirens ceased and the other women lay sleeping, Margaret lay on her bed and sorted through her turbulent thoughts. A reserved lieutenant occupied her mind—those incredible brown eyes and a sprinkling of tan-colored freckles. Finally Margaret turned to the only solace she knew, that of prayer.

Oh, God, I believe I acted rightfully in refusing to see Andrew again, but now I wonder if I'm being selfish. I can't get involved. Please don't ask me to give my heart to a man and then have him killed in this horrid war. I'm so frightened with all that goes on around me. Leave me in my shell, God. It's safer here.

The following day, Margaret transported several pilots to the hangars. She understood they were to be briefed on a special mission, and her orders were to wait until a commanding officer dismissed her. After awhile, she grew bored and exited the lorry to stretch her legs. Keeping her distance from the mechanics, she studied the planes waiting for takeoff: Spitfires with narrow noses and straight lines, known for their speed in fighting, and Hurricanes, the workhorse fighters. All stood ready, fueled up, and armed for their mission.

How many young pilots would come back? She wanted to believe the RAF could crush the Luftwaffe, but from her point of view, Britain's success looked bleak.

Hitler's military had cast terror into the hearts of all of Europe. She'd never whisper a hint of her fears to anyone. Yet sometimes she wondered if the newspapers stretched the truth about the British successes. Not that she'd ever doubt Churchill—"Winny" some called him. He kept up their morale with his hopeful speeches and spurred them on to continue one more day. Even so, the year 1940 had been a rough year for the men and women who fought for Britain.

She offered a prayer for the pilots' safety and turned back to her lorry. Climbing onto the seat, she saw a piece of paper. Curious, Margaret picked it up and found a sketch of a rose, perfect in petal and formation. At the bottom, a note had been carefully penned.

> *For Margaret:*
> *Never has a rose in England looked so fair. I wish I could have given you a real, brilliant red beauty, but none could compare to you—a royal flower amidst the ashes of London.*
> *Lieutenant Andrew Stuart*

Chapter 3

"Centuries ago words were written to be a call and a spur to
the faithful servants of Truth and Justice:
'Arm yourselves, and be ye men of valour,
and be in readiness for the conflict;
for it is better for us to perish in battle than
to look upon the outrage of our nation and our altar.
As the Will of God is in Heaven, even so let it be.'"
WINSTON CHURCHILL

Andrew didn't know why he'd sketched the rose
and left such a ridiculous note for Margaret in
the lorry, but he had. He didn't want to consider
what she might think of him after he'd followed his foolish impulse. Hadn't he resigned himself to steering away
from relationships until after the war? Of course, his
action could merely be his pride reacting to her refusal to
see him again. Or could this be something else? He
recalled her clear eyes, sparkling with laughter, and the
honesty in her voice.

Margaret, have you already pushed me from your thoughts?

Andrew realized he'd lost his common sense. After spending less than an hour and a half with the lady, he thought she might be the one God intended for him. What happened to his plans for friendship, a chum to share idle hours?

Lord, help me with this. Am I reaching out to Margaret instead of clinging to You? I'm wondering if I should be bothering You at all with my turmoil.

Andrew pushed aside the burdensome thoughts of the lovely Corporal Walker and considered his flight pattern for the day. He pulled his jacket around him in the frosty morning air and watched the ground crew load ammunition into the fighter's wing guns. This had to be done with expertise or the guns could fail during battle. Glancing about, he felt intense pride in being a part of the RAF. The foresight in camouflaging fighters and bombers from German planes was one of the reasons why the RAF still ruled the skies over England. Other European countries who had fallen in a matter of days had lined their air craft along the runways. Those planes had been perfect targets for airborne Germans.

Climbing into the cockpit of his Spitfire, Andrew pulled the hatch closed. The frigid air chilled him to the bone. Last winter while he flew for France, the weather had grown so cold he thought he'd never be warm again. He didn't look forward to another season like it.

With a heavy sigh, he glanced upward. The sky tinged a bit cloudy, but it did not hold the black, curling smoke of combat. Too many times he'd heard the burst of gunfire finding their mark in aircraft and heard the screams of falling planes. A smart man wouldn't want to take on these assignments, but he had neither the intelligence nor the will to be anything but bold and stubbornly courageous. He followed orders and his gut instincts, praying all the while for God to lead him in the right direction.

Some hailed Britain's pilots as heroes, but he laughed at those titles. The RAF did what it deemed necessary because it had no choice. In his estimation, the real heroes were the mechanics who bore the brunt of German fire to repair and patch the bullet-riddled planes. He certainly didn't want their job.

Margaret pondered Andrew's rose and poetic words for three days before summoning the courage to approach him about it. She'd written a proper note thanking him, but it seemed too proper and impersonal in light of his tender gift. She placed the picture under her pillow and studied it in her spare moments, putting his written words to memory and tracing the flower with her finger as though watching him draw it.

Through Beryl, who packed parachutes at the hangars, she learned Andrew's schedule. One evening she lingered outside the men's dining hall in hopes he sat inside. She'd planned a brief encounter, one to express her appreciation and not in any way commit her to seeing him again. But in the confines of her heart, another flower budded in a garden of secret dreams.

Margaret stood several feet back from the entrance of the dining hall, not wanting to attract attention from the other men. The pilots filed out, some laughing, some talking. The unmistakable lively voice of Corporal Harris swelled above the others and caught her attention. Beside him stood Andrew. Even the talkative corporal said nothing as Andrew sauntered toward her.

"Good evening," she managed through a ragged breath. She swept her tongue across dry lips and braved forward. "I wondered. . ." She studied her shoes to avoid the stares of the other men until they passed by. Glancing up into his face, she offered a faint smile. "I wondered if you would have a moment to speak with me."

"I do." Andrew jammed his hands into his trouser pockets. "We could take a walk."

"An excellent idea." A nip of icy air caught her hair and whipped it back from her face. She'd taken great pains to arrange it, but for naught.

"Winter is wanting to overtake us," he commented.

"I agree," she replied and wrapped her arms around herself, more from the undeniable emotions Andrew's presence gave her than the cold.

He pointed to an area shielded by buildings. "We can venture in that direction. It'll block the wind."

"Yes, thank you." Suddenly her carefully formulated speech escaped her.

"You wanted to talk to me?" Andrew asked.

She nodded. "The rose and your note were beautiful, and I wanted to tell you so in person."

"I got your post thanking me."

"But it didn't express my gratitude suitably. I was deeply touched."

He shrugged. "I'm pleased."

Silence overtook them, and she searched her mind for one of the million things she wished she could discuss with him.

"Have you eaten?" he asked.

She shook her head. "I didn't have much of an appetite."

"In better days, I'd have offered to take you to a fine restaurant."

"In better days, I'd have accepted."

He laughed then sobered. "Is that the problem, Margaret? Are you living in memories of pre-war England instead of reality, or do you truly not enjoy my company?"

His question stopped her colder than the November temperatures. "I did enjoy our walk and your company. I'm not certain I can explain my reluctance to see you. . . It's rather personal. . . Certain things need to be kept private, even sacred during war times."

"Some things are always sacred in God's eyes, no matter what is going on around us."

"Even if the time is not right?" Why did she feel like crying? Betrayed by her own fragile feelings, Margaret could not bring herself to look into his face.

"God's timing is always perfect."

She glanced at the building behind them, stone and hard. Sometimes she wondered if her heart had become the same. "Andrew," she began softly. "Do you know what happens when you plant flowers in the wrong season?"

He nodded sadly.

"They die for lack of nurturing," she finished.

"But not if they are sheltered within a greenhouse. The flowers still flourish, because the gardener tends to them."

"Do you believe this gardener decides which flowers will grow?" she whispered.

"No. I believe the flowers choose to live or die according to the riches of the gardener's care."

Margaret forced herself to look at him. "I'm afraid, Andrew." No longer could she conceal her tears.

He brushed away the wetness on her cheek. "I, as well. Remember, we Brits are known for not turning our backs on adversity and being prepared for hard times. Can't we begin as friends, Margaret, for isn't that how it should be?"

"All right," she finally said. "I can be your friend."

As the weeks poured into December, Andrew found every spare minute to spend with Margaret. He longed for her laughter and wit. She made him laugh with a single phrase, and she appeared to enjoy his company. At least she no longer refused to see him.

"Good news," Corporal James Harris announced one evening. "I see a new band will be entertaining the troops next week. Oh, it will be a jolly good time, don't you think?"

Andrew's mind raced. Margaret loved music. Perhaps she'd want to attend the event with him. "Are you sure about the band?"

"Quite," James replied, his mirth ringing through the roof of the barracks. He patted Andrew on the back. "Old boy, I see the light of love in your eyes. Have you fallen for the pretty corporal already?"

Andrew furrowed his brow. "It's only been four weeks, much too soon to be proper."

"Whoever said love had to follow socially acceptable timetables?"

"She's a friend, and that's all for the time being," Andrew said more gruffly than he intended. "We're a country at war."

"No need to get upset about it," James replied, "just making conversation."

Immediately Andrew regretted his rash words. "I'm sorry, old chap. Margaret is special, and I don't want to make light of her."

"Of course. All of us are a bit ill tempered these days. So would you like for me to get more information about the band? It's better than most of those they've had in the past."

"I surely would, and I'll ask Margaret about it as well."

James turned to go, but Andrew stopped him.

"Thanks for being understanding. With our missions increasing into Germany, my mind is torn between the war and Margaret."

"God is with us," James looked as stalwart as Andrew had ever seen him. "With all my talking and joking, I have faith we will prevail, and I believe God wants us to enjoy the friendships of those who bring us joy."

"Well said, James." Andrew took a deep breath and

reached for his fur-lined jacket. "How about a cup of tea and a game of Ping Pong? I'm in the mood to beat you."

"If you do, it will be a first in a long time."

Andrew knew James's observations about Margaret were true. He had fallen hard for her, something he hadn't planned to do. The logical side of him said his feelings escalated because of the loneliness and uncertainty of his job, but his heart told him otherwise. Every minute he spent with her seemed more splendid than the last. He appreciated what he saw and how she related to other women.

Andrew's thoughts returned to the day before when he and Margaret had returned from a lively game of darts at the Naffi. Beryl, Margaret's dear friend, met them along the way. Andrew hadn't thought Beryl looked ill, but obviously Margaret did.

"Are you all right?" Margaret had asked the woman.

"Oh, I'm very well, just out for a stroll," Beryl replied hastily, her gaze darting about.

"You need your rest." Margaret's face tilted and concern edged her words. "Don't overdue yourself."

"I won't," Beryl said with a smile. "A bit of fresh air will do me good." She glanced at Andrew. "It's good to see you, Andrew. Are you keeping Margaret out of mischief?"

He grinned. "I certainly try. You should have joined us. Corporal Harris asked about you, wanted to know if we all could do something together."

Beryl braced herself against the wind. "I think not, but kindly thank him for the invitation." Turning her attention to Margaret, she added, "I'll be going now. Cheerio."

Andrew watched her plod toward the dining hall. "Is her health not good?" Andrew asked once Beryl disappeared. "I mean she looks fit, and her cheeks are rosy."

"She's as well as can be expected," Margaret said. "Beryl hasn't been a widow long, and often his absence grieves her. Plus she has a young son living with family in Ireland. I'm afraid she doesn't take good care of herself, and with the winter. . ." Her voice trailed off.

"Don't neglect her," Andrew said. "I know I take up a lot of your time, but friends are important. Should I apologize for suggesting she keep company with James?"

"No, that's not necessary. I've told her what honorable men you are. She knows you mean the best." Margaret smiled appreciatively, while her gaze swept back to Beryl.

He saw a tear trickle from Margaret's eye, and once more he felt convinced of her tender heart. "Is there something else troubling you?"

Instantly her violet pools flashed into his. Did he see panic?

"Nothing I can tell you," she said. "I need to go inside where it's warm."

Andrew started to hurry after her but stopped. He understood Margaret enough to realize when she needed to work through things on her own. He wished she'd confide in him instead of running, but maybe he was the problem.

Chapter 4

A few days later, Margaret waited for Beryl to return from the nurse's station. Her friend had reached her sixth month and couldn't hide the rounding stomach any longer. Besides needing medical attention, Beryl needed to take care of her position with the WAAF and obtain a proper discharge.

A few days earlier, when Andrew stated Beryl looked fit and noted the color in her cheeks, Margaret feared he suspected the pregnancy. She'd heard the other women talking among themselves and whispering their suspicions. They felt sorry for Beryl—a new widow with two children to raise alone, but she needed to declare her condition.

One of the women approached Margaret; Jenny had

lived in the slums of East London before the war. A smile played on her lips, and she carried a piece of paper.

"How can I help you, Jenny?" Margaret asked. She motioned for the tall redhead to sit beside her. "You look more radiant than usual."

"My children are so happy." She sighed. "They tell me they love the country and want me to join them." She handled Margaret the letter. "Read for yourself."

Margaret took the note but sensed Jenny needed to voice more of her feelings.

"I know I'm lucky to know where they are and even hear from them, but my heart aches for 'em. My dear boy says he ain't never took so many baths, and he's gotten bigger since eatin' regular. My thirteen-year-old daughter says she can milk a cow and make good stew." Jenny clasped her hands together. "I couldn't offer them none of those things before, and look what they have now."

"Then it's God's provision." Margaret patted Jenny's hand. "He's taking care of them like we ask in our prayers. Isn't our God wonderful?"

Jenny nodded and a tear slipped from her eye. "Up until this very minute I doubted if a God really existed, but I see a miracle in my children. Matthew wants to always live in the country—doesn't want our tiny flat anymore." She toyed with a button on her shirt. "Of course the rats plagued us, and most likely it's blown to bits."

Jenny's story drew the attention of several others. The letter proved to be a blessing not only for Jenny but also for many women who pondered over the plight of their children.

Margaret pulled a handkerchief from her trouser pocket and wiped Jenny's cheeks. "See, the Germans did you a favor, and they didn't have the sense to know it. Got your children out of a bad situation and into a home where they're well-taken care of."

Suddenly one of the women began to laugh, and soon the others joined.

"I hadn't thought of the Germans doing any of us a favor," a thin young woman said. "When we chase them off once and for all, I'll get me a new house, and it won't have a thatch roof either to catch every fire spark."

"Me and my husband will have us a fine butcher shop again," another woman added, "without a bomb in the middle of it."

Soon they all were laughing and joking about their misfortunes. That's what Margaret liked the best about being British—strength and humor.

Beryl wiggled her way through the crowd to her cot. She wore a smile, but Margaret doubted if it held much substance.

"I have an announcement to make," Beryl said, waving her hands to quiet the others. She nodded at Margaret. "As much as I love all of you, I will be departing from your delightful company."

"Where ya going?" Jenny asked.

"To Patrick's family in Ireland. . .to be with my dear boy Christopher and. . .to give birth to another babe." She lifted her chin, while silence echoed around the barracks. "Would someone say something, please?"

A moment later, a dozen arms wrapped around Beryl,

and the hum of well-wishers sounded livelier than a beehive.

"When are you leaving?" Margaret asked, feeling immense relief for her friend but realizing how much she'd miss her.

"Shortly, I believe. Lieutenant Fitzgerald is making the arrangements." Beryl embraced Margaret and hugged her tightly. "Thank you for supporting me these months since Patrick died. I couldn't have made it without your God-given friendship and all of the wonderful ladies here."

Margaret responded with a nod. Later they could talk in private. Right then, emotion blocked her every thought.

"What will you name the babe?" Jenny asked.

Beryl smiled genuinely. "Patrick Winston if it's a boy, and Elizabeth Clementine if it's a girl."

"Ah," Jenny said. "For our Mr. Churchill and his wife."

"Bravo," the cheers rose. "To God and England."

"And His blessing on our families where'er they may be," Jenny added.

The conversation continued with names of children and mothers' fond memories of peaceful days. Without warning, the sirens sounded.

"Soon you'll be free of this," Margaret whispered to Beryl as they raced to the shelter.

"But a piece of my heart will always be here with you, my friends," Beryl said as they hurried to go, "and all of the RAF. Here is where Patrick and I found purpose to the lives God gave us."

🦋

Andrew watched Margaret and Beryl hug each other one last time before Beryl departed. A train would take her northwest to Liverpool where she would cross the Irish Sea to Dublin. Now he understood Margaret's concern for her friend and the reason she protected Beryl.

"So you'll be home for Christmas?" Andrew asked heartily. "I envy you with family and all."

Beryl laughed. "It seems like a fantasy come true." She clasped Andrew's hand. "Oh, I don't mean to sound selfish or shirk my responsibilities."

"Not at all," Andrew replied, peering anxiously into her eyes. "You have the responsibility to take care of another loyal subject. Motherhood is the finest profession I know."

Beryl tilted her head. "You are so kind, Andrew. I wish you the best, and take good care of Margaret for me."

"I will, be certain of that." Andrew winked at Margaret.

The conductor called for all to board, and Beryl glanced longingly at the train.

"Wait up," a voice shouted.

The three turned to see James racing toward them. He closely resembled a rugby player hurrying for the ball. "I wanted to see Beryl off," he managed between chilling breaths. He turned to her and removed his cap. "Hope you don't mind."

"Not at all. I'm humbled you took the time in this bitter weather," she said, drawing her coat around her bulging stomach.

The train whistle sounded.

He glanced up nervously. "God speed, Beryl. I wondered if I might write you."

She nibbled at her lip and glanced down at her suitcase

setting beside her. "I'd like to hear from you, Corporal Harris."

"Call me James," he said above the roar of the train.

She nodded and made her way up the steps. Turning, she waved. "Merry Christmas to you. I'll be praying for you and England."

Margaret stared after the train until it disappeared. No tears, only a trembling smile. *How wonderful for Beryl. May God bless her with a healthy baby and a good life.*

"Are you all right?" Andrew asked.

"Very well," she whispered. "Things will be fine for her. I'm sure of it."

He wrapped his arm around her waist and longed to take her into his arms and kiss her soundly, but he hadn't ventured past friendship yet. Christmas Eve he planned to tell her of his growing feelings, and he prayed she felt the same.

The winter seemed to be colder than usual, or perhaps the bleakness of the war held its own bitter temperatures. In London, a few fragile restaurants still stood and served four-course dinners—if one could pay for them—and the theatre still drew the attention of the elite. Although dust from the bombings fell on the stage; the "show must go on" philosophy kept the actors and actresses returning for repeated performances. English and Americans alike entertained the troops, often using the bomb shelters as a hotel.

"Wish I could find a small gift for Andrew," Margaret said wistfully to Jenny. The two had just finished breakfast and were walking back to the barracks.

"I understand," the tall woman replied. "With the cost of everything in London so dear and everything rationed, what can you do?"

Margaret contemplated the matter once more. She'd always sent much of her money home to Mum and Dad, and she couldn't justify not continuing to do so. "He says our Christmas will be celebrating the Lord's birthday and a carol-sing, but I wish for a token of our friendship."

"Friendship, aye?" Jenny asked with a soft laugh.

"Of course. We're good chums." Margaret knew she inched closer and closer to something more with Andrew, but she found it difficult to admit the truth to herself, much less confide in Jenny. At times Margaret's growing attraction angered her as if her heart had a will of its own. Other times she allowed the sweet bliss of love to envelop her like a garden of fragrant roses. She tried not to think about the many missions Andrew flew—only to be grateful when he safely returned.

Jenny leaned closer and whispered. "I know where you can get a chocolate bar."

Margaret nodded. "Perfect."

Unfortunately, on Christmas Eve, Margaret received orders to drive high-ranking officers to a special meeting and remain near the lorry until they finished. After she transported them to their destination, the air raid sounded as usual. She took shelter, then resumed her position and waited for the officers to finish. In the wee hours of Christmas morning, she returned to her barracks.

Christmas Day, Andrew flew an unscheduled flight. Margaret had learned he and James often flew these types of missions to take critical pictures for future bombings.

On the afternoon of December twenty-sixth, Margaret and Andrew were finally able to grasp a few moments alone to wish each other Merry Christmas.

"I have something for you," she said, pulling the rare sweet treat from her trouser pocket.

His smile warmed her like the fireplace at her mum and dad's home. "Hmm. I'll make sure James doesn't know I have chocolate. Thank you so much, and I have a gift for you. I hope you'll be pleased."

She held her breath, unable to image what Andrew could have gotten for her.

He carefully reached inside his jacket and produced a sheet of paper. She knew he had sketched something special, and judging by the rose he left in her lorry, she knew it would be magnificent.

The moment Margaret saw the drawing, she gasped. She touched her fingers to her lips to keep from crying aloud. There before her, a quaint, moss-covered cottage stood surrounded by a garden of roses. Some climbed the stone walls trailing up onto the roof, while smaller bushes and other flowers dotted the earth's floor. A winding rose vine arched the doorway, spreading blossoms over the entrance. In the middle of a pebble-laden path sat a young woman dressed in the manner of an eighteenth-century maiden. She inhaled the sweet fragrance of a rose and possessed a face identical to Margaret's.

"If I had my colored pencils, I'd have given her dark brown hair and violet eyes," he said. "I hope you're not disappointed."

"Oh, Andrew. This is the most extraordinary gift anyone has ever given me. Thank you ever so." She stared into his eyes and saw her own reflection and something else—the warm glow of love. The sensation both frightened and pleased her at the same time.

"Margaret," he began, "may I kiss you?"

She'd thought about his kiss—more than she cared to admit—but with this bridge between friendship and a relationship came a commitment. Could she brave forward?

"It's a step beyond. . .well, where we are now," she whispered, more for her own understanding than his.

"Yes, it is. I'm ready, but are you?"

She nodded and lifted her face. "I think so."

He wove his fingers through her hair and drew her close to him. His lips touched hers, gentle at first then deepening with his embrace. Trembling, she responded, desiring to hold back her own delicate emotions and yet losing the battle. With one hand firmly gripping the sketch, she wrapped the other arm around his neck and leaned into the curve of his body. She knew she'd given him her heart; no matter that the time seemed too soon and uncertainty lay around them. She could love him and he'd never know.

The kiss ended, and when they parted, Margaret traced her finger along his jaw line and lightly touched his lips. He gently caressed her fingers and kissed them lightly.

"Merry Christmas," he whispered, still holding her fingers.

She glowed from the inside out. "Thank you for making my holiday perfect."

"My pleasure, but the thanks go to you. You're all I need, all put together quite nicely in one lovely package."

Margaret could not reply. She wanted to say the thoughts wafting across her mind, but until Andrew made his declaration, she'd not have to respond. Truth be known, any feelings of love were best unsaid until after the war.

On Sunday, December twenty-ninth, Margaret was assigned to night duty delivering much needed medical supplies. The Germans' nightly bombing had continued to shake London, leaving their city collapsing in rubble and the injured storming the hospitals.

Britons refused to give into the siege against their capital and plodded on, unwilling to accept defeat as an option. The air raid shelters were full at night, while the cleanup and search for victims persisted by day. Some of those seeking shelter sank into wells of depression, while others spent their time singing songs and rallying England. The shared danger seemed to make them more sociable, or perhaps they learned to value those things money could not purchase.

Shortly after the medical supplies were loaded, the sirens sounded, and heavy air strikes began, stronger than she could remember in months. Instead of seeking shelter, she watched the bombs illuminate the night sky as if a demon had lit a giant torch. The incessant attack left her feeling empty and fearful. One prayer after another flowed from her heart.

As soon as the all-clear siren sounded, Margaret climbed into her lorry and drove toward the hospital, all the while wondering about the horrendous devastation.

This had to be the worst barrage since the Battle of Britain began in late August.

Fires raged in the distance. Their flames leapt into the blackness like giant tongues hungry for more. The attack appeared to concentrate its efforts on central London. Soon afterwards, she learned that in Westminster and the City regions, fires spread out of control and destroyed docks, factories, and offices.

Dear Lord, when will it all end? We can't take much more of this. I pray for those whose livelihood has been destroyed, for those who have lost loved ones this night, and for Britain to survive.

Chapter 5

*"Let us therefore brace ourselves to our duties,
and so bear ourselves that, if the British Empire
and its Commonwealth last for a thousand years,
men will still say, 'This was their finest hour.'"*
WINSTON CHURCHILL

High winds carried sparks from rooftops to melting stained glass windows, but Saint Paul's Cathedral towered erect as though the hand of God halted the bombs destroying everything around it. For Margaret, the magnificent church symbolized Britain's ability to withstand Germany's assault.

She leaned her head on Andrew's shoulder. Twelve hours ago, she'd watched in horror the sight of London plummeting into ruins thirty miles away. Yet, today, Home Guardsman and fire fighters worked diligently to extinguish the blazes and pull victims from the wreckage. The casualty count had been much lower than anticipated, since the areas hardest hit were commercial. In truth, it looked like the Germans had caught the British off guard by focusing their bombs on the heart of Britain's financial security district. News reports claimed it was the greatest fire in recorded history.

Beautiful old buildings—the pride of many Britons—had vanished beneath smoldering ashes. History in the making had destroyed the relics of the past.

"The Thames nearly ran dry," Andrew said. "Hitler chose to do his work during low tide. Can't put out such an inferno without water."

"What will Churchill say now?" Margaret asked, grasping his hand in the bitter cold.

His lips pressed firmly together. "I have no idea, but we are still here."

She fought the rage inside her over the violation of her homeland. "I shall not give up," she said. "Not as long as I can breathe."

He smiled and brushed a kiss in her hair. "We all feel the same. The more Hitler bombs, the more we rally onward."

"Do you suppose the United States will join the war now?" she asked, believing the Americans' entry would give Britain the edge to stop Germany.

"We already have many of their fine pilots joining our ranks." He sighed. "They're good chaps to volunteer and help us. Perhaps Churchill can convince them."

"I've heard speculation about Germany's plans," she ventured.

"I have as well. I believe Hitler would not stop at merely controlling Europe. He has even set his sights on the States."

Margaret felt a deeper cold seize her. "And would not Japan attack them on their west coast?"

"Who knows? We will not let it come to that."

Neither whispered a word for several moments.

"You and I are like England," Andrew finally said.

Puzzled, she merely stared up into his face.

"We can withstand any adversity. Nothing can separate us. We'll make it through this war and live to tell about it."

She smiled sadly, not wanting to consider the fact that every time he flew, the odds increased of his not returning.

He began to hum "There'll Always Be an England," a popular wartime tune. Together they softly sang the chorus.

> *There'll always be an England,*
> *And England shall be free*
> *If England means as much to you*
> *As England means to me.*

The winter persisted with work and missions halting when the pilots were hampered by ice and snow. Germany eased the intense bombing that had occurred during late August through the end of 1940. It appeared the island had passed the test for control of England.

Spring arrived, and Andrew wanted to take Margaret to the country. He felt they would gain new hope in the midst of fresh air and the landscape unscathed by bombs.

"I'd like to take a few days to go see my mum and dad," he announced one March morning. "I'm sure I could help with the extra children, and I want to see my nephew before he's walking."

"Splendid idea," Margaret replied. "You need a break."

"Would you care to join me?" he asked, all the while praying she'd agree. "My mum has plenty of room, even with the children."

"Are you sure? I mean it sounds wonderful."

"Positively." Oh, how he treasured the joy of the woman beside him. "The garden will be blooming in spring color, and there's a special spot I'd like to show you."

Because Andrew and Margaret had not taken any passes for several months, their arrangements were quickly made. The end of March, he escorted her to London, where they boarded a train to Northamptonshire. From there they'd take bicycles to Andrew's family estate.

The moment London lay behind them, he felt his spirits lift, much like in his schooldays when he traveled home for a holiday. So many things he needed to tell his parents. With no end of the war in sight, they should hear of his love and respect for them. Andrew also wanted them to meet Margaret. He knew they would love her as much as he did.

Andrew hadn't revealed his true feelings for Margaret. He prayerfully waited for the right moment. In the confines of his heart, he feared she might not share the same feelings. Whenever he spoke of the future, she veered from the subject and irritation took over her demeanor. He knew her commitment to the war and her apprehension about his dangerous position, but her eyes betrayed her. He'd seen the love; he'd guessed her feelings.

In Northamptonshire, they purchased bread and cheese for a picnic and secured bicycles for the remaining distance to the Stuart Estate. He was anxious and excited, wanting to leave the dark months of war behind and enjoy three days of peace. Glancing at Margaret pedaling beside him, her hair flying free, he saw the weary lines vanish from her face and her cheeks grow rosy in the chilly air. They sang songs and teased the other over forgotten words to the tunes, and laughter rang from the budding trees. He stole a kiss, which nearly wrecked them both.

Once they walked their bicycles so they could hear the birds, although he believed the lilt of her laughter far sweeter than any sound of nature. The lightheartedness reminded him of a proper courtship, the way it should be.

"Up ahead is home." Andrew pointed to a huge manor rising in a clearing behind ancient stone walls.

"Oh, Andrew, it's beautiful. I had no idea it would be so grand." She stopped her bicycle to view the rugged estate.

"I want to show it all to you." He shielded his eyes from the sun. "Have I gone daft, or do I hear children?"

She lifted her chin and turned in the direction of the merry sound. "I hear them. How many are your parents keeping?"

"A dozen, I believe, in addition to my nephew."

Over the ridge, an army of small children filed in a haphazard line. They clung to shirttails and hems of dresses while marching like miniature soldiers. Their little voices echoed like fairy-tale magic.

"Oh, Andrew. It's been so long since I've seen or heard little ones. I want to hug them all." She peered at the group hiking down a grassy knoll. "I believe there's closer to fourteen than twelve."

"My word," Andrew breathed. "There's my dad and Mr. Hardy, the gardener."

Abandoning his bicycle, Andrew called out to a white-haired gentleman taking up the rear of the procession. "Father!" Andrew waved and raced toward them. He didn't care if he looked like a child himself, for at that moment the war lay far behind.

Margaret studied each child seated around the long wooden table. She recalled Jenny commenting about her son's letter—how he loved the country and never wanted to leave. She envied Jenny's children and the precious hope of Britain's future.

Mr. and Mrs. Stuart had trained the children well, especially since most of them had come from poverty-stricken areas. Andrew's mother had told her in private the sad condition of some of them: lice infested, dirty, underfed, and without manners. Even with the rationing, Mr. and Mrs. Stuart had provided for them all. Their bright eyes held the glow of promise.

"I simply mother them and enjoy every minute of it," Andrew's mother had said, her ample cheeks swelling with pride.

Andrew looked more vibrant than Margaret had ever seen him. He laughed more, and she appreciated the gentle way he dealt with the children. She felt at peace with herself in a way she couldn't remember since before the war, maybe not even then.

"Would you like a bit more stew?" Mrs. Stuart asked, interrupting Margaret's contemplations. The older woman brushed back sandy-colored hair, the same shade as Andrew's.

"No, thank you, Ma'am. I'm simply admiring all of these precious children."

"Oh, they can be a handful," Mr. Stuart said, lifting his knife to emphasize his words. His voice rose above the cherub voices. "Not so loud, children. Our guests will think we're not proper." He feigned a stern look at the brood, in particular one little girl who had not ceased laughing.

A boy about eight years old asked if there would be sweets tonight.

"Possibly," Mrs. Stuart replied with a smile. "When everyone has eaten their stew, I might find a treat. In fact, I believe Mrs. Hardy made gooseberry tarts today sweetened with honey."

The children cheered, and those who had not finished their stew and bread hastened to clean their bowls.

After dinner Margaret helped Mrs. Stuart and some of the older children wash and dry the dishes. Once the wet towels were draped over the sink, the older woman announced bath night.

"How do you manage to bathe them all?" Margaret asked, mentally calculating how long the task would take.

"Mr. Stuart and I split them up—girls and boys. Then he heats one tub and I the other. It doesn't really amount to a long time, and the older children help the younger ones undress and dress."

Andrew marched into the kitchen carrying his nephew on his shoulder. "Tonight it will go twice as fast, for we intend to help. Right Margaret?"

She grinned and laughed at another toddler tugging on his trouser leg. What a lovely day. A part of her wanted it to go on forever—or maybe she wanted to live in this make-believe world with Andrew forever. Margaret forced her feelings for him from her mind. The memory of her brother's death and Beryl's circumstances still shadowed her heart. Perhaps when Germany ceased to plague the world, they could talk of a life together.

The following morning, after breakfast had been eaten and the kitchen scrubbed spotless, Margaret and Andrew offered to entertain the children until lunch. Normally his parents and Mr. Hardy took over those duties while Mrs. Hardy busied herself in preparing the day's food.

"We will go exploring," Andrew announced to the children. "Who knows what we might find?"

The children's voices mounted as each tried to tell Uncle Andrew their most prized find. A short while later they proceeded in single file across the hillsides, grasping shirt and dress tails, just as Margaret and Andrew had observed the previous day.

"Why is it you have the little girls after you?" Margaret called to Andrew while they hiked along a brook's edge.

"I have no idea, but the boys appear to like you best," he replied and lifted a wee girl to his shoulders.

"True. I must be prettier," she teased, feeling the sweet weight of two little boys pulling on her arms.

He swung a grin over his shoulder, mesmerizing her with his tender glance. "This afternoon I'd like to show you the garden. Perhaps just after tea?"

"Wonderful," she replied, visualizing a lovely array of spring color. Everything about Stuart Manor filled her senses with beauty and delight.

Andrew and Margaret enjoyed tea in delicate demitasse cups, poured from a family heirloom pitcher and served on a silver tray. They added a precious lump of sugar and ate cucumber sandwiches and biscuits. She tucked away every memory to open like a treasured book when the days ahead sought to overwhelm her.

❧

"Close your eyes and let me lead you," Andrew coaxed, once they'd left the manor. "I want this to be a surprise."

"I might peek," she said with a giggle.

"Ah, fair lady, then must I blindfold you?"

"Probably so."

He reached into his pocket and produced a clean, white handkerchief. She nodded approval before obediently turning for him to secure it over her eyes.

Andrew couldn't resist and lightly kissed her neck. He detected a shiver. "Cold are you?" he asked.

"Not exactly." A smile played on her lips. "How far are we going?"

"Miles, my lady. Just hold tightly to my hand."

On they walked, beyond the back of the manor and dark yew hedges to a place where dreams were made. He drank in the earthy smells and watched the light splay through the tree limbs. Never had he truly appreciated the garden's beauty and Mr. Hardy's labor until today.

"Here we are," he whispered, stopping several feet in front of a winding brook beside a small, stone cottage. Andrew removed the handkerchief from Margaret's eyes, watching every movement on her face.

She held her breath and tears fell from her eyes. "It's my picture, my Christmas picture." She studied each delicate spring flower, fern, and grass. She stepped across a rock path to the bubbling brook, then bent to examine a patch of daffodils and red tulips. As though in her own world, she noted each blooming array of primrose, crocus, and white narcissus. A light laugh sprang from her lips as she gingerly scooped up a cherry blossom petal that had fallen among the grasses.

As if a symphony played in the background of rustling water, Margaret slowly stood and approached the cottage.

"The roses." She closed her eyes. "I can only imagine all this paradise when they're in full bloom."

Andrew felt his heart race at the sight of his beloved Margaret posed at the threshold of the small structure.

"In summer the scent of the roses mixed with honeysuckle will take your breath away," he said, choosing to join her.

She touched the moss-covered wall. "And the beauty of them, just as in my picture."

"Nearly as lovely as you."

She blushed, and her gaze followed a vine trailing up

the side to the roof. "Thank you," she said, so quietly that her voice blended with the gentle sounds of nature. "This is a sacred place. Surely Eden could not have been more colorful and alive." She whirled to face him. "Oh, Andrew, God is here; I can feel Him."

"That's why I've chosen this place to tell you how I feel." His heart pounded and his mouth felt dry, but he dare not lose courage now. Lifting her chin with his finger, he gazed into those beloved pools, more radiant than the blossoms from spring and summer combined. "I love you, Margaret. I want us always to be together. Marry me and let me take care of you."

Her face paled, and she stepped back. "Marry you. . . while the war rages around us?" Her gaze darted like a trapped animal.

Andrew's heart plummeted. "This war will not last forever."

She shook her head. "I can't. I can't possibly marry you. What if I lose you like my brother? Or how Beryl lost Patrick? Forgive me, Andrew, but what you ask is impossible. Perhaps after the war. . ." Her voice trailed off, and in its wake her sobs broke the spell of the garden.

Brushing past him, Margaret rushed toward the house beyond him and the call of the garden.

Chapter 6

"This is a war of the Unknown Warriors;
but let all strive without failing in faith or in duty."
WINSTON CHURCHILL

Margaret raced from the garden toward the Stuart manor, her tears falling uncontrollably. She needed to leave this place and get back to London where she belonged. There in the real world, she had duties and responsibilities that mattered. Andrew had tricked her into coming to Northamptonshire. He knew she'd never agree to marriage while on base. By taking her to the country, he'd played on her sentiments. How selfish of him to ask her to wed when pilots faced death every moment they were in the air. Andrew had taken her affections for him and used them to his advantage.

"Margaret!"

She hurried faster.

"Margaret!"

Anger laced every syllable.

Before she could consider a reply, he grabbed her arm and forced her to face him.

"You're a coward," he shouted. Blood pumped its power through his face and neck. "Life doesn't give any guarantees, Corporal Walker. What will your excuse be after the war? I might get sick? I might get hit by a trolley? I might choke on a poached egg? England's weather doesn't suit you?"

"You have no right to talk to me that way." She shook loose his hold and took a step back. Their fury split the picturesque countryside. What happened to her quiet lieutenant? "You don't understand."

He raked his fingers through his hair and expelled a heavy sigh that seemed to come from the soles of his feet. "Oh, I understand perfectly. Do you think you have the market on heartache? Look at the thousands of children living without their parents. Think of the parents who have no idea of their children's living conditions. What about Beryl and Patrick? Do you think they stopped loving because Hitler decided to wage war?"

"Leave me alone," she said through her tears.

"First tell me you don't love me." He intensified his demand with a piercing stare.

"You don't deserve an answer. You brought me here under false pretenses, thinking the country and its garden would twist my mind and heart into seeing things your way."

"Since when is the love God gives a man and a woman something to be reckoned with like a formidable enemy?"

She balled her fists, more angry than she could

remember. "He instructs us to be discerning," she spurted through a ragged breath.

Andrew lifted his chin. "It is you who cannot perceive what is clearly before you. How sad. You cannot make a commitment, and you're using anything you can clutch as an excuse." He paused, then stiffened. "Tell me you want me out of your life." His voice softened. "Tell me now, and I won't ever bother you again. I give you my word."

A lump settled in her throat. Her lips quivered and she swallowed hard. She turned and raced back toward the house.

"Go ahead, run," he called after her. "I won't come after you. You've made your choice."

Sunday morning, Andrew rode the train back to London alone. Margaret had gathered up her things on Saturday afternoon and left the house before he'd walked off his anger and talked to God.

He'd been prepared to apologize for losing his temper, and when he found out she'd left his parents' home, he wanted to go after her. But he held onto his pride. He recognized it, and still he could not humble himself to make amends with her. She'd tested him once too often. Margaret would have to come to him.

As he buried himself in the RAF—flying at a moment's notice and often several times during the day or night—Andrew attempted to cast aside his love for her. He avoided the places they'd ventured together, believing he could tuck her memory into a remote corner of his heart. A few times she'd driven the lorry transporting the pilots to the hangars, but he refused to look her way.

Bitterness erupted when he least expected it like a land mine, damaging his relationships with other flyers. He apologized and the others said they understood, but it didn't stop the guilt.

A month later, Andrew settled his plane into formation with other Spitfires above the waters of the English Channel. Radar had indicated German fighters en route to Britain's shores, and the fighters churned their engines to meet them. The RAF planes flew twenty thousand feet above the clouds, making them invisible until the right moment to swoop down behind the unsuspecting German Messerschmitts.

Andrew waited until he knew the enemy swarmed beneath them before ordering the fighters to separate, turn, and dive for the attack. Sadly outnumbered, the RAF utilized their offensive position to fire the enemy from the skies.

The surprise attack left black swirls of smoke and the decimated end of many German planes. Andrew saw two of his friends' planes burst into flames; one pilot parachuted out. The other man now rested in God's hands.

Angry at the loss of his friend's life, Andrew flew down through the middle of six German fighters and pumped bullets from every angle. He knew he took too many chances lately, and although he'd earned the title of a relentless fighter, he understood his daring came from his wounded heart.

One enemy aircraft met his demise and two others took on heavy damage. He quickly lifted his plane above the clouds to strike again.

Within seconds, he detected three enemy fighters rapidly moving in from his rear.

"You think you have me?" he shouted. "We'll see who wins this round."

The hair on his neck bristled when a fighter zoomed in faster than Andrew anticipated. He pulled his Spitfire up, narrowly missing an onslaught of bullets. Beads of sweat trickled down the side of his face despite the winter temperatures.

"Lord, I need Your help," he said.

Through the white veil concealing him, Andrew spotted a Messerschmitt looming behind. Andrew lifted the plane higher and quickly swung to the right. He aimed his wing guns, fired, and watched the enemy aircraft disappear in an explosion. Another fighter appeared just ahead. Andrew ascended on the plane and sent it spiraling downward.

He no sooner recovered than the third German fighter trailed after him. Andrew used the same maneuver, except this time he swung to the left. The enemy stayed on him as though sensing Andrew's moves. Again he lifted his Spitfire and repeated a wide turn to the left.

The Messerschmitt followed, now within firing range. Enemy bullets ripped into Andrew's fighter.

Lord, this German is smarter than I am. I need You to direct me.

Following his instincts, Andrew sank below the Messerschmitt and prayed for guidance. He glanced at the amount of fuel remaining and accessed the damage done to his plane. He wondered if the right wing guns would work at all. Taking a deep breath, he moved from under the enemy and twisted to the right, but not before taking a bad hit to the side.

Pressing on, he finally secured a rear position and pumped all he had into the German fighter. The aircraft exploded, but the Spitfire would never make it back to base.

Thank You, Lord. Please be with the other pilots as well.

Andrew parachuted out and saw his landing would be on English soil and not the water. He breathed a prayer of thanks, for he had no inclination to drop into the icy waters of the Channel or set up a rescue boat as a target for air-borne Germans. He cringed when his fighter plane crashed into the coastal terrain long before his feet found safety. He rather fancied that little fighter, but like Margaret, all had been lost.

On May tenth, Andrew picked up his Bible and read through Isaiah forty. He had long ago put the verses of twenty-nine through thirty-one to memory and often prayed through them in flight. This morning the Scripture held a different meaning. He closed his eyes and allowed the words to flow through his body and soul.

"He giveth power to the faint; and to them that have no might He increaseth strength. Even the youths shall faint and be weary, and the young men shall utterly fall. But they that wait upon the Lord shall renew their strength; they shall mount up with wings as eagles; they shall run, and not be weary; and they shall walk, and not faint."

Andrew felt as though a knife had thrust through his heart and twisted. ". . .*the young men shall utterly fall.*" His pride was destroying him. For weeks he'd been depleted of strength, not the strength required to fly his Spitfire but his ability to hold onto the Lord. His broken heart had stopped him from forgiving Margaret and apologizing for losing his temper. The time had come to stop asking God why she'd refused him and accept he might never know until he saw God face-to-face. For now, God had allowed this upheaval in his life, and He did know best.

Forgive me, Father, for my hard heart. I will find Margaret today and apologize. Thank You for caring enough to point out my sin and for providing a way for me to seek forgiveness. You know my love for her, and now I see my love must be unconditional, like Yours.

Andrew closed his Bible. He did not have to fly until tonight. He'd make amends with Margaret and not go another day with the shame tormenting his soul.

"I'm praying for you, Chum," James said from his cot. Their friendship had grown to the point where oft times neither had to speak a word to sense the other's mood and thoughts.

"Thanks, James. I've been a fool not to patch up things. At least Margaret and I could be friends. At times I can't help but wonder if I'd gone after her that afternoon things might have ended differently."

"No word from her at all?"

"Nothing, but I haven't tried to contact her either." Andrew shrugged. "I misjudged her feelings and then judged her myself." He glanced up. "I've had a nasty disposition lately, but I promise things will be different."

"We all know it's been rough."

"No excuse for taking out my wounded pride on you and the other chaps. I'll make sure I talk to them today."

After apologizing to the other pilots and assuring them that God had dealt with his bad temperament, Andrew scoured the camp for Margaret but couldn't find her. He asked some of the women at her barracks, but none knew where she could be found. He prayed he'd have an opportunity to speak with her before heading to the hangars.

As the day drew to a close, he prepared himself for flight. Although his heart felt the burden of not righting things with Margaret, he sensed a peace. Laughter came naturally; optimism for the future returned.

When the call came to board the lorry, he filed out with the others pilots. If only Margaret drove, but he couldn't see the driver's seat from the vehicle's angle.

"Did you see the driver?" he asked James once they were en route.

" 'Tis Margaret," James replied. "I spoke to her, and she acknowledged me. She looks as unhappy as you."

Andrew felt a spark of hope. "I'm going to do my best to have a word with her once we get to the hangars."

"Jolly good idea."

Once they reached the aircrafts, one of the pilots cornered Andrew about a downed plane from the preceding day in which a pilot lost his life. "Sir, about yesterday, the pilot confided in me about a concern he had with his fighter."

Andrew lifted a brow. "Did he discuss it with a mechanic?"

"Not to my knowledge."

"Let's talk inside and see if we can pinpoint the problem."

As they stepped into the wooden building, the lorry drove away. Regret washed over him, but safety for his pilots came first.

Shortly before darkness wrapped its blanket over England, the fighter pilots were summoned to the skies. Andrew raced to his plane and pulled the canopy over his head. He felt the familiar adrenaline pump through his veins as he waved to James beside him and mouthed tally-ho. Taking his position on the runway, Andrew breathed a prayer before lifting his Spitfire into the air.

🦋

Margaret's misery increased every time she thought of Andrew. She missed him terribly and despised their harsh words. So many times she wanted to go to him and apologize, but in doing so she feared he would press her about marriage. Couldn't they love each other until the war no longer existed, then discuss a future?

Today she'd transported him to the hangars. It took all of her control to avoid him. She wanted to ask how he fared and seek the warmth in his deep brown eyes. A part of her realized his feelings for her had vanished. She'd ruined it in Northamptonshire—the day in the beautiful garden when he proposed. Admittedly, Margaret didn't know what she wanted, nor did she know what God intended for them. All she knew was the ache in her heart for Andrew. Perhaps her misery stemmed from the fact she refused to seek God's will. Her heavenly Father might ask more of her than she could give.

She'd told her friends in the barracks not to breathe a word of her whereabouts if Andrew came looking. He'd done so today, and now the pain ravaged her heart.

Early evening, Margaret delivered a document to one of Churchill's advisers in London. Within minutes, she climbed into the lorry to head back to base. Evening had drifted into night, and along with the darkness came the sirens alerting London of imminent German bombing.

They never give up.

She glanced up at the skies as the warnings assaulted her ears. Sometimes she simply didn't care when it sounded; other times she prayed for those who would be affected. Praise God Britain had the early detection radar, for without it they'd have fallen months ago.

Margaret picked her way along the road, avoiding deep crevices and rubble resulting from previous bombings. In the war-torn city, she felt uneasy, trapped by the probability of falling bombs and collapsing buildings. She'd feel much better once safely away on base.

She heard the roar of enemy planes above her and the zoom of their engines cutting through the darkness to drop their destruction. To Margaret, there appeared to be more than usual, reminding her of December twenty-ninth's raid. Bombs fell like a shower of hail, igniting fires that burst into yellow-orange flames. They raised their fiery fingers to the sky as though paying homage to the German bombers.

An apartment building exploded in front of her, sending shattered glass through its walls directly into her path. A man, obviously wounded, emerged from the fiery mass and stumbled in her direction. Pulling the lorry to a halt, she rushed to his side.

"I'll get you to a hospital," she said above the deafening roar. As the fire lit up his face, she saw blood stream down his forehead and cheek.

He leaned heavily on her until she fell. Together they struggled to their feet and inched their way to the lorry.

"My wife's inside," he said, attempting to gain his breath.

She helped him onto the seat and patted his shoulder. "I'll look for your missus."

He uttered a feeble thanks as she shut the door.

Margaret scanned the burning area but saw no one. The heat nearly took her breath away. Why hadn't the couple gone to a shelter? Another bomb crashed on the same building, eliminating any chances of the woman's survival. Margaret needed to get the injured man to the hospital and away from the fire. Even the street was laden with fire.

She rushed to the driver's side and in one fluid motion slammed the door and stuck the key into the ignition. "I'm sorry, Sir, but I don't see your wife, and I can't get inside the building to find her." No need to tell him it had been destroyed. She hoped her words sounded compassionate, but in truth fright tore through her senses.

With trembling hands, Margaret jerked the lorry into gear. She backed up, all the while taking in the devastation. The man slumped against the passenger's door and moaned before whispering something inaudible. She wished she could have helped his wife, but only God could deliver the woman now. Terror gripped Margaret as she steered away from the site.

The burning mass disguised the normal landmarks, and she wondered what street to take to the hospital. An explosion in front of them caused her to slam on the brakes. She screamed as a mighty force pulled her from the vehicle and threw her into the inferno.

Chapter 7

"Never in the field of human conflict was so much owed by so many to so few."
WINSTON CHURCHILL

Margaret opened her eyes. Fires blazed, while the deafening sounds of falling bombs echoed around her. From where she'd been thrown, she could see her lorry in flames. She called out for the injured man inside, knowing full well the futility of her cries. A moment later she prayed he'd been tossed from it as well.

Her mind dulled to everything around her except her tormented body. She felt as though every bone had been broken, but a fierce determination to survive compelled her to move. Every muscle and nerve screamed out in protest, and blood trickled into her eyes. Fighting the pounding in her head, Margaret tried to lift her right arm to find the source of the blood, but excruciating pain hindered any movement. Her head dropped back onto a rock.

I have to see the rest of my body. Oh, dear Lord, I'm scared.

She tried to suck in air, but the smoke caused her to choke and sputter. After several long minutes, she slowly raised her head and studied her body sprawled out on a mass of rubble. The lights from the fires showed what she suspected. Her left leg curled in an awkward position away from her torso. She had to lie there until one of the fires tasted her body and devoured her.

Listening to the crackling and crashing going on around her, Margaret prayed for strength to endure whatever happened. Although she tried to stay alert, she drifted in and out of consciousness. Sometime during the night, she awoke and her thoughts turned to Andrew.

Dear, sweet Andrew who only wanted a chance to love her. She'd been so cruel to make light of his feelings.

I can't ever tell him how sorry I am for that afternoon in the country; never tell him how I wanted to spend the rest of my life with him and be the mother of his children. He'll never know how much I truly love him.

Her past harsh words spilled across her mind like ink blots. In the recesses of her heart, she knew he'd been right. She was a coward—afraid of getting hurt and being left alone. She was paralyzed by the memories of her brother, Beryl loosing Patrick, and the countless faces of pilots who never returned. Other women in her barracks grieved the family members who gave their lives in the war effort. Margaret didn't want to think about being in the same situation. She didn't have the courage to love a man no matter how hopeless the future.

But with God all things were possible.

She well knew this Scripture. Why hadn't she remembered it before? Guilt for her inability to be bold and courageous assailed her heart and mind.

Precious Lord, forgive me for not seeking Your will about Andrew. I know I'm going to die, and all of this time my fears were for him. The irony of death, Lord. I've been such a fool.

A wave of blackness drew her back into its web.

Later she woke again to the sound of German bombers still releasing their fury on London. Opening her eyes, she strained to see a hint of daylight, but a thick film coated her eyes. With the searing pain invading her body, she prayed for death's release.

Andrew wearily opened his eyes. Throughout the previous night he'd flown repeated missions until at last the Germans ceased their attack that morning. Glancing at the clock, he noted six hours had gone by, and he felt like sleeping another six.

"I see you're awake," James said from his cot.

"Trying to be," Andrew replied. "How long have you been up?"

"About an hour."

Andrew swallowed hard. "So what's the word?"

"Gloomy, at best."

He stared at his friend. "How bad?"

"I heard nearly seven hundred acres of London burned." James stared at the ceiling. "This is the first time I've really felt low about the war—asked myself why go on."

"I've felt the same way from time to time, more so when a chap parachuted beside me and still didn't make it." Andrew hesitated. "Tell me more about the bombings."

James expelled a heavy breath. "A number of places were hit: Scotland Yard, Westminister Abbey, most of the City, and all the bridges across the Thames. None of the telephones are working, and I'm sure there's more, but I heard enough to know the Germans must have dropped every bomb they had on us."

"What about casualties?"

James's gaze appeared to bore through Andrew. "I'd hate to speculate. Fires raged for miles."

Andrew prayed for all those innocent people and for England. "We only lost one fighter plane and shot down fourteen of theirs. At least that was the count this morning."

James nodded. "Our radar has helped tremendously, and I know we did well last night, but the devastation is horrible."

"Are you praying?" Andrew asked.

His friend gave him a faint smile. "I have to. Without God, we are nothing."

Their conversation ceased when a pilot stood before their cots.

"Lieutenant, a woman is waiting outside to speak to you."

Andrew reluctantly rose to his feet. Suddenly the possibility of Margaret seeking him out brought a new surge of energy.

Outside his door, he recognized Jenny, one of

Margaret's friends. Although disappointed, he would not reveal it.

"You wanted to speak with me?" he asked. He saw the tension in her face, and it alarmed him.

"Yes, Sir," Jenny replied. She glanced nervously about and back to Andrew. "Margaret has been seriously injured. She was caught in the bombing last night."

Andrew felt the color drain from his face. "Is she here at the hospital?"

"Yes, Sir. I'm on my way now. I thought you might. . . well, might want to join me."

"Not my Margaret," he said, his stomach threatening to retch.

He rushed back inside for his jacket and to ask James to pray. A moment later, Andrew and Jenny rushed to the hospital. If only he knew the extent of Margaret's injuries. The thought of losing her had a strangling hold around his neck. He hadn't been able to apologize, and now she lay injured in the hospital. His pride, his stubborn, foolish pride.

Dear Lord, hold her in the palm of Your hand. Heal her body.

Inside the busy hospital, Andrew located a nurse and asked for assistance in finding Margaret. She directed him to a women's ward at the far end of the building. Another nurse met him outside the room.

"I'm Lieutenant Stuart. We're looking for Corporal Margaret Walker," he said. "I understand she's in this ward."

The nurse nodded. She wiped a loose strand of hair

from her face with her arm. Blood had splattered her apron. "She drifts in and out, Lieutenant. You can visit, but she needs her rest."

"Thank you. We won't stay long," he said, peering anxiously into the room.

The nurse hurried down the hall, then spun around. "Lieutenant, is your first name Andrew?"

Startled, he stared at her a moment before replying. "Yes, it is."

"Good." She smiled. "Corporal Walker has repeated your name several times."

Tears welled in his eyes, and he hastily blinked them back. "I've got to see her." He stepped aside for Jenny to enter, although it took all of his might to uphold his proper upbringing.

Margaret's bed sat midway down the ward in a room filled with injured women. His pace couldn't get him to her side fast enough. At the sight of her, Andrew again swallowed his emotion. In his worst expectations, he didn't think she would look so battered. A bandage wrapped around her head, and her swollen face revealed a mass of bruises, making her barely recognizable. A cast encased her right arm and another wrapped around her left leg. He prayed there were no internal injuries. She appeared to sleep, but Andrew wondered if she lay unconscious.

"Margaret," he whispered. When she didn't respond, he spoke her name again.

"Do you think she hears us?" Jenny asked, reaching out to stroke Margaret's arm. Instantly she drew back her hand. "Poor lamb. I'm afraid I'll hurt her."

"If she's asleep, then she's not in pain," he said. Andrew could only stare into Margaret's face. "Jenny, do you know any of the details of what happened?"

"Not much more than what I already told you. She had to deliver something into London and got caught in the bombing. Lieutenant, I'm not surprised Margaret called out your name."

He raised a brow.

"She's been miserable since you two stopped seeing each other." Jenny sighed. "Oh, yes. I don't know why you two decided to go your separate ways. . . Guess it's none of my business."

Andrew chose not to reply. So many things needed to be said to Margaret, and even then he wouldn't want to discuss their relationship, or rather the lack of it, with anyone else.

"Andrew," Margaret uttered though her eyes were still closed. "Is it really you?"

He bent to her face. "Yes, it is." He wanted to hold her, kiss away the bruises and cuts. "Don't try to talk, just rest."

"I'm so sorry," she said, her voice barely above a whisper.

He held his finger a hair span above her bruised lips. "Hush. You just concentrate on getting better. I'll visit you tomorrow and every day until you're well. Jenny's with me; she needs to say a word with you."

He stepped back for the woman. "Hello, Love. Please do what Andrew says and listen to the doctor. All of us will be praying for you."

Margaret wet her lips and her face relaxed.

For the next three days, he visited Margaret at every

opportunity. On occasion Jenny and a few of the other women from the barracks accompanied him, and sometimes he went alone. The doctors kept Margaret sedated, and he knew she rarely comprehended his presence. While he sat and waited by her bedside, he watched her lovely face and longed for the day when she would be well. He couldn't help but allow his thoughts to drift toward dreams of Margaret by his side forever.

Margaret stirred. Had she been in another world, or had Andrew actually been there? She glanced about and realized she lay in a hospital. With her uninjured hand, she felt the bandage on her head and noted the casts on her arm and leg. Instantly her mind reverted to the night of the bombing: the wounded man, the fires, and the explosion throwing her from the lorry.

Thank You, Lord, for sparing my life. I pray the injured man fared as well.

Glancing about her, she saw the crowded beds and the women occupying them. Margaret could only imagine the stories they had to tell—tales of tragedy and heroism. When she felt better, she'd talk to those patients and make sure they had a relationship with Jesus.

Something drew her attention to the door. She must be hallucinating, for she believed Andrew stood there, looking more handsome than she could ever remember. As he approached her bed, tears sprang to her eyes.

"Andrew, for a moment I thought I might be dreaming." She reached out her left hand, and he took it firmly into his.

"How are you feeling today?" he asked in the same quiet tone she remembered. And those incredible brown eyes were only a few feet from her.

"Much better, I think. I know where I am and the pain has subsided."

"Good, then my prayers are answered."

"Thank you for coming to see me."

He smiled. "I've been here every day since the accident."

"You have? I had no idea." She took a deep breath. "Andrew, I'm sorry for the things I said to you in the country. You were right. I'm a coward, and I did make excuses to not commit myself."

He shook his head. "I'm the one who needs to apologize. I lost my temper and demanded things you weren't ready to give."

She allowed her stinging eyes to close for a moment and asked the Father for the courage she desperately needed. Forcing them open, she continued. "I love you, Andrew. I don't want to ever lose you again—I mean, if you'll still have me. It took the accident and believing I was going to die in my foolishness to make me realize how much I love you."

He bent over her, his arms on each side of the bed. "Oh, my sweet Margaret, I never stopped loving you. My pride got in the way."

Gazing up into his beloved face, she wept.

"Don't cry, Darling. We'll work this out. The war can't last forever," Andrew said, brushing away a tear with his finger.

"It's not the war," she replied. "I'm happy, Andrew.

When I get these casts off, would you? I mean, if you still want to. Would you marry me?"

In August of 1941, beside a moss-covered, stone cottage outside the city of Northamptonshire, Lieutenant Andrew Stuart and Corporal Margaret Walker held hands on a pebble-laden path lined with white lilies and pink phlox. In the midst of vibrant pink and red roses, the flowers' sweet scent mingling with the fragrant honeysuckle, Andrew lifted her hand to his lips. Margaret smiled and blinked back a joyous tear that threatened to glisten her cheek. She dared not gaze anywhere but into the eyes of her Andrew for fear this wedding blessed by heaven might disappear.

They both wore their blue-gray dress uniforms, and she carried a bouquet of the garden's pink and red roses. Never had she known such happiness.

The moment came when the minister raised his hand and pronounced them man and wife. She realized they were so much more than a wedded couple—foremost children of God, loyal subjects of England, and fighting members of the Royal Air Force dedicated to preserving the freedom of their country.

Epilogue

January 1946

Andrew shifted the bouquet of vibrant red roses and hurried down the long corridor of the London hospital. He slid between an empty bed and a metal cart of medicines without slowing his pace. A nurse called for him to slow down, but he ignored her.

Finally he stood outside Margaret's door. Taking in a deep breath, he steadied his exhilaration and stepped into the room. Not since the day he and Margaret were married had he felt such pride and thankfulness to his Father God.

Margaret glanced up and met his gaze. A smile graced her lips and held him spellbound.

"Come see your daughter," she whispered. "Have you decided on a name?"

He nodded and laid the flowers on her nightstand. Kissing first Margaret and then his tiny infant daughter, he pulled a chair closer to the bed.

"Thank you for the flowers, Sweetheart. They're

lovely," she said, her face as radiant as the day they wed in the garden.

"You and our daughter are no match for them," Andrew replied, gently brushing his finger over the baby's hand. "I'm one lucky man."

"And the name?" Margaret asked. "Oh, Andrew, I can't wait any longer to hear what you've chosen."

He grinned and straightened his shoulders. "I want to call her Audra Rose. Audra means noble strength, and I want our daughter to never forget the strength and courage God gave us to save our England."

DIANN MILLS

DiAnn lives in Houston, Texas, with her husband Dean.
They have four adult sons. She wrote from the time she
could hold a pencil, but not seriously until God made it
clear that she should write for Him. After three years of
serious writing, her first book *Rehoboth* won favorite
Heartsong Presents historical for 1998. Other publishing credits include magazine articles and short stories,
devotionals, poetry, and internal writing for her church.
She is an active church choir member, leads a ladies Bible
study, and is a church librarian. She is also an active board
member with the American Christian Romance Writers
organization.

Robyn's Garden

by Kathleen Y'Barbo

*"Let my teaching fall like rain
and my words descend like dew, like showers on new grass,
like abundant rain on tender plants."*
DEUTERONOMY 32:2

Chapter 1

Robyn Locksley slid her hand over the torn papers and broken wires strewn across her desk and said a silent prayer of thanks that she hadn't been in the building when the intruders arrived. They'd come like the proverbial thieves in the night. Still, she felt as violated as if she'd let them in herself.

As befitting the docent of the Lowingham Manor gardens, her office held more books on horticulture than most libraries. Thankfully, those had been spared. Obviously the thugs did not read.

Stepping over debris, she ran her hand over the well-loved spines of *Lindley's Ladies Botany*, *Handbook of British Flora*, and *Letters on the Elements of Botany addressed to a Lady*, then turned to stare at the disaster in her office. Her computer, the phone, and fax machines were all replaceable. The children's money, however, was not.

She sighed as she rang up the Cotswolds Special Needs Day School in nearby Malmsbury. A lovely gentlewoman, Anna Lawrence had run the day school for three decades, two years longer than Robyn had been alive. Thankfully Miss Lawrence answered the phone, although the school had been closed for hours.

"Dear me," Miss Lawrence said when Robyn finished her story. "So there's nothing left?"

"No," she whispered, waving away Nigel Sudbury, the elderly chief of security who stood in her office doorway. "I'm sorry but everything in the safe was taken, including the money intended for the children's trip."

During the brief silence that followed, Robyn watched Nigel shrug and disappear down the hall. She'd obviously offended him with the dismissal, and she'd have to make amends later.

"I suppose I will have to tell the children," Miss Lawrence finally said. "It won't be easy. They worked so hard."

Robyn's heart sank at the thought of the disappointment the loss of their Seeds of Love fund would cause. After all, these special and amazing mentally challenged children had put in so many long hours in the garden to raise the fruits and vegetables that had provided the cash. It had taken them the better part of two years to reach the lofty goal of paying for summer camp.

How could she now tell them their efforts had been in vain? Surely something could be arranged to replace the money.

"Would it be possible to delay the announcement?" Robyn asked, nursing the gem of an idea as she toyed with the telephone cord. "Perhaps the money will be returned."

"I suppose," the older woman said slowly. "But do you honestly believe this?"

"I believe the Lord can make good from any circumstances," Robyn said as she thought of the precious students who made weekly trips to the castle for gardening and fun. "If the Lord wishes those children to go, He will see that it happens."

"Indeed," Miss Lawrence said, "but you understand time is of the essence. The deposit has been made, and the remainder is due within the week."

Robyn forced a smile to her voice. "Then perhaps we should both pray for Him to hurry."

Miss Lawrence chuckled. "Dare we?"

Again an almost ludicrous idea surfaced. The useless medieval longbow hanging above her mantel might be worth something after all. Father deemed it priceless, an heirloom passed from father to son since the first Locksley took it into battle at Hedgeley Moor in 1464. Scholars from nearby Oxford had authenticated it as one of only six remaining longbows from the Renaissance period.

She just called it ugly.

Its wood, a primitive yew, was rough and gnarled, and it looked positively ghastly hanging over the lovely Laura Ashley floral wallpaper she'd splurged on when she first moved into the flat. More than once she'd considered hanging the horrid thing back in the rafters of the barn where it had been hidden during the last world war.

Of course, as much as she disliked the piece, she'd never think of allowing it to leave the family. At least not permanently.

But perhaps a certain discreet antiquities dealer in London might give her a brief loan on it—just until the children's money could be returned by the magistrate.

Among her former circle of friends, the Simpton-Wright Gallery in the Notting Hill district was often called upon as the solution for overextended royals with temporary cash flow problems. At any given time, his Portobello Road shop was filled to the sixteenth-century rafters with treasures gone unredeemed by the gentry.

But she wouldn't have to worry about the bow landing in the shop window. The magistrate's office would have the children's money returned to her by then, and the bow would be safely back above her fireplace—or perhaps safely tucked back into the protective custody of the barn.

"Miss Lawrence," Robyn said with renewed confidence, "I'll ring you tomorrow with something a bit more definite, but perhaps there is another way."

"Dear," the other woman said slowly, "do I detect a ray of hope?"

The ray of hope followed Robyn on her visit to the castle gardens. It settled into something more when she shucked her office attire in favor of dungarees, soft leather gloves, and her most comfortable straw hat to dig in the fertile soil of the walled in area the children had named Robyn's Garden.

Tomorrow the boys and girls, all fourteen of them, would descend and utter chaos would reign, but today only the occasional bird's call interrupted the peace. Robyn attacked a particularly rocky patch of ground at the edge of the garden with her hoe and listened with satisfaction as metal dashed against soil in rapid succession.

The muscles in her arms began to burn, and despite the moderate temperature, a trickle of perspiration made a path down the center of her back. Still she continued to hack away at the contrary soil, forcing it into submission as she tried to do the same with her worries.

Too soon they caught up with her in the form of the security chief she'd so easily dismissed earlier. Ignoring him proved impossible when he settled onto the low stone wall enclosing the garden, adjusted his frayed jockey's cap, and began to whistle.

According to castle legend, Nigel Sudbury had been quite a successful jockey in his day, and a hit with the ladies as well. While he still retained his slight jockey's frame and the hat and silks he'd worn in victory as well as the rare defeat, his skills as a ladies' man were long past.

For that matter, his skills with anyone left something to be desired, although Robyn had long since learned to overlook his eccentricities most of the time. Any other day, perhaps Robyn might have found the security chief a welcome distraction. Today, however, the man who perpetually wore tweed with his racing silks was the last person with whom she wanted to speak.

For that matter, she really hadn't planned to speak to anyone but the Lord until she had her problems firmly in hand. One look at Sudbury, however, and she knew he'd planned a long visit.

Robyn stabbed the hoe into the ground and leaned against the wooden shaft. "Good day, Mr. Sudbury," she said as she wiped her brow with the back of her gloved hand. "I trust you've brought news."

"Aye, indeed I have." He removed an ancient pipe from his pocket and proceeded to tamp a spot of tobacco into the bowl. "And 'tis news you'll be liking." Watery blue eyes looked up from his task. A smile tugged at his ancient lips and twisted into full form.

Irritation worked at her manners, causing her to wish she'd not been taught to respect her elders. Finally, when she realized he would say nothing more without prodding, she gave in. "And the news you've brought would be what?"

He looked up at her through the thick silver fringe of his eyebrows and winked. "The demons have been snagged, Lass. Caught 'em halfway t'Milford Haven."

In a split second Nigel Sudbury's stock had risen dramatically. Robyn grasped the old man's hand and shook it with vigor. Tiny specks of tobacco ash landed like confetti on Sudbury's tweed trousers and marked several spots on the brilliant gold stripe of the racing jersey he preferred on Mondays.

"That's marvelous," she said. "Simply marvelous. Now the children will have their trip to camp after all." Robyn lifted her eyes to the pale gray sky. "Thank You, Lord, for Your bounteous mercy." Ignoring Sudbury's harumph, she offered a smile instead. "When will the money be returned?"

The security chief slipped the pipe between his teeth and lit it. The warm vanilla smell of Sudbury's favorite tobacco drifted toward Robyn as the old man crossed his legs and made himself more comfortable.

"Never said it would be returned. Only said they found it."

Her heart sank. "Oh," she managed as she yanked the hoe out of the ground and picked at the clumps of mud on the blade. "I'd hoped things would move swiftly once the criminals were detained."

"Now, don't you worry." He removed the pipe and inspected the tobacco in the bowl, then fished a slip of paper out of his jacket pocket and thrust the paper in her direction. "These things generally settle quick enough."

"Do they?" Robyn pushed her straw hat back farther on her head and squinted to decipher the old man's scrawl. After a moment, she had the name and telephone number.

"Told 'em you'd ring forthwith to claim your money."

"Of course." She stared at the paper and allowed her hopes to take flight. Dare she believe the Lord had actually answered her prayers as quickly as she'd wanted? "I've need of the money for the children in less than a week."

Sudbury rose from his spot atop the wall and chuckled as he emptied the contents of the pipe onto the marigolds. "Lass, nothing's done in a week," he said. "Takes that long t'fill out the paperwork."

"Oh dear."

"Rest assured, Miss Locksley," Sudbury said. "You'll see your money in due time." He straightened his cap and looked off toward the east. "If you'll excuse me, I've an appointment, although why the earl insists on a specialist, I haven't the foggiest."

"What sort of specialist, Mr. Sudbury?"

He frowned. "Some Yank. Private security man or some sort of rot, and a waste of time if you ask me."

"I see." The wind kicked up and threatened to lift her hat. "Before you go, could you venture a guess as to how long the authorities will hold the children's money?"

"Expect a fortnight." Sudbury tucked the pipe into the pocket of his jacket and shook his head. "Anything less'll be a miracle. Take that up with Him, not me." He stuck his chin upward toward the heavens.

Robyn smiled and clapped her hands together to loosen the dirt on her gloves. "Thank you, Mr. Sudbury. I believe I shall."

As soon as Sudbury had ambled off, Robyn did as he suggested and landed on her knees in the fertile English soil to thank the Lord. She rose and dusted off the knees of her overalls, then cast a final glance at the garden. Overhead the sky had begun to darken and rain threatened, but conversely, her mood had lightened considerably.

Her stomach grumbled a protest as she walked back to the storage room to put away the hoe and her gloves, and she thought of the remaining bit of shepherd's pie in the staff kitchen. While Mr. Sudbury kept the staff in confusion as to what he actually did around the manor, Mrs. Sudbury's talents left no room for question. Her job was being the best cook that had ever graced the Lowingham Manor kitchens.

Shoving the gloves into place on the shelf above the tools, Robyn dropped her hat atop it and cast one last glance at the disgraceful appearance of her clothing. Dare she appear in the office this unkempt?

"Perhaps it's not so bad," she said, turning the new shovel around to its shiny side.

In the shovel's reflection, corkscrew curls in a horrid shade of red shot out at odd angles and what little style she'd managed to put into her hair had long since fallen. Her very proper mother would have called her a fright. Quickly Robyn put the offending shovel away before her image in it became any clearer.

"All right, so I looked abysmal," she said under her breath as she closed the shed door soundly behind her. "But fashionable or not, a girl's still got to eat something."

And that something absolutely, positively had to be shepherd's pie a la Sudbury.

Outside the sky rumbled along with her empty stomach and the first few drops of rain began to splatter the stone walkway. Still the pie beckoned. A quick glance at her watch told her that all but the most foolhardy staff members should be home at their hearths by now.

The hearty potato and meat pie couldn't be good for her hips. Better she dine on salad and a slice of crusty bread. She jammed a fallen hairpin back into her unruly mop and tried to think. Two more pins fell out and landed at her feet, where she left them without a second thought.

Suddenly the smell of rain in the air rearranged and became the scent of savory roast and creamy white potatoes. If she left off the sugar from her tea, perhaps the savings would make up for the difference.

Weak as a lamb in the face of her desire for Mrs. Sudbury's heavenly concoction, she strode quickly across the courtyard and pressed the ancient doors to the former gatekeeper's house where the staff offices currently resided.

The low rumble of men's voices rolled along the thick walls toward her, so she quickly slipped into the stairwell leading to the south tower.

"No, it's quite the mystery. Nothing's amiss in the manor house and the staff apartments. Even the more rare pieces were left untouched," she heard Sudbury say as two pair of footsteps came closer. "Only the cash and computers were taken. Of course, the demons did substantial damage in the process." He chuckled. "Looks like London after the war, if I do say so."

Deep laughter echoed down the hall and bounced around the bell tower entrance. "So they passed on the real treasures and went for the replaceable items?"

The voice, lower than Sudbury's by an octave, sounded slow as molasses and nearly as sweet. Instantly Robyn thought of the American actors she'd seen at the cinema. When the stranger spoke again, Rhett Butler came to mind and stuck there.

"Frankly, Mr. Sudbury," Rhett said, "I'd hoped you would offer. I know in my line of work I'm not supposed to play favorites, but I've got a soft spot for medieval weapons. Imagine being able to document the ownership back nearly six centuries. But then I suppose that's. . ."

The Yank's voice faded and somewhere nearby a door closed. Robyn peered around the corner and found the hall clear. She leaned against the wall and closed her eyes.

Surely a proper English lady like herself wouldn't dare slink around like a common criminal, especially when there were visitors about. Logic and good breeding told her to take the nearest exit and the walk to the safety of her apartment above the mews.

Hunger, however, drove her to square her shoulders and start for the staff kitchen. Rounding the corner she pressed as close to the wall as she could in her race to the last door on the left. Twice, she looked back over her shoulder to make certain she hadn't been spotted.

Finally, with the door in sight, she slowed to a walk and breathed a sigh of relief. Then the doors crashed open, and she ran directly into a wall of denim and black leather. The last thing she saw before the lights went out was two red-haired Medusas reflected in a pair of silver mirrored sunglasses.

Chapter 2

Robyn shook her head, and the leather-clad image swirled and faded, replaced by a sharp pain centered directly above her left eyebrow. Somehow she rose of her own accord, pulled to her feet by a strong tug.

"Forgive me," she muttered as she extricated herself from the stranger's grasp and took an inventory of the damages. Other than her pride, she seemed to be intact and no worse for wear. Who would have thought a simple wish for shepherd's pie would end in such a kerfuffle?

"It was my fault, Ma'am." The Yank folded his mirrored frames and slid them into the pocket of his jacket. Startling blue eyes twinkled with what looked like amusement. "I get in a hurry sometimes. Bad habit of mine."

Stunned, Robyn reached for the hairpin that dangled near her nose and pushed the tangled mass of hair away from her face. Somehow, though her hands shook, she managed to capture her curls into some semblance of order. As she stared at the stranger, a memory danced nearer. She pressed it away and jabbed the hairpin into the thick of her ponytail.

"Miss Locksley, this is the specialist," Sudbury said, jangling his outrageously large key ring. "Meet Mr. Gentry."

The American thrust a hand toward her. "It's a pleasure, Miss Locksley."

"Pleased to meet you, I'm sure, Mr. Gentry." Robyn clasped his hand in what she hoped would pass as a firm handshake while she cast about for an exit from the unpleasant scene.

"The pleasure is all mine," he said. "And call me Travis."

The words flowed warm as honey and curled into a tight ball in Robyn's stomach. Her empty stomach. Somehow, even after the collision and corresponding headache, she still felt famished. But mostly, she felt quite the fool.

"Lass, are you ill?"

"I'm fine, Mr. Sudbury," she lied. Her gaze collided with the Yank's, and her knees threatened to give way. Strange, this silliness she felt. Must be for want of Mrs. Sudbury's pie.

"Are you sure you're all right? Do you want Sudbury to fetch a doctor?"

Again the man's voice did strange things to her insides. Again, she blamed it on being totally humiliated and completely famished.

"Really, that won't be necessary, Mr. . . ." The name she meant to say evaporated as she felt her legs turn to pudding.

He smiled. "Gentry, but you were going to call me Travis."

Somewhere on the edge of Robyn's vision, Nigel Sudbury cleared his throat. "Yes, well, since you seem to be unharmed, perhaps later you'll allow Mr. Gentry to take a peek at the famous bow. He fancies himself quite the collector, and yours is a fine specimen."

Robyn tried to think, tried to look away from the endless pools of blue. She failed miserably at both. "Bow?" she whispered.

"The family treasure," Sudbury said quite impatiently. "Surely there is only one Locksley bow."

"Of course."

Again, she'd acted the fool. What in the world was wrong with her? These feelings, this silly behavior went against all she held dear. The mere act of standing this close to one so masculine broke more than one promise she'd made to herself and to the Lord.

"I'd be forever in your debt if you'd just give me a few minutes," Gentry said, and she wanted right then to give him all the time in the world.

"I can't," she said, as much to him as to the Lord.

"I understand," they both seemed to answer at once.

Tears threatened as another blue-eyed man crept into her memory. Shoring up the dam before the waters burst through, she tried to muster an answer that would send Sudbury and his specialist packing. Unfortunately, her good intentions couldn't be forced into words. The old familiar urge to lean into him and test the width of his shoulders against the length of her arms rose instead.

Father, help me. Lead me not into temptation. Not again.

"Nonsense. We'll be up to give it a look and be gone in two shakes, Lass," Sudbury said.

Up? Shakes? Robyn allowed the picture to crystallize

and saw no good in it. "No," she said. "My flat looks a fright."

And so do I.

"Sudbury, I believe the lady's answered us," he said.

Her gaze left his blue eyes and flitted over a pair of cheekbones chiseled from the finest granite, finally settling on lips nearly full enough to be feminine. And yet, the effect when viewed askance stood the test of masculinity quite well.

Sudbury rattled his keys. "Ahem, yes, well, if you'll just let the lad loose then, Miss Locksley, we'll be on our way."

Robyn looked down at her hand, horrified to see she still held tight to the darkly tanned fingers of the American. "Oh, forgive me, I—"

She mumbled a few more words, then made a hasty retreat out the back door. Just past the end of the building she paused to collect her thoughts. With heat singeing her cheeks, she picked her way down the familiar garden path toward the solitude of her flat. At least the rain had ceased, and the twilight of the evening was upon her.

Only the motion of a lantern shining in the distance diverted her from her mission to hide from the world. Along with the light came a soft sound, something akin to metal striking newly plowed dirt.

"Miss Locksley, is that you?" came the soft voice of Annabelle Priory, the eldest among the group of children at the Special Needs Day School and the most likely to wander off at all hours. Thankfully, she lived nearby and had only a brief walk up the lane to be home.

"Annabelle, Darling," Robyn called as she veered off the path, "have your parents any idea their daughter's roaming about in the night?"

"Miss Robyn, do you fancy a bit of digging in the garden?"

The girl's wide smile and unabashed innocence combined to make a lovely package. If only she realized the effect it had on others—especially males. At nearly fourteen, Annabelle's blossoming attributes had been attracting quite the attention from the local youths.

Robyn knew too well what sort of action that reaction brought about. She also knew the consequences.

"I will ask again," Robyn said sternly. "Do your mother and father know where you are?"

"Aye," Annabelle said as she dropped the trowel. "I told 'em I had a yen to pick carrots for the mutton stew."

A second voice, this one an octave deeper, joined in the laughter. "I might not be from around here, but I think you'll have trouble if you put those in a stew."

The American stepped out of the shadows, and Robyn gasped. Alarms rang loud in Robyn's mind, and she had to force herself to walk and not run toward Annabelle.

"Mr. Gentry, I really don't appreciate you bandying about and frightening innocent persons."

"Oh, he didn't frighten me at all, Miss Robyn. Actually I think he's quite the looker."

Annabelle attempted a step toward the Yank, but Robyn held her in place. "I hardly think that an appropriate answer, young lady," she said. "We shall speak of this at length on Thursday."

The Yank moved forward and held his hands out as if to surrender. "Hey, I didn't mean to scare you two," he said. "Just checking the perimeter."

Checking the perimeter? What sort of idiocy was that?

Once more Annabelle tugged at her arm. "He sounds like a movie star, don't he, Miss Robyn?"

"Doesn't he," she corrected.

"Do I?"

Her gaze connected with the enigmatic Mr. Gentry's, and even in the dimness of twilight, the collision rocked her to her toes. Shaken, she turned her back on the intruder and offered a quick prayer for strength.

"Let's set this to rights, Darling," she said as she ignored the Yank, "and then I'll see you get home safely."

Annabelle knelt and began to dig at the soft soil with her hand trowel. "I'll repair this straight away, Miss Robyn," she said. "It'll be good as new. You'll see."

"Actually it looks like she picked something you didn't want growing in a vegetable garden anyway," Mr. Gentry said. He stepped between them to retrieve the muddy lump.

"Oh," emerged from her lips like a mouse's squeak as she identified black nightshade, the pesky plant she'd been fighting since the spring thaw. "I didn't realize."

"Miss Robyn says we're farmers because we provide food for people." Annabelle offered the American another grin. "Would you care for a bunch of carrots or possibly some beans of some sort for your dinner?"

The Yank chuckled. "No, thank you," he said as he set a toppled tomato cage upright. "I'm still on Texas time."

"Are you a farmer too?" Annabelle asked.

Gentry's broad grin could have lit the sky had the

moon not done it for him. "Darlin', that's the last thing I'll ever hope to be again. I'm one hundred percent city boy now."

With her free hand, she poked Robyn's arm. "I knew it. You are a movie star. My mum took me to the cinema and I saw a—"

"He's a specialist, Dear. He's helping Mr. Sudbury." Robyn tightened her grip on Annabelle's hand. "Now let's leave him to his work and get you home, shall we?"

Annabelle fell into step beside Robyn and began chattering on about movies and farming as they left the garden area and headed for the lane. Only the strongest of wills and a continual recitation of the Twenty-Third Psalm under her breath kept her focused on the path ahead.

As their feet left the soft grass and began their walk down the cobblestone lane, Robyn realized there were three sets of footsteps rather than the two there should have been. She turned to see Mr. Gentry trailing them and froze. Annabelle continued to skip ahead, her giggles echoing in the quietness of the evening.

Turning on her heels, she placed both hands on her hips and gave him her most authoritative stance. "Surely you've other duties to attend, Sir," she said.

"No."

In three long steps, he passed her. She whirled about in time to see him take Annabelle's outstretched arm. Before she could react, he'd seen the girl to her gate and bade her good evening. With a wave, Annabelle skipped off toward the door, oblivious to the trouble she'd caused. Trouble in the form of a darkening sky, the golden glow of lamplight, and the tallest, handsomest Yank Robyn had ever laid eyes on.

He didn't walk toward her but rather stalked like a panther on the prowl. His face lay hidden in shadow, but her memory served to fill in the blanks darkness hid.

A feeling began to bubble just beneath the surface, settling into a rhythm not unlike the pounding of her heart. "No," she whispered as she did the first sensible thing that came to mind.

She ran for home.

The moment the door closed behind her, she set about turning on lights and brightening the flat, as much from necessity as from lingering irritation. Before she shed her filthy clothes and stepped into the tub, she made certain the bathroom door was locked, even as she'd been careful to bolt the front door.

While the warm water washed away the garden grime, she allowed prayer to begin the process of removing the fear of defeat. Moving away from the city and all its temptations had kept her on the straight path. Now that temptation had come strolling in, she could only pray and turn the rest over to Him.

But the rest loomed every bit as large as an oversized blue-eyed Texan with a knack of knocking the breath out of her, both literally and figuratively.

"How big is your God, Robyn?" she said aloud. "Turn Mr. Gentry and all that goes with the sight of him over to the Lord. Let God do with him what He will."

This she did and felt His loving kindness flow over her, even as she dressed in her most comfortable Oxford rowing club T-shirt and leggings. Padding to the kitchen with bare feet, she washed the teapot and put water on to boil. Somewhere between hello and humiliation, the dual encounters with Nigel and his specialist had left her quite without appetite. Perhaps a spot of tea would be just the thing to settle her stomach and allow her to sleep.

While she waited, she brushed the tangles out of her hair and caught as much as she could in a hasty braid. The rest she said another prayer over and left alone.

Unbidden, the thought of the Yank returned. "Oh, my, I played quite the fool," she said aloud as she poured hot water over the tea leaves and set the tray on the table. Slowly, while the liquid darkened, she gave the matter a bit more thought.

A man is a man is a man, her mother used to say. Until you meet the right man.

Robyn had certainly become an expert in the former, at least before she'd begun her walk with the Lord. As for the latter, she had her doubts.

"Preposterous," Robyn declared as she sipped gently at the too-hot liquid and listened to the tick of the mantel clock.

Releasing a pent-up breath, she swirled the spoon about in her tea and watched the leaves dance in the amber liquid. Robyn took another sip and turned her thoughts to a more cheerful topic, that of the children. She'd have to have a stern discussion with Annabelle, and there would definitely be some weeding to be done in the garden, but overall the class's regular Thursday visit looked promising.

Tomorrow morning she'd ring Miss Lawrence to inform her the money had become available. The Day School director need not know the temporary removal of the famed Locksley bow to the vault of the Simpton-Wright Gallery would be financing the trip.

The clock struck nine as Robyn washed the pot and put away the tea tin. Already her eyes felt heavy, as if the weight of the previous few days sat squarely upon her eyelids. Still, she felt too restless to sleep.

"Perhaps I'll watch a spot of telly," she said as she turned off the kitchen lights. As an afterthought, she nabbed a raspberry pastry to fend off the hunger pains. "Just until I feel ready for bed. After all, it's not too late."

❦

"Are you sure we're not here too late, Mr. Sudbury? Maybe she's just gone to bed."

The old man shook his head. "I make it my business to know the habits of people here, and this one burns the lamps late into the night. I say if she's not answering, there's trouble." He gave Travis a long look. "Pure luck the cab hadn't arrived to take you back to London."

"Indeed."

Travis leaned against the ancient oak beam that ran the length of the upper floor and watched the funny little man try to play security guard. He thought about the pretty redhead and the smudge of a bruise he'd seen forming on her otherwise pale forehead.

Maybe she'd been hurt far worse than she let on. After all, she'd behaved a might strange out in the garden. Could be a head injury. A defensive tackle in high school had hit him hard, and when he came to, he didn't even remember he'd been at the football game.

She could be lying on the other side of the door unconscious at this very moment. His instincts went on alert, and his gaze scanned the perimeter for another means of entry.

"Aye, looks like we have a winner," Sudbury said as he fit yet another key into the lock.

Travis looked away and decided he'd give the man five minutes to prove his worth before he put his own size thirteen boot to the door and broke it down. As the moments clicked away, the second thoughts began.

What an idiot he'd been. If he'd been paying attention instead of thinking about the legendary weapon, the pretty girl would never have been run over like a rookie in a Pro Bowl game.

The least he could do was check on her—and take a look at the bow before he left for London. He cast a quick glance at his watch and tried not to calculate the time back home in Texas and the jobs being left undone by this side trip.

He had big plans to expand his business and less than three weeks to finish his work in England and get back to Texas to take the first step in that direction. He'd have greater challenges and all the work he could manage if this deal went through. The way he looked at it, joining forces with Daniels Security would only bring more revenue; and that meant more for the Lord too.

After all, the Lord had given him his talent. Surely He meant for him to do more with it than to protect rich, pampered clients who couldn't keep their doors locked.

"A moment more, Mr. Gentry," Mr. Sudbury said. "I'll have this latch open in two shakes of a pony's tail. Oh, my." He jammed another ancient skeleton key into the door lock and tried in vain to turn it, then repeated the process on another of the multitude that hung from his giant metal ring. "Mayhap this key will do the trick."

Travis sighed. At least this one knew how to keep her doors locked.

This Miss Locksley, what was her first name? He searched his mind and came up without a clue. He'd been too busy fighting the urge not to touch her curls and stare into the depths of those green eyes to remember mundane details.

"Ah, here we are," Sudbury said as he turned the key and pressed against the ancient door. This time it creaked and groaned like sound effects in a bad horror movie before it swung open.

"Right this way, Lad. The Locksley bow's over the mantel on your right." He froze. "Oh dear, and it appears things are worse than I anticipated. Is that blood?"

Chapter 3

A raspberry pastry.

Travis smiled as he leaned away from his desk at the London offices of Gentry Security Specialists, Inc. and pictured the moment all over again. Had it already been two weeks since the incident at Lowingham Manor?

The ancient security guard had almost come unglued when he found the pretty horticulturist curled up under an old blanket with a smear of red, later determined to be raspberry jam, near her lower lip. She'd been plenty mad, the sleepy little English redhead, and for all her fussing, he'd been lucky he hadn't been hauled off to the dungeon for trespassing.

His smile broadened as he remembered her saying those exact words, and he whispered the word in the same way she had, "Tres-puh-sing." Funny, he'd never much appreciated spunk in a woman until he came across this one. Funny too how she'd only paid attention to his "tres-puh-sing" and not old Sudbury's.

It was almost as if. . .

"Forget it, Gentry," he said under his breath as he powered up his computer and typed in his password.

After a half-hour of work, someone came around with a box from the bakery on Bond Street. Two bites into a raspberry-filled pastry and the little redhead was back in his mind all over again.

To move his thoughts in a more productive direction, Travis decided to place a couple of E-mails to a few of the dealers he'd done business with before. If he couldn't have the Locksley bow, maybe he could locate a substitute before he flew home tomorrow.

Before he sent the E-mail, he hit delete. To a man who demanded perfection, there would never be a substitute for the Locksley bow.

Disgusted, he stood to stretch out the kinks. Every time he made the trans-Atlantic trip, jet lag hit him a little harder. It seemed as though he'd just about get rid of it in time to get on the plane and develop it all over again. That must be why, even after three weeks on English soil, he couldn't think straight. It had nothing to do with Robyn Locksley and her missing money.

That he'd put off important work to check out a heist that turned out to be punk kids and petty theft was a minor irritation compared to the reason he remained in London. Three times he'd tried to make a reservation, only to have it canceled. A client had offered his plane only to withdraw its use at the last moment due to mechanical trouble. It seemed as though God wanted him in London instead of back home in Texas.

Finally, a commercial flight had been secured for

tomorrow morning, and as a back up he had a private jet on standby, an extravagance he rarely allowed but deemed necessary given the looming meeting with the Daniel folks. In the meantime, he'd taken a corner office and decided life, and his work, must go on. London was a beautiful city, if you could get past all the old buildings cluttering the skyline.

Without warning, thoughts of Miss Locksley drifted past like the clouds outside his window. He pushed them away with a shake of his head. Tomorrow he'd be on his way home, God willing, and she'd be an ocean apart. Why this mattered to him was a mystery, and more than once during his time in London, he'd thought of phoning her.

He hadn't, of course. He had neither the time nor the inclination to strike up a friendship with anyone, least of all a British beauty with an obvious dislike of men.

Besides, she lived out in the middle of nowhere.

Life in the big city was about as sweet as it could be, and Travis had no plans to leave it. He'd lived in nowhere before. No way would he ever go back. That would be like admitting defeat, something a Gentry would never do. Besides, his brothers would never let him live it down.

The icon on his desktop computer began to flash, indicating an incoming E-mail with an attachment. He ignored it in favor of the last few bites of his midmorning snack and a quick peek at the first few pages of the next thick file on the stack. Before he knew it, he'd plowed through that stack and gone on to another.

The intercom buzzed, and he reached for it.

"Gentry," he said as he double-clicked on his flashing E-mail icon.

"Sir, will you be needing anything further?" his London-based secretary asked.

A list of E-mails scrolled across the screen. Buried between one from a contact at the Bureau and a reminder of his meeting with the Daniels brass, he found one with an unfamiliar E-mail address and a subject line that sparked his interest.

Who could be e-mailing him about the Locksley bow? Surely not old Sudbury; he didn't seem like the Internet sort. After the debacle with Miss Locksley, he doubted she would give him the time of day, let alone send him an E-mail.

Still, he could hope. As fast as his fumbling fingers could move, he double-clicked on the envelope to read the post. Strange, the sender was a London antiques dealer on Portobello Road from whom he'd bought a few pieces in the past. Stranger still that this man would contact him about the redhead's family heirloom.

"Mr. Gentry? Did you hear me?"

His secretary's voice buzzed in his ear as the words on the screen registered. "Just a second, Constance," he said. He read the message again and shook his head.

Travis eased back in his chair and stared past the last rays of the sun to the dusk settling on the high rises. The fiery sparks of gold on the mirrored windows reminded him all over again of the redhead.

Why in the world would she pawn one of the most valuable pieces of medieval weaponry known to exist in its original state? It was one of only six in the world, and its origins could be traced back to the fifteenth century. Could the thieves have struck again, this time taking the real valuables from Lowingham Manor?

Anger throbbed at his temples at the thought of someone invading Robyn Locksley's apartment to rifle through her belongings. And what if she was there when they came to steal the bow? No, he wouldn't accept that possibility.

He had tried to tell the earl that his country home needed a fully updated security system instead of Nigel Sudbury and his oversized key ring. Travis's mind jumped from the English aristocrat to his comely chief of plants and gardens. *And weeds*, he thought with a chuckle.

"Sir, I really must go. Do you need anything before I leave?"

"Yeah," he said as he clicked to answer the message with a vague statement of interest, "have my car brought around and reschedule tomorrow's flight back to Houston for the red-eye. I gotta see a man about a bow."

He walked out of the office with a real purpose for the first time in weeks.

For the first time in weeks, Robyn felt like she had a purpose. She'd signed the agreement and seen the bow off safely to Mr. Simpton-Wright and today met with Miss Lawrence and the Day School children for their last session before camp. As usual, Annabelle garnered most of the attention with her antics while, the rest of the children worked heartily to rid the patch of the most stubborn nettles and briars.

"Mind the stinging nettles," Miss Lawrence called. A chorus of "yes, Ma'am's" answered her.

"Once you return from camp, we shall begin to make ready for our next project," Robyn said, envisioning the lovely plants that would replace the empty dirt.

"I shan't go to camp," Annabelle said. She giggled and tossed a handful of dirt in the air. "It's dreadful boring there."

"Mind the dirt stays in the garden," Robyn warned as she gently guided Rupert, one of the youngest charges, toward the pail labeled "weeds." "And I must disagree."

"That's right, Miss Robyn," Rupert said. "Me mum says I shall swim like a porpoise when I return." He punctuated the statement with a broad grin that showed him to be minus his two front teeth. "Perhaps I'll have a go at the Thames. Maybe even swim to France like that chap on the telly."

Robyn chuckled. "I advise you ask your mum first, young Rupert. She may have a different opinion."

"Still, I think I shall stay here," Annabelle said. She cast a dreamy glance over her shoulder toward the ornamental hedges and the garage beyond. "It's ever so much more fun."

As Annabelle drifted toward the pail of weeds with a handful of something green, Miss Lawrence slipped up beside Robyn. "Quite the young lady, that one," Miss Lawrence whispered.

Nodding, Robyn watched Annabelle take Rupert by the hand and patiently show him how to pull a weed out by the roots rather than the stems. He made several attempts before finally succeeding, and when he finally did, the two of them collapsed in a fit of giggles, the weed already forgotten.

"She is quickly coming of age," Miss Lawrence said.

Robyn's mind flashed back in time to the escapade in the garden. "I've noticed."

"She's so innocent, and the world is not."

A shaft of regret mingled with concern speared Robyn's heart. "I pray she will not learn right from wrong the hard way," she said. *Not like I did.*

Miss Lawrence leaned toward Robyn and nodded. "I will speak to her mother and father, and I'll ask you to keep a close eye on her whereabouts until she's off to boarding school in a month."

Robyn offered a weak smile of agreement and turned her gaze back toward the children. At least her own moment of temptation had passed with the permanent exit of the enigmatic Texan.

"Lovely afternoon, isn't it?" she said to seal the end of her reverie.

The rest of the afternoon passed quickly, and too soon the children had washed up and boarded the bus back to the Special Needs Day School. Annabelle, ever the straggler, came bounding off the bus at the last moment and wrapped her arms around Robyn's shoulders.

"I shall miss you greatly, Miss Robyn," she said with a giggle.

"Why Annabelle, are you going to camp after all?"

Annabelle nodded. "Aye, Rupert tells me all the boys will be there."

Father, You are the light of my life. I need no one else. Help this precious girl to know this as well.

"Miss Locksley," Rupert shouted from his window seat on the bus, "you have a visitor."

"Do I?"

"Afternoon, Ma'am," the familiar voice drawled.

Robyn whirled around and slammed into a wall of denim and black leather, then landed in a heap on the soft ground. As she looked up into twin red-haired medusas reflected in mirrored sunglasses, she realized Travis Gentry had knocked her off her feet for the second time.

Chapter 4

She wore green, the color of apples in the spring, and her eyes were a shade darker. Travis tried hard not to compare her to all the other females he'd ever come in contact with because he knew she'd win. Instead of thinking on this, he offered her his hand. She ignored his gesture of help and glared at him instead.

"Sir, I will thank you to announce yourself next time," the redhead said as she stood and knocked the dust off her jeans.

Travis fought a grin as he decided he liked the way she referred to a "next time," not that he would take her up on it. No matter what, come tomorrow he intended to be on the next plane toward Houston and home; no way could he miss the big meeting. He'd had enough of England to last him a lifetime.

"Perhaps you've lost your way, Mr. Gentry," she said. "I'm sure Mr. Sudbury could arrange transport for you to the airport."

Staring up at him, she looked as crotchety as his grandma's old mule and as cute as a new puppy all at the same time. He decided to choose his words carefully lest she bolt and run again.

"Forgive me, Ma'am," he said in the tone he generally reserved for Sunday school class and visiting with elderly relatives. He tipped his Stetson at the kids and old lady on the bus. "You all have a good time at camp, you hear?"

The girl from the garden nearly fell out the window wishing him a good time as well. Then she pointed at Robyn. "Are you going to kiss the American, Miss Robyn? In the cinema the lady and gentleman always kiss at the end."

A round of laughter erupted from the bus, and the old lady looked like she swallowed a bug. Travis turned to watch Robyn Locksley stalk toward the vehicle with fire in her eyes.

"Annabelle Priory, I shall speak to you this instant."

A moment later, the kid climbed off the bus like a prisoner on her way to the executioner. Robyn Locksley looked good and mad, and this girl seemed to be the cause.

Or was she?

Travis smiled. Could his presence have affected her any? Maybe the lovely Miss Locksley was just in a tangle because old Gentry was back in town. He cast a glance to the right and then to the left. Okay, so town was a few miles back and it barely qualified, but still the thought appealed to him.

"Naw," he said under his breath as he watched her whirl around and stalk toward him. "This gardening gal's as cool as a cucumber to you, Pal, so stick to business."

The bus roared away in a cloud of dust and diesel fumes, and for a moment he felt like he was back in Houston standing at the Metro stop outside his building. He coughed as he waved to the children peering out the back window at the spectacle he and Miss Locksley must have made.

"Mr. Gentry, if you please." She gave him a stiff nod and marched right past him toward a shady spot in the garden.

Like a puppy following a bone, he trailed her. "I guess you're surprised to see me again," he said.

She slid a hand over her curls and looked less agitated and more confused as she settled onto an iron bench beside an azalea hedge. "Surprised does not begin to describe it," she said.

Just like beautiful doesn't begin to describe you.

Warmth began to creep up Travis's neck, and he gulped down the need to apologize for words he hadn't even said aloud. "I had some follow-up questions to ask," he finally managed to say. "About further attempts on the manor's security system," came out in a choke of stale words.

Her face registered neither surprise nor acknowledgment. "I'm sure Mr. Sudbury will be happy to answer them. Shall I point you in the direction of his office?"

"No," he said far too quickly. "Actually it was you I was hoping to speak to."

"Really?" She inclined slightly to look up directly into his eyes. One rust-colored brow rose. "What could I possibly tell you?"

A list most inappropriate to the conversation rose in

his mind, and he quickly squelched it. What was wrong with him? He'd gone toe-to-toe with four knife-wielding fugitives in a Moroccan desert without breaking a sweat. Since when did one scrawny Englishwoman make him act like a tongue-tied kid?

Since I've decided she's the one.

Travis turned to find the source of the voice and found no one there. Only Miss Locksley and he remained in the garden. *Oh no, Lord, not her,* he pleaded. The warmth inched another notch up his neck, surely reaching his chin and jawbone.

Without warning, the object of his thoughts rose from the bench and breezed past, leaving the scent of flowers in her wake. "Join me for tea," she said as she marched across the lawn toward the old stone building where the manor's staff offices were situated. "I've a schedule to keep, and unfortunately lolling about in the garden isn't on it."

"Yes, Ma'am," he said as he tipped his Stetson in mock salute.

A few minutes later, Travis found himself wedged onto a stiff sofa between an uncomfortable pile of fancy flowered pillows and a stone wall decorated with ancient family photos. He recognized a small shot of the queen holding the Locksley bow and leaned over to study it. The man in the picture must be Miss Locksley's grandfather, the fifth earl.

Robyn obviously inherited her looks from the other side of the family.

While his hostess looked away to pour the tea, he

tossed two of the ruffly things behind him and watched in dismay as a third landed on the floor at Miss Locksley's feet. Their gazes met, and a moment of silence passed. Travis felt a knot tangle in his gut, and everything in his realm went crooked and out of focus.

Then she smiled, and the whole world righted again.

"Perhaps you'd prefer to sit at the desk." She pointed to the Louis IV campaign desk piled high with seed catalogues and documents bearing the logo of the National Trust. In the center of it all sat a small silver laptop computer. From his vantage point, Travis could see a scrolling marquee with a verse from Deuteronomy he'd learned at his father's knee.

" 'Let my teaching fall like rain and my words descend like dew, like showers on new grass, like abundant rain on tender plants.' " He realized he'd spoken aloud only when Miss Locksley smiled.

"You know the verse, Mr. Gentry?" she asked.

Travis nodded. "Being a farm boy I was well acquainted with that one." He avoided her steady gaze by staring at the picture of the bow instead. "Took me until I was grown to get the real meaning, though."

"And that would be what?"

He shrugged and chanced a glance in her direction. "As a kid, I always thought it meant that if the crops needed rain, you ask and the Lord provides."

She took a lady-like sip of tea. "And did He?"

"Generally," Travis said.

"And now?"

Her eyes looked so innocent and her smile so faintly

amused that Travis could only guess whether she actually wanted an answer. So many times he'd talked about his beliefs to a woman only to find out the last thing the lady had on her mind was the size of his Bible knowledge. Better to be brief than boring.

"And now I know He will provide, although not always in the way we think He will."

His hostess leaned her head to one side and looked as if she were considering his statement. "Interesting," she said in a near whisper.

Travis could only nod. *Interesting? Yes, she was. Very.*

"So you grew up on a farm?" she asked. "Where?"

"Central Texas," he answered slowly, "little town called Independence."

"Really?" She smiled. "And did you have any siblings, Mr. Gentry?"

He nodded. "Two brothers. I'm the youngest."

"And these brothers. Are they farmers too?"

The inquisitive look on her face told him she had no idea she'd been stomping on tender ground. "Sort of," he answered, keeping it short and sweet. "What about you? Any more like you back home at the castle?"

Her smile faded a notch, and her gaze flitted past him to the window and the world beyond. "Just me," she said. "I'm the single Locksley heir." She rested her cup and saucer on the arm of her chair. "Father and Mother wanted more, I'm sure, but the Lord had other plans."

"And His plans are perfect."

"Yes," she said. "I suppose."

Again silence lapsed between them. The air grew thick around them, and Travis realized he'd spent so much time assessing the situation that he hadn't even tasted his tea. Tossing two lumps of sugar into the dainty glass, he watched them sink to the bottom and begin to dissolve.

Travis swirled the melting sugar with his spoon and took a healthy sip of tea. "This is good," he said. "What kind is it?"

"Earl Grey." She leveled him a direct look. "Mr. Gentry, you haven't come all this way to sip tea with me or to talk about Bible verses. To what do I owe the honor of your visit?"

"Just checking out a lead I got yesterday."

"Oh?"

He watched her carefully. "An item came on the market, and it's my job to make sure it's legit."

"I see." Her hand shook as she tasted her Earl Grey. "Are you at liberty to say more?"

He took another long look before allowing himself to reply. "Nope."

Her lack of response baffled him. Setting the teacup on the nearest table, Travis winced when the cup clattered against the saucer and nearly fell.

The gardening gal reached to catch it, and their hands grazed. Travis jerked his away like he'd touched a hot iron, and the cup and saucer went with it. What looked to be expensive china now lay shattered on the polished wood floor.

"I am so sorry." He reached to clear the mess and stabbed his hand with a piece of the saucer.

"Don't move," she said with some authority as she tossed him a soft white tea towel. "Wrap it with this, and I shall see to bandages."

Travis complied without a word. Miss Locksley stepped over the mess and disappeared into the hall, only to return a few seconds later with tape, a roll of gauze, and some sort of medication in a tube.

I'm fine, really, he should have said. *It doesn't hurt a bit,* would have been the truth.

But when she leaned near enough to smell the flowers again and took his hand in hers, all he could do was whisper, "Ouch."

Startled green eyes met his. "Did I hurt you?" she asked.

"No. . ."

Of course the pain hadn't come from the squeeze she'd given his hand or even from the sting of the foul smelling ointment she'd applied to his cut. It had come directly from the jolt she'd given his heart. He stared in hopeless silence, while she went back to work totally unaffected by the situation.

Too soon she finished her ministrations. "Are you all right, Mr. Gentry? You look a bit flustered."

Travis yanked his hand away and cleared his throat. "I'm fine, really." His words sounded like a squeak. He stood to shake off the lingering effects and tried his voice again. "The Locksley bow." He leveled his best professional interrogation stare at her. "I'd like to see it."

Prim Miss Locksley looked like she'd been socked in the stomach with a shovel. Her face went pale, and her eyes widened. A second later, she recovered enough to clear her throat and meet his gaze.

"That won't be possible," she said. "It's not. . .that is, I haven't. . ."

The former lawman in him went on alert. If the Locksley bow had been stolen, the last thing the woman would be doing would be trying to hide the fact.

"Are you saying it's not here?"

Again she cleared her throat. This time she added a shrug, then rose to stand inches away from him. "I said nothing of the sort, Sir."

"So I can see it?"

Her shoulders went from stiff to slumped in a split second. "I'm afraid that will be impossible," was all she offered before she swept from the room like a queen dismissing her subject.

Travis felt shards of china crush under his boots as he stalked across the room and out into the hall. Robyn Locksley's retreating form disappeared into the bright morning sunlight. "Oh, no, you don't," he said as he raced after her.

Chapter 5

The feelings swirled about and flustered Robyn, causing her to seek out the nearest hiding place, notably the arbor or perhaps the boxwood maze. Ideally she could have fetched the hoe and shovel and worked out the issue by her favorite method. Like her Lord, praying in the garden seemed a most foolproof way of doing away with her worries.

With the specialist on her trail, she could only wish for a quiet moment to consider the possibilities. Had the American found out her secret? Dared she imagine that the Locksley bow had been sold?

"Impossible. Mr. Simpton-Wright is an acquaintance of Grandfather's and a holder of the royal seal. He's been in business for a quarter of a century; he wouldn't dare do something illegal," she said under her breath.

Straight away she must ring up Mr. Simpton-Wright to investigate. In the meantime, she had more pressing business. She must fend off the inquisitive Mr. Gentry without causing suspicion.

But first she must consult the Lord.

She looked about for the American and found him nowhere in sight. Ducking into the maze, she pressed herself near the edge of the boxwoods and closed her eyes. "Father, I've quite the problem here."

"What were you planning to do with it?"

Robyn's eyes flew open, and she whirled around to confront the man who had somehow followed her into the hedges. Where had he come from? Only moments ago she'd been alone.

Standing like an old west gunslinger, the specialist slowly brought his arms up to link them across his chest. All denim and attitude from the tip of his boots to the top of his American cowboy hat, the man looked positively intimidating.

Old fears surfaced along with the need to run. But where? Travis Gentry stood between her and freedom, and the opposite end of the maze lay too far away to consider.

Trust him, a gentle voice said. She cast about for the source but found only the American in attendance. *He is My child,* the voice whispered. *Trust him.*

"I'll repeat the question," he said as he inched a bit closer. "What were you going to do with it?"

"It?" Robyn took two steps back and collided with the prickly leaves of the boxwood hedge. The need to escape still rode high in her mind, but the voice continued to whisper a litany of calming affirmations.

The American moved a bit closer. "The Locksley bow."

Fear once more ran cold in Robyn's veins, obliterating the bite of the boxwood against her arms and the gentle voice in her ears. "What do you know about the bow?" she managed.

"Past, present, or future?" he asked slowly.

She shook her head. "Excuse me?"

"How bad did you need the money?" he asked. "Do you drink? Or maybe you've got a problem with gambling. It wouldn't be the first time I've seen something valuable lost to vice."

"Of all the. . ." The ability to speak left her, and she stood mute before the specialist. Finally she sank to the ground, defeated. "It was for the children," she stammered before she dissolved into tears.

Tears. Travis gulped. He could handle just about anything else, but not a woman's tears.

"Hey," he said softly. "Stop that."

The redhead looked up, her eyes bright and glittering. Even now she looked every bit the aristocratic English lady, and it was all he could do not to scoop her into his arms and promise her anything just to get her to smile again.

"Forgive me. I'm hardly a woman who bursts into tears without. . ."

She swiped at her eyes and ducked her head. Rust colored curls obscured her face, but her heaving shoulders gave away the fact she hadn't stopped crying. Before good sense could stop him, Travis knelt and pushed back the curtain of hair hiding her face to reveal a beauty that took his breath away.

His knuckles grazed her jawbone and traveled across

the softness of her wet cheek as he searched for the words to erase her sadness. To his surprise, she nearly fell backward in her scramble to escape him.

He saw an almost primal fear in her eyes when she tilted her head. Travis took a quick glance over his shoulder to be sure he was the one who caused it. He looked back in time to see her disappearing around the corner at the end of the hedgerow.

"Hey, come back here," he shouted into the empty expanse of leaves and dirt.

Only the sound of retreating footsteps answered him. The gentleman in him said to let her go and cry in peace, but the investigator said to hunt her down and ignore her tears. He decided to compromise and pray for her while he followed her path. Asking for discernment and advice seemed to be the right thing to do, but a map of this human trap might come in handy too.

Again the clatter of footsteps on hard packed dirt rushed past, this time sounding like it came from the other side of the hedge. Travis thrust his hand, shoulder, and right leg through the greenery only to have its sharp branches and pointy leaves bite back. The footsteps slowed, then picked up speed again, and Travis realized she must have seen him try to take the short cut.

"Ouch," he mumbled as he checked the damages.

Other than a couple of minor scratches on his good hand and some leaves stuck in his hair, only his pride had been hurt.

Then he made a request for patience; the one prayer he soon came to regret. As the sun slipped higher overhead and several hours passed, he walked deeper and deeper into the oblivion known as the Lowingham maze.

Even stopping to stand on the occasional stone resting-bench gave him no idea where he was. The hedges stood twice his height, and in some places their limbs met overhead, obliterating the sky. Going through them had already proven both dangerous and impossible, and using his generally keen sense of direction had proved useless.

Finally Travis sank onto a bench to reconsider his options and once more consult the CEO of his life. In a rush of thoughts, he began to pray and ask God's guidance on the situation.

As he waited, he remembered the bow sitting in his safe at the office, wrapped in brown paper and packed for mailing. He considered the redhead and tried not to dwell too much on her shimmering green eyes. Last of all, he stared at the endless walls of prickly plants and the lengthening shadows on the dirt.

The sound of the soft afternoon breeze became a roar in his ears, and he could almost feel the bite of the green branches as they tore between the layers of protection he'd worn so long. A feeling long gone yet never forgotten came rolling toward him, and he had to stand and dart past it to keep from a sure collision.

Being stuck in a maze in the middle of the English countryside was trouble enough without borrowing more. The last thing he needed to consider was the past; his little problem was something he would handle someday when he had time. But how would he take care of the present?

The answer came in the form of an unexpected chirp from his cellular phone. Travis stared down at his pocket and laughed aloud through three rings, then answered on the fourth.

"Mr. Gentry, this is Constance. The courier is here from the embassy. Shall I have him take the package?"

A voice not his own nor his secretary's whispered in his ear. *Yes.* He repeated the word to his secretary, then swiftly ended the call with trembling fingers.

"Was that You, Lord?" he asked aloud, fully aware that the package in question contained the Locksley bow.

By nightfall the weapon would be halfway to New York in a sealed embassy pouch, and by tomorrow afternoon, it would be stored in the vault at GSI headquarters awaiting further instructions. For better or worse, the Locksley bow was his, and the Locksley lass was. . .

Yours to love as well, the voice said.

Travis nearly fell off the bench. His phone clattered to the ground, and he reached to pick it up, stuffing it into his pocket as he scanned the perimeter for signs of life.

The soft words hit him like a linebacker at the goal line. He shook his head. "But I only wanted the bow."

That's not true.

"Look, I've been meaning to talk to You about this. What's all this 'she's the one' business? She is not the one because I know absolutely nothing about her other than that she's afraid of me, likes plants, and lives in the middle of nowhere."

But I know her.

"Okay." Travis searched his brain for a rebuttal. "Regardless, You and I have never discussed women before."

That's not true either.

He paused to think.

"Okay, I'll admit I've had a thought or two about being lonely since I hit the down side of thirty."

A time or two?

Travis shrugged. "Well, You know more than I do about that."

Yes, I do.

"I figured You'd take care of it by bringing me more work."

You have more than enough work.

He scratched his head and pulled a piece of the hedge out of his hair. "Well, what about another Sunday school class to lead to get me out of my predicament? I mean when I thought of companionship to fill my time, I never expected. . ."

A vision appeared at the end of the row and moved slowly toward him. He rose on legs that barely held him upright.

"Miss Locksley?"

"Yes."

Late afternoon sunlight dappled shadows across her face and lit up her sweater with pinpoints of bright apple green. Travis tried not to remember what it had done to her eyes earlier in the day. He also tried not to remember the conversation he'd just had with the Lord.

Unfortunately he failed miserably on both counts.

"Lord, are You sure?" he whispered as the redhead approached.

I am.

Travis studied the woman and wondered if, for the first time in recorded creation, God had made a mistake. Beauty she had, of this there was no doubt. But exceptional outer beauty had never been a big draw, at least not after his hormones settled and his walk with the Lord matured.

An errant thought flew past, and he captured it, mulling it over as he watched the sunlight wash over soft curls and pale skin. *I could get used to her, maybe, but could she get used to Houston?*

He pushed away the idiotic musing and turned his mind to more concrete thinking. *You're going to have to show me a sign before I make a move like this.*

Again the soft voice tickled his ears and blew past him on the breeze. *She is a Christian woman, Travis. She will rescue you from your predicament.*

The horticulturist held her hands out as if to fend him off. "I am a Christian woman, Sir. I am merely here to rescue you from your predicament."

Travis said something. He must have because she nodded a response and turned to walk away. When she disappeared into the hedges, he hurried to catch up.

"Sorry, am I losing you?" she called over her shoulder.

Travis fell into step with her and shook his head. "Nah," he said, "I'm kind of hard to lose."

She actually smiled. "Too bad."

"Oh yeah?" Travis shook his head. "I didn't think I'd

ever get out of here. When my secretary called I. . ." The words he meant to say were lost as he remembered his reasons for being at Lowingham in the first place.

The mysterious sale of the Locksley bow.

He stopped short and tugged at her hand, bringing her to a halt. "There's a matter I'd like to clear up before we part company."

She narrowed her eyes and stared at him as if she knew a secret. "The bow."

Travis nodded. "Do you know where it is?"

She looked away, only to swing her gaze back to meet his. "I don't know how you found me out, but I suppose your being a specialist had something to do with it."

He gave her no indication of an answer. This seemed to spark anger and something else. Could it be fear again?

"The bow is on loan for a specified period of time. I've the papers to prove it, but I dare say I shan't fetch them to show the likes of you."

"Oh, I believe you," Travis said. "But you don't have to fetch them. I've already read them."

Her face paled. "What do you mean?"

"You were paid a sum of money in exchange for the Locksley bow." He shrugged. "As a collector of these things, I'm interested in knowing why you would let it leave the family."

"It's not leaving the family. I had an agreement with—"

"Mr. Gallagher Simpton-Wright."

She gave no sign of what the name meant to her. Then the veneer cracked, and she shook her head. "I rang him up. He's on holiday."

This came as no surprise to Travis. Before making the appointment with Simpton-Wright, he'd had the man thoroughly checked out. The first thing he'd learned was that the antiques dealer had already booked a flight out of Heathrow to Dubai. A connecting flight would take him to Lagos, Nigeria, then on to Mexico City.

From there, the reservations paper trail ceased, but he had his best guy investigating the possibilities, something he'd be doing himself if he hadn't been out in the middle of nowhere wasting time on the redhead. He shook his head and pressed the irritation away.

"And?" he said.

A flustered expression crossed her face. "And since the magistrate's postponed the return of the money, I assumed this gave me a bit of leeway in the time I had to. . ." She paused as if to gather her thoughts. "My family bow has been sold, hasn't it?"

He braced himself for the tirade, then spoke the truth in as spare a way as he could. "Yes."

Before his eyes, her backbone straightened, and the confusion and concern left her face. Only a look of determination remained. "Tell me what you know."

"I've said all I intend to."

"Fair enough." She turned on her heels and stalked away. "Then I've led you as far as I intend to." In a flash, she slipped between the hedges and disappeared.

Travis set off after her, trying in vain to follow the retreating footsteps. "That's right," he shouted over the sound of blood boiling in his ears, "run away again. You're really getting good at that."

No answer.

Travis took a deep breath and said a quick prayer to subdue his anger. He chose his next words carefully and picked a tone of voice designed to soothe and not to beg.

As soon as he opened his mouth, however, all his careful planning went out the window and he shouted the first thing that came to mind. "Surely you're not going to leave me out here. It'll be dark soon."

"You're the specialist," she called from what sounded like a great distance away. "Perhaps you should scan the perimeter and investigate the possibilities."

Chapter 6

Three phone calls and more than an hour later, Robyn stormed into the maze and practically dragged the American out by his ears. She said nothing of what she'd learned from the authorities—in fact she said nothing at all. The wheels had been set in motion for the return of the family bow and the incarceration of Mr. Simpton-Wright—and quite possibly Mr. Gentry as well.

She might have been a bit late in obtaining the funds to retrieve the bow, but the contract she signed required the antiques dealer to inform her of any pending sale so she could match the offer. Simptom-Wright had conveniently forgot this bit of detail.

Torch lights flickered along the path to the manor house, spreading tongues of golden flame against the purple-blue sky. A single star twinkled in the north, with the promise of more to follow. In all, it should have been a beautiful sight.

Unfortunately, Mr. Gentry's presence prevented it from being so. Rather than tell him this, she opted for a more generic farewell. He stood perplexed while she, trembling in anger, found the path toward her flat above the mews.

"I have the bow," he said in the Rhett Butler voice that had charmed her not so long ago.

Robyn whirled on her heels and stared at him in disgust. "Then return it, and I shan't seek prosecution."

"Prosecution?" He shook his head. "What're you talking about? I checked every detail. The sale is legal and binding."

"Here's a detail you missed, Mr. Gentry." She looked past him to where a slender moon held court at the edge of the night sky. Around it lay a scattering of pinpricks, the first of the constellations that would soon fill the heavens. Slowly, she turned her gaze back to the American. "I've a solicitor in London ready to prove that you were in collusion with Mr. Simpton-Wright to defraud me, and the magistrate in Malmsbury agrees."

Utter shock registered on his face and for a moment, Robyn felt the old fear return. He easily could hurt her, this man. He could also, under other circumstances, cause her to hurt herself.

"That's a lie."

"Is it?" She didn't know, although believing so made disliking the American easier. And disliking the American made everything else easier. "We'll leave it to the solicitors to sort through then."

The specialist pulled a cellular phone from his pocket and began punching numbers into the dial. All the while he kept his gaze directed on her. After a few terse statements into the phone, obviously directed toward someone's answering device, he rang off and shoved the phone into his pocket.

"You're pretty well connected for a gardener," he drawled. "I've got a message on my voice mail telling me my passport's been pulled and my tickets for home tomorrow are no longer any good. Seems I'm wanted back in London for questioning on a matter of the utmost importance."

He said the last few words in a mock British accent, complete with the appropriate barrister's serious scowl. If the situation had been less grave, she might have laughed.

"Then I shan't keep you, Mr. Gentry. Mr. Sudbury's making the arrangements, so I suggest you report to him forthwith for your return trip."

"Under the circumstances," he said in an even slower drawl than before, "you might as well call me Travis."

An inkling of trouble worse than the loss of a family heirloom tickled the corners of her mind. "Under what circumstances?"

He reached for her elbow and guided her toward the path leading to the mews and the door to Sudbury's office. "If I'm going, you're going with me, Robyn." He flashed her a rather out-of-the-ordinary smile. "I can call you Robyn, can't I?"

Butterflies took flight in her stomach, while her head worked through the scenario Travis Gentry had just threatened. She began to pray, asking the Lord to do something about the American and his demand.

As if God had heard and answered, the trip to London

proved unnecessary. Sudbury phoned well-placed chums of his with assurances that Mr. Gentry would remain in his custody until the situation was resolved. An empty pensioner's dwelling had been readied on the property, and Mr. Gentry was sent there with instructions not to flee upon penalty of incarceration.

As Robyn worked to restore order to her office and try to forget the disorder that was her life, Mrs. Sudbury rang up.

"The earl's dinner over t'the manor house's been canceled, and someone has to eat this," she said in her singsong cook's-in-charge voice.

And eat they did, dining in grand style in the cozy staff kitchen at the far corner of the mews. Robyn picked at the potatoes and thick slice of rye bread on her plate as she watched the American go at his second helping with gusto while discussing with Sudbury the merits of certain breeds of horses.

So much for the deprivation due a prisoner of the manor.

"Not hungry, are you, Lass?" The cook's voice drew her out of her thoughts.

She turned her gaze to Mrs. Sudbury. The older woman's wide brown eyes narrowed slightly as she leaned toward Robyn in a conspiratorial gesture. "It was that way with Nigel and myself, you know," she whispered. "One minute a body can't get enough meat and potatoes, and the next you only have eyes for 'em and the food's gone stale and cold."

Robyn cast a quick glance over her shoulder to make

sure the men were still deep in discussion. "What are you talking about?"

Mrs. Sudbury touched Robyn's arm and chuckled. "It's as plain as the empty spot over your hearth, Child," she said. "The man's got it bad for you and you for him, and this situation with the bow is the Lord's doing for sure."

Robyn felt the warmth fly up her neck and into her cheeks. "That is preposterous," she stammered as she collected her plate and pushed away from the table. "Now if you'll excuse me, I'll go warm this a bit."

Cold.

That's what Travis felt every time he looked across the table at Robyn Locksley. He shook off the feeling with a roll of his shoulders and returned to the conversation with Sudbury, a conversation that hadn't lagged a bit despite his immersion in thoughts other than horses.

As he watched the pretty English lady slip out of the room, he felt his heart go with her. Stupid, he realized, since he knew very little about her beyond the fact that it seemed as though the Lord had determined they should be together.

His cellular phone rang, intruding into his thoughts but not into Sudbury's monologue on the new sod covering the pitch at the Guards Polo Club in Great Windsor Park. He excused himself to answer, then suppressed a laugh when Nigel barely noticed the interruption.

By the time Travis had finished speaking to his London solicitor, Robyn had returned. Sudbury had moved on to talk about next year's Royal Ascot and the assorted horseflesh in competition for the title.

"Good news, Mr. Gentry?" Sudbury's wife asked.

Travis slid the phone into his pocket and pointedly ignored the bored look on Robyn's face. "Not really. It looks like my passport's not going to be returned until this mess has been resolved." He turned to stare at the prim redhead. "So in the meantime, I'm stuck in the middle of nowhere, and my business is going down the drain."

The cook pointed her finger at him. "The Lord knows your troubles, Mr. Gentry. Lay them at His feet."

"I already have, Ma'am."

But had he?

In the days that followed, while he wandered around the castle grounds with little to do but think, Travis pondered the question at great length. Ultimately, as he lay beneath the cherubs and clouds of an eighteenth-century frescoed ceiling in one of Lowingham Manor's three pensioners' houses, he realized he'd only played at trusting the Lord.

Climbing out of the bed, he landed on his knees and lowered his head until his brow touched the feather mattress and his eyes slid shut. For what seemed like an eternity, he listed all his worries, from the potential ruin of his deal with Daniel Securities to the worry over the Locksley bow to his inability to find comfort in the peace and quiet of the countryside at the feet of his Savior Jesus Christ. Then, one by one, he let them go.

All but one.

The next morning, that last trouble arrived at the breakfast table in apple green, the same sweater she'd worn in the maze. Travis glanced up from his plate of ham and Scotch eggs to watch her pour a cup of tea before he returned his attention to his breakfast. Finding the chair farthest from him, she dove into the *London Times* without so much as a "good morning to you." In return, Travis tried to muster up all the reasons why he shouldn't care, starting with the extension he'd gained on the Daniels Security deal.

Each day after started and ended the same. Even Sunday morning brunch after early church services had brought no end to her silence. To think she would still carry a grudge after listening to a sermon on bearing with each other in love.

By Monday morning, their game had driven Travis to distraction, forcing him to take up manual labor to work off his frustration. That afternoon he dragged the gardening tools into the patch of weed-choked vegetables named after his tormentor. In short order, he had the weeds pulled and several rows ready for fall planting.

Funny how it didn't seem like farming when he dug in the dirt with Robyn Locksley in mind. Tuesday morning at breakfast he still hadn't figured it out.

"May I join you?" she asked.

Travis jerked up to stare into the face of the object of his thoughts. "Sure," he said with a shrug of nonchalance as false as Nigel Sudbury's teeth. "Take a load off," he added for effect.

Take a load off? Where had that lame statement come from? He fought the urge to cringe, covering his embarrassment by filling his mouth with a fork full of eggs.

The redhead settled into a chair on the opposite side of the table, nearest to the door. Without actually looking him in the eye, she pointed to the sugar bowl and muttered something about passing it to her. At any moment, Travis expected her to bolt and run.

When he leaned forward to press the delicate porcelain piece in her direction, their fingertips touched and scalded a path on his skin. He snatched his hand back and upset the creamer, littering Mrs. Sudbury's floral tablecloth with spilled milk.

Righting the crock, he grabbed for the napkin in his lap and dabbed at the spot. Through it all, his companion sat silently, watching his shame with eyes that gave away nothing of her thoughts.

"I must apologize," she said over the rim of her cup. "You've certainly not shirked hard work during your stay, and I've been remiss in saying so."

Travis bristled at the reference to his forced house arrest. The woman acted like he'd checked into a bed and breakfast. The part about her apologizing softened the rest, but only slightly.

"What is it you Yanks say?" she continued. "You've got a green thumb. I'm suitably impressed with the quantity of work you've accomplished."

He shrugged and waved away the compliment with the napkin in his hand. Best not let her know how well her words fit in his ears and in his heart. "Hard work's cheaper than therapy."

A hint of a smile touched her fresh-scrubbed face, and she pushed back an errant strand of red from her forehead. "Do you find yourself in need of therapy very often, Mr. Gentry?"

"Call me Travis and I just might answer that question."

She tilted her head slightly as the smile dawned bright, illuminating the room despite the grayness of the morning. "All right." She paused to take another sip of tea. "Travis, it is."

He nodded his approval. "So, Robyn." He tested the taste of her name on his lips and decided he liked it just fine, so he said it again. "Robyn, I don't recall the need for therapy before I met you."

"Nor did I need a solicitor."

He winced. "Touché."

Their gazes met and locked. For a moment, the room shrank until all the ancient timbers and crumbling plaster walls were gone, leaving a set of sparkling green eyes that he could have easily become lost in—just like the maze. Only the ring of his cell phone broke the silence.

"Yeah," he grunted into the object of offense.

"Mr. Gentry, this is Constance."

Reluctantly he allowed his gaze to leave the redhead and fall on the window behind her so he could think straight. "Yeah, what's up?" he asked even though he knew.

"The embassy courier has arrived. Shall I have him transport the package to the authorities in Malmsbury?"

"No," he said much too loudly. He quickly offered Robyn a weak smile and watched her return one much more dazzling. "That won't be necessary."

"But, Sir, I thought you were anxious to have this matter settled. Are you sure you want the package to go back to the vault at the embassy?"

He watched Robyn rise to reach for the pot of tea on the sideboard. She topped off his cup and then her own, sliding back into her seat with the poise of a beauty queen. Even watching her pour sugar into her cup was like watching grace in motion, just like how she stirred her tea without spilling a drop.

"Sir?" Constance's voice nagged at his ear and forced his mind back to thinking of things of which he wanted no part. "Your passport's arrived. Once you deliver the bow, you can go home."

She paused, possibly waiting for him to respond. Instead Travis tightened his hand around the phone and watched Robyn's fingers slide across the table to place her spoon on the saucer.

"Sir, did you hear me?"

"Yes, Connie, absolutely." He'd heard, all right, but Constance hadn't been the first to deliver the news. Yesterday his London solicitor had phoned to tell him he had been released pending the return of the bow to Lowingham Manor. A determination would be made on its ownership via transatlantic wrangling.

Little did his breakfast companion know she owed her beautifully groomed garden to his frustration over that fact. With a promise to call soon, Travis ended the conversation and offered Robyn a shrug.

She shared his smile. "Problem?"

He faked disappointment with a shake of his head. "Looks like I'll be here indefinitely.

Chapter 7

I ndefinitely?

Robyn covered her confused feelings with a bland smile. "Then we shall have to find something productive for you to do," she said. *Something that will get you out of the garden and away from my thoughts.*

"Aye, and I give a hearty second to the lass's motion," Mrs. Sudbury said from the doorway. "You like the garden, don't you, Mr. Gentry? Seems quite a pleasant opportunity for the two of you to work together."

A range of responses played across Travis's face, each fleeing as quickly as it appeared. Robyn watched in fascination while the Yank turned his charm on the cook:

"The garden's fine, Ma'am," he said in that Rhett Butler drawl of his, "but I think I'd prefer peeling potatoes to planting peas."

"Now stop your teasing." Mrs. Sudbury punctuated the statement with a giggle and a light toss of her cleaning cloth. "You'll do nothing of the sort, will he, Lass?" She turned narrowed eyes toward Robyn, all sign of giddiness banished.

Robyn refused to be intimidated by the meddling cook. "Perhaps Mr. Sudbury's got something for him."

"Pish-posh, Girl," she said. "My Nigel's a dear, but he's not got enough t'do on his own. I'll not be surprised if he doesn't announce his retirement soon. You know he'll be eighty in a few weeks." She shook her cloth as if to wave away the subject. "Now scoot, the both of you or it'll be time to serve lunch before the breakfast dishes are washed."

"I'm sorry, Ma'am," Travis said as he pushed away from the table and tossed the napkin next to his empty plate.

Only a sprig of parsley and the slightest smudge of mustard mixed with paprika showed the man had dined there. Robyn mentally counted the calories and cholesterol and decided the Texan was a walking time bomb if he ate this way all the time.

"Perhaps you could take a stroll while I busy myself with the work I've been neglecting," she suggested.

Mrs. Sudbury shot her a warning look. "Now what were you saying, Mr. Gentry?"

"I said your cooking's so good I forget myself. Do you suppose you could show me how you make those Scotch eggs? I've been just about everywhere, even had breakfast at Kensington Palace once, and I've never tasted anything so good."

Once again, the normally staid and solid Mrs. Sudbury giggled as she began to describe her special process of rolling the stuffed boiled eggs in a certain sausage available only at the market in Tetbury. All the while, Travis hung on her every word, giving the impression that the cook's egg recipe was akin to the secrets of the mummies' tombs. Robyn resisted the juvenile urge to roll her eyes in favor of the more mature reaction, none at all.

A quick glance at the clock over the mantel showed her how very late the hour had grown. "If you'll both excuse me," she whispered, hoping to make a quick exit.

"Oh, no, you don't, Lass." Mrs. Sudbury's iron fingers pinched her just above the elbow. "I'm sure the gentleman would—"

"Miss Robyn, Miss Robyn," Annabelle shouted from just outside the large open window.

"Please quiet yourself," Robyn said as she leaned against the sill to stare down at the flustered girl. "I'm sure no business is so important that it must be conducted through the window. Please have a seat on the bench, and I'll see to you shortly."

Turning to face the other two occupants of the room, Robyn smoothed a strand of hair off her face and offered a weak smile. "If you'll excuse me, I'll just be off."

She brushed past the cook and headed down the hall toward the exit, partly upset at Annabelle's behavior and partly thankful that she'd been given a reason to leave. By the time she reached Annabelle, she'd all but forgiven the girl for her brash behavior.

"Now, Darling," she said as she ignored the two faces at the window and sat beside the girl, "what's the matter?"

Annabelle turned a flushed face toward her and pointed toward the east. "Come quick, there's a dead fellow in the maze."

Before she could respond, Travis Gentry leaped from the window like one of those chaps in the cinema. "Get in the house, ladies," he shouted in midair. "I'll take it from here."

Robyn watched her breakfast companion change from personable to predatory before his boots hit the ground. Beside her, Annabelle began to whimper.

The girl hid her face and dissolved into full-fledged tears. "If only I'd not fancied him."

If only.

Travis heard the words but refused to think of what they meant. The old habits kicked in hard, and in the time it took him to reach the maze, emotions were forced out by instinct.

He'd been lost in the green monster before, so he took a second to get his bearings. With the sun at his back, he crept slowly into the leafy jungle, taking note of where he stood and where the shadows lay.

A sound just around the bend stopped him in his tracks. Too soft to be words and too distinct to be anything but a man in pain, Travis balled his fingers into fists and readied himself to strike. Either the guy wasn't dead or there had been more than one of them. In either case, Travis had no plans to walk into a trap.

As he scanned the perimeter, he took note of two sets of footprints in the hard-packed dirt. Again, the sound drifted past him. Travis cast a glance over his shoulder to be sure he hadn't been followed. The redhead hardly seemed like the type to take orders. Thankfully, she'd obviously made an exception this time.

Moving soundlessly to the edge of the opening, he said a brief prayer for safety and discernment. A moment later, he stormed around the corner to face the source of the sound.

To his surprise, a gangly fellow barely on the far side of puberty lay crumpled in a ball on the ground. Blood trickled from his nose and a small garden trowel lay beside him. His fair hair was laced with green leaves and dirt, and his disheveled clothing looked worse. The patch on his white shirt pocket gave him away as a member of the staff. Beneath the manor's coat of arms, the name Nick was embroidered in scarlet script.

At the sight of Travis, the teenager began scrambling backwards until he wedged as far as he could beneath the hedge. "She's crazy, that one," he said as he swiped at his nose.

"Am not."

Travis whirled around to see Annabelle standing beside Robyn. A picture of what had transpired here began to form. He reached for the kid's hand. "Let's hear your side of the story first, Buddy," he said as he pulled him to his feet.

The teenager used his shirttail to wipe the blood from his nose. Before he could speak, Annabelle broke free of Robyn's grasp and made a grab for the shovel. Only Travis's quick thinking and even quicker reflexes kept the boy from being pounded again. He pressed Annabelle in the direction of Robyn and held tight to the shovel.

All the while, the kid just stood there looking confused.

Robyn, on the other hand, looked fit to be tied. Unless he missed his guess, he'd best keep the shovel out of her reach too.

"You said I looked like a cinema star, Nicky."

Annabelle planted her fists on her hips and seemed to be daring the boy to speak. Behind her, Robyn's face looked redder than her hair.

Travis stabbed the shovel into the dirt and shook his head, then turned his best interrogator's face on the kid. "You brought her in here to take advantage of her."

The teenager's lower lip began to tremble, but righteous indignation shone on his face. "I didn't bring her in here, Mister. She caught me taking a break."

Annabelle kicked at the dirt with her sneaker. "You told me you would kiss me like those American blokes."

"Did you tell her that?" Travis asked.

Nick looked distinctly uncomfortable. "I might have."

"You did," Annabelle said.

"All right, so I did but then I realized that it was wrong to take advantage of her. I mean she's. . ." He paused to pick a leaf off his shirt. "Anyway, when I didn't kiss her, she whacked me well and good," Nick said. "Beamed me over the head with that there, she did."

Annabelle made a grab for the boy, but Travis yanked him back just in time. "Whoa there," he said. "You all right, Nick?"

The kid nodded. "Just a little blood." He held his hands out in a show of surrender. "I'd like to go about my business now."

Travis gave him a sideways look. "You sure?"

"Aye." He ducked his head and a few errant leaves fluttered to the ground. "It's my fault for sleeping on duty and fraternizing with the guests, Sir. I shan't be forgetting this lesson any time soon."

He clasped a hand on the kid's skinny shoulder. "I believe you. Now go on, get out of here." The boy complied, giving Annabelle a wide berth as he raced past.

"Come back here," the girl called as she attempted to run after him.

Robyn caught Annabelle by the wrist and pulled her close. "This is beyond belief."

Annabelle stuck out her lip and looked more like a little girl about to cry than a nearly grown woman who'd just committed assault with a deadly weapon. "But I just did what you said."

Travis whirled back to face Robyn. "Did you tell her that?"

The color had drained from Robyn's face, and only a shocked look remained. "But I only meant to protect you from. . ." The words trailed off as her gaze flitted from Annabelle to the back of the fleeing kid.

Then Travis saw them.

Tears.

He gulped. One became two and then three until they blended together to slide down her cheek. When Annabelle saw Robyn crying, she joined her.

Standing glued to the spot, the only thing Travis could think to do was pray that God would send him a way out. He had two females in tears and nothing to say to make them stop. Worse, if he tried to beat a hasty retreat, he'd get lost for sure.

"Oh my," Robyn said with a sniffle, "this has become quite the kerfuffle, hasn't it?"

Send me an answer quick, Lord. I can't handle this alone.

"Nothing the chief of security can't handle. What will you people do when I'm no longer around?"

Never had Travis been so glad to see Nigel Sudbury. "I'd be much obliged if you would escort the young lady home, Mr. Sudbury."

The elderly fellow's watery gaze fell first on Robyn, then on Travis. Finally he turned his attention to Annabelle. He produced a white handkerchief out of his jacket pocket and handed it to the girl. "Your mum's waiting in my office, Miss," he said gently. "Shall we go see what she wants?"

"Thank you, Nigel," Travis said as he breathed a sigh of relief.

He seemed to consider the statement a moment before nodding. "Away with you then," he said to Annabelle.

The girl nodded and skipped off a few paces ahead of Sudbury, totally oblivious to the trouble she'd caused. Too soon Travis found himself alone with Robyn. At least she'd stopped crying.

Travis eased his way toward her, stopping short of arm's length. His cell phone began to ring, but he ignored it. Finally it stopped.

"Robyn," he whispered, "let's get out of here."

She only stared. "Don't you see what I did? An innocent young man was hurt because of me. Because of my fear of—"

Travis completed the sentence for her. "Men."

To his surprise, she shook her head. "No," she whispered. "Of myself."

The tears started again. This time he took action.

Releasing her wrist, he wrapped her in his arms and let her have a good cry. While she cried, he prayed, sending pleas to the Lord to let Him know he'd been mistaken about Robyn Locksley and His plan for the two of them. Soon her sobs had subsided and his shoulder was soaking wet, but the Lord had remained silent.

"I should go," Robyn said softly, although she made no move to leave. "Annabelle might. . ."

"Shhh." Travis lifted her chin and wished away the sadness in her eyes.

Then, just like in the movies, he kissed her.

Chapter 8

Wow," was all he could manage when the kiss
ended.

"Indeed," she whispered.

A moment more glorious than he could put to words
unfolded between them as he stared down into eyes
fringed with lashes still wet from her tears. A second later
the phone rang and the feelings evaporated.

Without a word, she slipped out of his grasp and
walked right past him. The phone sounded again.

"Answer your phone." She turned the corner and disappeared. "If you'd like to see the Tetbury Market, meet
me at the car in half an hour. I've a party to plan for the
children's return."

Travis jerked the shovel out of the ground and scrambled to catch up. He answered on the fourth ring to hear
the managing partner of Daniel Securities promise to exercise his option to pull out of negotiations if he missed
Friday's board meeting. Travis placated the CEO with a
promise to take the red-eye to Houston on Thursday night,
then followed up with a call to place his reservations.

A third call was to Constance, who failed to answer. Leaving instructions on her voice mail, he severed the last tie between him and Robyn and released the bow for delivery. As soon as his secretary got the message, the artifact would be on its way home and so would he. If he missed the flight, he knew he'd never leave.

With a heavy heart, Travis shook off the nagging thought that he'd somehow let the Lord down and went off in search of Robyn Locksley. If today were going to be his last one in England for awhile, he should at least make the most of it.

From the car ride up the A429 to the magnificent scenery, Travis soaked up the sights. But mostly he enjoyed Robyn's company. She'd laughed as they passed through the village of Malmsbury, claiming that only two things had ever happened in the sleepy town in all its years of existence. The first was the death of the unfortunate Hannah Twynnoy at the hands of a tiger from a visiting menagerie in 1703, and the second was the loss of the abbey to a weaving business.

Five miles past the town, they turned onto the cobblestone streets of Tetbury and parked near the seventeenth-century Tetbury market. Travis stared at the ancient stone buildings, each one nestled against the other, their exteriors covered with the gray of a multitude of centuries of use. Only the occasional modern gutter or light fixture gave proof the Renaissance had ended. He thought of the bow, surely winging its way back to Robyn at this very moment, and smiled.

Yes, it belonged here in England and not back in his

loft apartment in downtown Houston.

As do you.

Travis shook his head. No use arguing with the Lord on such a beautiful day.

❧

There was no use arguing with the Lord on such a beautiful day. A hint of fall lay in the breeze, and soon she would have to think of things more important than lolling about on a picnic with Travis Gentry. But for now God seemed to be in His heaven and all looked right with the world. The fish and chips weren't bad either.

Robyn dropped the chip into the folded paper and stared past Travis to the green hills beyond Tetbury. *What a lovely spot for a picnic.*

"What are you hiding, Robyn?"

She swung her gaze to look at Travis. "Excuse me?"

He leaned close and removed the remains of her lunch from her hands, setting it beside her. "Something happened, and you've never told anyone."

Warmth crept up her neck and into her cheeks. No answer formed. Finally she managed a weak, "How did you know?"

"You're afraid," he said simply.

Something changed between them, a slight shift in the world that made all things new and different and yet so familiar.

"Why should I share this with you?"

He looked thoughtful. "Because you need to tell someone. I'm a safe bet because I'll be gone soon."

Sadly, she could see no argument in this. "Very well then. I shall reveal my secret if you give over yours." She smiled when she realized she'd startled him. "You go first."

For a moment, Robyn felt tempted to relieve him of his obligation and launch into her own story. Instead she vowed to wait him out.

"Gentry men have farmed in Texas since before it was a state." He paused. "I just picked another profession."

Robyn braved the intimacy of touching his fingers and did not pull away when he wrapped her hand in his. "No," she said carefully, "there's more."

Eyes as piercing blue as the Cotswolds sky looked her direction. For a moment she thought he might change the subject, possibly force her hand on the issue of her own secret. Instead the hard lines in his face softened and he seemed to be far away.

Back in Texas.

"I didn't know they would sell the place."

Those words, so straightforward, seemed to loosen something he long held close. His fingers tightened around hers, the only reminder that he knew she still sat at his side.

"You loved the family farm then?"

Abruptly he released his grip. "No." He shook his head. "Yes." Again he reached for her hand. "I don't know. I do know that something good, solid, and true is gone because of pride."

She captured his gaze. "I don't understand."

"I went to college and promised myself I'd never live like backwoods country people again. Didn't even want to be part of the inheritance when the folks passed on." Anger flashed across his face, swiftly replaced by sadness. "Guess I proved my point because my brothers jumped at the first chance they had to sell the farm. Now there's a neighborhood sitting on the same spot where I used to listen to my grand-daddy tell stories."

With care, she leaned into him, allowing their shoulders to touch. "And your brothers, are they happy?"

A wry smile turned up the edge of his lips. "Delirious. One's a missionary in Chile, and the other's got a glass-bottom boat business in the Cayman Islands."

"Then all's as it should be." Gently she nudged his shoulder. "Guilt is not of the Lord, Travis."

He turned toward her, bringing them dangerously close. She watched his lips, remembering how they'd felt on hers. Obviously the Lord had ignored her pleas to rid her of the memory. Instead, He seemed to encourage thoughts of the Texan.

"Say that again, Robyn. I need to hear it."

"Guilt is not—"

The lips she'd been dreaming of touched hers in a gentle, almost chaste kiss. Too soon, and not soon enough, it ended.

"Thank you," he said, and she hadn't the courage to ask whether he spoke of the kiss or the advice.

She reached for the remains of their lunch and began to crumple the papers. "We should go," she said as she stood to toss the bundle into the trash receptacle.

Before she could accomplish her mission, Travis hauled her back beside him. Fish, chips, and paper littered the grass where she'd dropped them. "Oh, no, you don't. No more running."

Father, please.

She could think of nothing more to add to her futile prayer. Squaring her shoulders, she cast about for a way to tell the tale she'd told no one but the Lord.

"Very well. There was a man," she began, "I was young, not yet twenty."

Words seemed to tumble out one after the other until she'd told Travis Gentry her most ghastly secrets. There had been so many parties, so many alcohol-induced stupors and morning-after hangovers. In horrid detail, she told him all the things she'd hidden, things even now she could barely believe.

All but one.

Only the Lord would know about the other set of blue eyes that still haunted her. The one she'd given her heart to.

Travis cradled her cheek with his hand, a touch so light for a hand so rough. She leaned against it and closed her eyes. For a moment she almost forgot the pain of baring her shame to this near-stranger.

"Robyn?"

She opened her eyes but said nothing.

"The man you haven't told me about. Do you still love him?"

Robyn recoiled in fear, tumbling backward out of his reach. Somehow she stumbled to her feet, blindly scrambling for the car and freedom. How had he known? Had he seen to her very soul?

Tell him. The gentle voice pierced her heart and stilled her feet. *Trust him with everything.*

The truth, a bitter pill to take, now sat lodged in her throat. The choice to swallow it rather than expose the worst of her sins bore hard on her. Reluctantly, she trusted and obeyed.

"No, I have no feelings left for him." She paused to settle her thoughts and turn them into words. "I thought it to be love, and he encouraged the idea." Slowly she turned to face him, carefully avoiding his gaze. "I was young, too young to do what I did."

"You didn't understand."

"That's not true. I knew perfectly well and chose freely." She paused to head off the tears threatening. "I gave him what a woman has only one chance to give. He soon tired of me and moved on." She wrapped her arms tight around her waist and forced out the last of her admission. "From thence, I had no trouble giving myself casually to whomever came along. I'm ashamed to say I rather fancied it. Three years ago, I gave my life over to the Lord and left London and the person I was behind."

Finally she mustered the courage to face him and saw no trace of loathing there. For that she could be grateful.

Attempting a smile, she shrugged as if she hadn't a care. "So now you know my story and I know yours."

He nodded. "And you're determined to ignore God's promise of forgiveness."

She leveled him an even stare. "As are you."

"Touché." He gathered their lunch leftovers and tossed them into the trash bin. "We should get back."

Of course he would be anxious to be rid of her. How could he bear to be in the presence of someone so. . . ?

No term seemed vile enough. When Travis strode toward the car, she followed in silence, and when he said something about the lovely picnic, she muttered an agreement. Eventually, they left Tetbury behind and were flying down the A429.

In Malmsbury, she stopped for petrol, allowing Travis the male role of working the pump. While he filled the tank, she slipped into the loo to check her face. Once more, she looked a fright. Splashing on cold water helped a bit, as did refreshing the braid in her hair. When she returned to the car, Travis stood waiting.

"How about I drive the rest of the way?" He paused and seemed to study her as she handed over the keys. "You're beautiful," he said.

Thank You, Lord.

"Enjoy the ride, Robyn," he said before she could comment. "It's over too soon and life is too short to run away."

If only she'd listened.

❧

The next morning, with children arriving in a quarter-hour, she stumbled over a package set squarely in the center of her office floor. More than two meters in length and wrapped in brown paper covered in official looking seals from several government agencies, it could only contain one thing.

The Locksley bow.

Attached was a note from Travis, just two lines thanking her for the patience and hospitality she'd shown him during his stay and telling her of pressing business in Texas. "The continued existence of my firm requires me to say a final good-bye, although I won't soon forget you." Robyn read the last line and willed herself not to cry.

A moment later, the clock chimed, reminding Robyn there would soon be children in the manor who wanted a back-to-school party, even if she did not. Tossing the note into the wastebasket, she rang up Sudbury's office.

Someone had to fetch the bow to her flat or the children would trip over it.

"Aye, Lass," he answered when she outlined her request for help. "So the lad's off, is he?"

"Yes," she said. "He's gone home to Texas."

"Most interesting if I do say so," was his final comment.

With no time to spare before the children's arrival, Robyn ran a hand over the treasured volumes on her bookshelf, then reached for her grandfather's Bible. It fell open to the book of Deuteronomy 32:2, the same chapter and verse she knew by heart. This time as she recited the words of comfort, she heard them not in her voice, but in Travis's, and as he spoke, she prayed through the tears.

Then, as if called out by her prayer, she saw him. Standing in the door with a leather bag slung over one shoulder and a smile on his face, Travis Gentry looked like a traveler about to depart. As he well must be.

"What are you doing here?" Stupid words, spoken like an idiot. She added to them with more idiocy. "I thought you had business."

"I did." Travis dropped the bag and took a tentative step toward her. "See, in business as well as in life, I take my direction from the Lord. This morning, He helped me close what just may prove to be the deal of a lifetime." He moved another step closer. "You don't look happy for me."

"Oh, I am, really," she said as she surreptitiously removed a tear. "Do tell me all about it."

Closing the gap between them, he stood close enough to touch. With difficulty Robyn kept her arms at her side and her eyes on the Bible in her hand.

"It's a high level position," he said, leaning toward her. "Very nice location with total charge of security and no more jet lag."

She gave him a sideways look. "Where?"

"Here." A smile touched his face. "Sudbury's retiring and I've agreed to take his place." He reached for her hand. "I'm coming to live permanently at Lowingham, Robyn, and I'd like to see where the Lord leads our relationship." He paused, looking charmingly unsure of himself. "Say something."

What could she say? "I think I shall like it very much."

"That's it?"

Another tear threatened. "No, there's more but perhaps we should discuss this later when we've a bit more privacy."

"So aren't you going to kiss her?" Annabelle's voice rang loud and clear from the doorway. Behind her a chorus of giggles joined in.

Miss Lawrence peered over Annabelle's head. "I'm afraid she's correct. The gentleman always kisses the lady in the closing scene."

Travis gave Robyn a smile that promised much and gave away nothing. In lieu of an answer, he quirked a brow and slid one arm around her back. His other arm rested at the base of her neck.

"Oh my," she heard Miss Lawrence say. "Do proceed."

"We can't disappoint the audience," Travis said.

And he didn't.

Secrets from Mrs. Sudbury's Kitchen:

Shepherd's Pie a la Sudbury

3 cups chopped cooked
   lamb or beef
1 large clove garlic,
   peeled
1 small onion
1 cup each diced celery
   and carrots

1 teaspoon rosemary,
   crumbed
4 tablespoons butter
2 tablespoons flour
¾ cup beef or lamb broth
salt and pepper to taste
3 cups mashed potatoes

Combine meat, garlic, vegetables, and rosemary and chop fine. Melt butter in a skillet and stir in flour. Add broth and stir continuously, allowing the mixture to cook at least five minutes before adding the lamb mixture. Season with salt and pepper to taste and spoon into pie dish or deep casserole. Spread mashed potatoes evenly on top all the way to edges of dish. Make crisscross design with fork and bake at 350° for 35–40 minutes until meat mixture is bubbling hot and potatoes are browned.

Travis Gentry's Favorite Scotch Eggs

1 pound ground
   sausage
5 hard-boiled eggs,
   peeled

1 raw egg, lightly beaten
1 cup breadcrumbs
1 tablespoon milk

Wrap sausage around each of the five boiled eggs. Dip each into mixture of milk and raw beaten egg, then roll in breadcrumbs. Place on rack in pan and bake at 350° for one hour. Cool and cut into quarters. Garnish with mustard and sprinkle with paprika.

KATHLEEN Y'BARBO

Kathleen is an award-winning novelist and sixth-generation Texan. After completing a degree in marketing at Texas A&M University, she spent the next decade and a half raising children (four) and living with her engineer husband in such diverse places as Lafayette, Louisiana; Port Neches, Texas; and Jakarta, Indonesia.

She now lives with her nearly grown brood near Houston, Texas, where she is active in Fellowship of The Woodlands Church as well as being a member of American Christian Romance Writers, Romance Writers of America, and the Houston Writer's League. She also writes a monthly column in the local RWA chapter newsletter and lectures on the craft of writing at the elementary and secondary levels.

A Letter to Our Readers

Dear Readers:

In order that we might better contribute to your reading enjoyment, we would appreciate your taking a few minutes to respond to the following questions. When completed, please return to the following: Fiction Editor, Barbour Publishing, Inc., P.O. Box 719, Uhrichsville, OH 44683.

1. Did you enjoy reading *The English Garden?*
   - ❑ Very much. I would like to see more books like this.
   - ❑ Moderately—I would have enjoyed it more if _____

   _____

   _____

2. What influenced your decision to purchase this book?
   (Check those that apply.)
   - ❑ Cover
   - ❑ Back cover copy
   - ❑ Title
   - ❑ Price
   - ❑ Friends
   - ❑ Publicity
   - ❑ Other

3. Which story was your favorite?
   - ❑ *Woman of Valor*
   - ❑ *A Flower Amidst the Ashes*
   - ❑ *The Apple of His Eye*
   - ❑ *Robyn's Garden*

4. Please check your age range:
   - ❑ Under 18
   - ❑ 18–24
   - ❑ 25–34
   - ❑ 35–45
   - ❑ 46–55
   - ❑ Over 55

5. How many hours per week do you read? _____

Name _____

Occupation _____

Address _____

City _____ State _____ Zip _____

HEARTSONG
PRESENTS

If you love Christian romance…

You'll love Heartsong Presents' inspiring and faith-filled romances by today's very best Christian authors…DiAnn Mills, Wanda E. Brunstetter, and Yvonne Lehman, to mention a few!

When you join Heartsong Presents, you'll enjoy 4 brand-new mass market, 176-page books—two contemporary and two historical—that will build you up in your faith when you discover God's role in every relationship you read about!

$10.⁹⁹

Imagine…four new romances every four weeks—with men and women like you who long to meet the one God has chosen as the love of their lives…all for the low price of $10.99 postpaid.

Mass Market:176 Pages

To join, simply visit www.heartsong presents.com or complete the coupon below and mail it to the address provided.

- -

YES! Sign me up for Heartsong!

**NEW MEMBERSHIPS WILL BE SHIPPED IMMEDIATELY!
Send no money now.** We'll bill you only $10.99 post-paid with your first shipment of four books. Or for faster action, call 1-740-922-7280.

NAME _____

ADDRESS _____

CITY _____ STATE _____ ZIP _____

MAIL TO: HEARTSONG PRESENTS, P.O. Box 721, Uhrichsville, Ohio 44683
or sign-up at **WWW.HEARTSONGPRESENTS.COM**

ADPG05